# GAINING INTEREST

"That's not too bad," he said, admiring the work of Piet Mondrian. "I see how someone could see a four-sided polygon as art."

"The other works are just as exquisite. Especially if you see them in a museum."

He turned the page, narrowing his eyes at another Mondrian. "Fine, it's a date."

She hesitated, unsure whether he was joking or not. He wasn't. She could now understand why Elissa, her cat, had been purring. He had a heat that exuded from his large frame, conflicting with his cold eyes. She abruptly shut the book, eager to escape the wicked temptation he presented. Puzzles always had a special allure.

Eric covered her hand before she could move. "Don't run."

"I wasn't going to," she lied.

He hadn't moved, but somehow he felt closer, his warmth creeping up the length of her skin, igniting all her senses. She couldn't voice what she was feeling, yet she couldn't move away.

He was going to kiss her; she wasn't going to stop him.

# BOOK YOUR PLACE ON OUR WEBSITE AND MAKE THE ARABESQUE ROMANCE CONNECTION!

We've created a customized website just for our very special Arabesque readers, where you can get the inside scoop on everything that's going on with Arabesque romance novels.

When you come online, you'll have the exciting opportunity to:

- View covers of upcoming books

- Learn about our future publishing schedule (listed by publication month and author)

- Find out when your favorite authors will be visiting a city near you

- Search for and order backlist books

- Check out author bios and background information

- Send e-mail to your favorite authors

- Join us in weekly chats with authors, readers and other guests

- Get writing guidelines

- AND MUCH MORE!

Visit our website at
http://www.arabesquebooks.com

# Gaining Interest

## Dara Girard

**BET Publications, LLC**
http://www.bet.com
http://www.arabesquebooks.com

ARABESQUE BOOKS are published by

BET Publications, LLC
c/o BET Books
One BET Plaza
1900 W Place NE
Washington, DC 20018-1211

All Kensington Titles, Imprints, and Distributed Lines are available at special quantity discounts for bulk purchases for sales promotions, premiums, fund-raising, and educational or institutional use. For details, write or phone the office of the Kensington special sales manager: Kensington Publishing Corp., 850 Third Avenue, New York, NY 10022, attn: Special Sales Department, Phone: 1-800-221-2647.

First Printing: May 2004
10 9 8 7 6 5 4 3 2 1

Printed in the United States of America

*To Mum and Dad, whose spending
habits inspired the idea for this book.*

# One

Eric Henson listened to the loud crack of a tree snapping, its limb an unfortunate victim of the harsh October weather settling over the city and slapping a crisp wind against his office window. The tree's destruction echoed in his ears. He had to remind himself that the sound wasn't his patience snapping in two.

He stared at Adriana Travers across the broad mahogany desk. She didn't meet the disbelief reflecting in his serious, speculative gaze. She was too busy buffing her nails, casually tapping her foot. He wasn't angry, he reminded himself, letting his gaze fall to his desk. He didn't let himself get angry. She had obviously misunderstood his suggestions.

It was perfectly understandable that she be confused about his recommendations regarding her finances. She didn't seem the type to take much interest in financial matters. The dreadful state of her books was a good indicator of that. He wanted to help her, but doubted he had the fortitude to do so. Most times he hoped he would glance up and she would disappear like a bad dream. However, she was real and in his office looking as out of place as two commas in a tax return.

She had the color and vibrancy of a hummingbird and was completely incongruous with the serene gray of his office. Her curly black hair fell around her face in a crazy array that seemed to suit her carefree personality. A long

purple skirt draped her legs while thick-heeled black boots
peeked from underneath. A shimmering jacket completed
the look, but her silver earrings caught most of his attention. They constantly twirled and he couldn't understand
what law of physics allowed their continuous motion.

He pulled his gaze from them and focused on the problem at hand. He was a professional and needed to handle
the situation in a calm and tactful manner. He would not
insult her intelligence and put her on the defensive. He was
used to her type. He'd met a few in his line of work and
knew they required a patience his other clients didn't need.
He sat forward and clasped his hands together, ready to address and dismiss any of her concerns.

"Did you hear what I said?" she asked, clearly annoyed
by his silence.

"Yes. What do you mean by 'no'?" His voice was soft,
laden with a hint of steel. Usually his tone gave a person
pause. She, however, presented him with a brief, disinter-
ested caramel glare and continued to buff her nails.

"It means that I disagree with you," she clarified. "It
means that I think your suggestions are poorly thought out
and most of all illogical."

Eric adjusted his glasses, a small bit of temper beginning
to claw around him. He prided himself on being logical. He
was always logical. What did she mean he . . . He loosened
the grip on his pen and took a deep breath. She did this on
purpose to provoke him. In the three years he had known
her they had never been able to speak without annoying
each other. He had thankfully seen her only a few times
since her best friend had married his brother. They were
usually spared the aggravation of being in each other's
company. Until now.

When he had heard she needed financial counseling,
he had wanted to help. So for once in all his practical years
he had—in a moment of temporary insanity—done something he never did. He'd been impulsive. He had called her

up and offered his services. To his surprise she had accepted. He glanced at her now as she wiggled her fingers in front of her. He was too tired to kick himself for that brief lapse in judgment.

"What did you find . . ." He searched for words. "Unacceptable about my suggestions?"

She leaned forward, took the budget from the desk, and tapped each item. "No, I will not eat regular nameless foods, cut down my visits to the salon, stop my cable, or put my cat to sleep."

He blinked. "I never suggested that."

"You probably would if you knew how much I spend on cat food and kitty litter."

He sat back and folded his arms. *Patience,* he reminded himself. "I think your cat is a necessity, an essential part of your life. You probably consider it a family member as many pet owners do." He paused, thoughtful. "Ultimately, the cat likely serves some purpose. I've read that it's healthy to have a pet. Usually they refer to dogs because they force you out on daily walks, but I'm sure cats offer some sort of healthy regime." He shook his head. "No, I would never suggest you get rid of your cat."

Adriana crossed her legs and tapped the buffer against her knee. "How generous of you," she said in a dry tone. "I was completely unaware of my cat's many benefits until I met you. She's not just a beautiful, friendly, and furry companion, but she's also a good health investment."

The brown eyes flickered. "There's no reason to be sarcastic."

Adriana hid a tiny grin. She was beginning to get to him. She didn't know why the thought cheered her, but it did. It was nice to know the unflappable Eric Henson had a temper. Perhaps he had a heart as well.

He was eerily too much like his office. Cool, elegant, and intimidating. There were no pictures on the wall, not even a plant to give color to the gray decor. Just a pathetic

vase of plastic lilies that sat high on a bookshelf, turning
gray from the gathering dust. She measured him in one
quick glance, wondering how often he needed dusting. The
dark blue of his tie and shirt complemented the brown of
his skin. It was an unremarkable light shade with all the di-
mension and warmth of a piece of cardboard.

She would not call him handsome. His face was too serious for such a clichéd label. His features were firm,
undeniably male in structure with eyes as warm as petri-
fied wood, offset by round, gold-framed glasses. He didn't
have a mouth that entertained a smile or laughed very often
and his hair was pitch-black and cut almost cruelly short.

She didn't know why she was here. She inwardly
groaned. That was wrong. She did know. She had been impulsive. It was a terrible fault of hers and usually landed
her in trouble. She remembered when Eric had called her
one late afternoon while she was flipping through a Vic-
toria's Secret catalogue. After overcoming the shock of
hearing his voice on the other end, she heard herself saying yes to his seemingly reasonable offer, forgetting whom
she was saying yes to.

The beginning of the meeting had been cordial until he
started taking charge of her spending habits like an
overzealous hospital nurse. He had angered her by treating
her as if she had no common sense. She knew his type— a
pulse-free intellectual who thought he had the sole mo-
nopoly on brain function. Yes, she liked to tease him. She
wanted to show him that he was human and emotional like
the rest of the ordinary world.

"Do you have a pet?" she asked.

"No."

"Not even a cold, dull goldfish swimming dizzyingly
around in a bowl on your windowsill?"

"No."

"Remind me to get you one. A tiny one so that it won't
be too much of a bother to you."

He glanced out the window. "As I was saying, your cat Elena—"

"Elissa."

"Right. Elissa is part of regular household expenses. However, the other items I listed are easily dispensable. For example, you could do without going to the salon."

"No, I could not."

He met her gaze. "Then go to a cheaper one."

"Would an owner of a Mercedes send his car to a Saab dealership for repairs?"

"We are not talking about cars."

"No, we're talking about me. My skin, my body."

Ah, hell, now why did she have to mention that? He tried to keep his eyes from the satin beauty of her dark coffee skin. He knew she thought of him as an automon, but he was a *male* automon.

"My visits to the salon are part of my monthly maintenance," she continued.

He waved the receipts. "Only a person with severe physical deformities needs to spend this much money on maintenance." And she had absolutely no physical deformities from where he was sitting. She was not a beautiful woman but her caramel eyes were captivating and she had a full mouth that on more than one occasion occupied his mind with purely male distractions. He put the receipts down, gathering his thoughts, when he found himself staring at her lips.

"It's part of my job."

He wanted to laugh. Now how was she going to explain this expenditure as a necessity? He leaned back in his chair instead. "Explain this to me. I can't seem to make the connection."

She spoke slowly. "I can't sell my merchandise if I look unkempt. I sell a fantasy and I have to look the part."

"At these prices you'll have to sell a lot more than a fantasy. You spend over a hundred dollars every visit and you go twice a month."

She ignored the implication. "Going to the spa relaxes me."

"Find a hobby."

"It is a hobby."

"I thought your hobby was club hopping."

She narrowed her eyes at his tone. "That's under entertainment."

"Isn't that Keith's role?"

"That's none of your business." Her voice was ice.

He shook his head, pushing his glasses to the bridge of his nose. He knew he was treading on dangerous territory, but he liked the feeling. A part of him liked the whisper of warning that came with risk. He didn't care if she got angry as long as he made his point. "You have spent nearly three thousand dollars on him. That is my business."

"Don't make it sound so vulgar," she snapped. "He's an artist and needs supplies."

He rested his chin in his hand and studied the list of supplies for a moment. He looked up at her and raised one eyebrow, softly mocking. "Seventy-five dollars for one brush?"

"It's of excellent quality. Haven't you ever wondered why paintings are so expensive?" She glanced around his bare walls. "No, I guess you don't. The fact is Keith is really very good and once he's made his big break he'll pay me back."

"His big break," Eric murmured. He shut his eyes for a moment. Adriana was more naive than he thought. He hated Keith's ability to capitalize on that. She was flighty and vexing, but she was kind and he would not let her get used.

He softened his tone, trying to sound indulgent. "Has he displayed his work?"

"Yes." For the first time that afternoon, she actually

smiled at him, excited by his interest. "Actually, I'm wearing one of his prints now. Would you like to see it?"

He nodded. Inside, his gut clenched. He hoped Keith showed some marketable talent.

She opened her shimmering jacket, displaying a black dress shirt with splatters of red, yellow, and pink—like one would find on a baby's bib—accentuated by white dots.

He squinted at the design. "What is that supposed to be?"

"It's not supposed to be anything. Keith says it's just a conveyance of emotion. Anger versus despair versus hope."

Eric lost his patience. "Why don't you get him a paint-by-numbers set and invest in him when he learns how to draw?"

Adriana glared at him. She shoved the buffer in her handbag and stood. "Thank you for your advice," she said stiffly.

He silently swore. He had pushed her too far. "Sit down, Adriana," he said. "I'm not finished."

"Yes, you are." She rested her hands on his desk and leaned forward. "All you've done is waste my time and insult me. I'm not a complete half-wit although you have done your best to make me think so. You've insulted my lifestyle, my job—"

"I never made fun of your job."

"No, you just smirked. My lingerie boutiques are excellently run and very profitable."

He nodded. "Yes, I agree you make a handsome income."

There it was again, that arrogant, condescending tone that implied his surprise at her fortitude. She'd had enough of him, his unreadable dark eyes and cool, mocking voice. She had made a mistake, but she would not make it again. She turned on her heel and headed for the door.

Eric was there before she could open it. She gaped up at

him, surprised. For his placid, calculating ways she hadn't expected him to be so swift or so large. His size always came as a shock. One wouldn't expect a mathematical robot to tower over six feet with a powerful, intimidating presence. She looked at his pressed shirt, amazed at how it clung to his wide frame. While not overly muscular he was anything but scrawny and moved with a sinewy, catlike grace. He leaned against the door looking mildly regretful. "I apologize."

She shrugged, mollified by his apology. "What for? It was my mistake for coming here."

"No, it wasn't. It was bold of you to come and I haven't made it easy for you." He stared at the floor. A tiny frown formed between his brows. He was trying to be gentle. She found the attempt endearing. The soft whisper of a Jamaican lilt accented his words. "Talking about money is always difficult. It represents much more than our financial status, it reflects our habits, our personalities, our fears, our goals . . . It takes a lot for my clients to be as honest with their spending as you have been. People feel more comfortable talking about their sex lives than debt."

"Would you rather talk about sex?"

His eyes captured hers. "Are you offering?"

Her heart began beating an odd rhythm. He was quick for a nerd. "No."

He pushed himself from the door and took her arm. The grip was loose, but she knew escape was impossible. "Sit down. Let's see if we can come to an agreement."

She sat and stared at him in wonder.

"What?"

She rested back, impressed. "You're very good."

He frowned.

"I was prepared to storm out of here, bristling with indignation, and somehow you convinced me to stay. Amazing."

"It's because you realized—"

"No, you're just very good at reading people." She tilted her head to the side, trying to read his dark eyes. "Pull any cons when you were a kid?"

He gathered some receipts. "About the spa—"

She sighed. Why did she even try with him? "I like to go," she cut in. "I like being pampered." She looked at him. The poor man was trying, but he still didn't understand. Before he could argue she said, "Isn't there something you like to do? Something that relaxes you and makes you feel so good that you couldn't imagine life without it because it's part of who you are?"

His dark eyes flickered with genuine amusement. He nodded. "Good argument. Okay, once a month."

She let out a breath in relief, then frowned. What hobby couldn't he do without? She couldn't even picture him with a hobby. What would he find entertaining? *Business Week*, CNN, a scientific calculator? She knew it was no use asking him. What he didn't offer he wasn't willing to share.

He wrote something down on a Post-it. "Let's see what other adjustments we can make to this budget."

The phone rang. Eric glanced at his watch and answered. "Henson."

Adriana watched in amazement as his face softened. Not into a smile, but something close. She knew at once who was on the line: her best friend, Cassie.

"Thank you. Yes, I got them." He nodded and glanced at her. "Yes, she's still here. Would you like to speak with her?" He nodded again, then handed her the phone. "It's Cassie."

"Hi," she said as she watched Eric discreetly leave the room. Once he closed the door she asked, "How do you do it?"

"Do what?"

"Get the statue to soften."

Cassie sighed. "How many times do I have to tell you that your opinion of him is all wrong?"

"Until I believe you, I suppose."

"He is one of the sweetest, most gentle men I know."

She reached for the Post-it note he had written, but his handwriting was too illegible to read. "You're just biased because he's your brother-in-law."

"If he's so horrible, why did you ask for his help?"

She pushed the pad away and toyed with his pens. "I didn't ask for his help, he offered and I accepted out of desperation. Believe it or not I would really like to get my finances in order."

"Well, Eric can definitely help you do that."

"So why did you call?"

Cassie hesitated. "He didn't tell you?"

Adriana straightened. "Tell me what?"

"I guess it's his business. He doesn't have to share if he doesn't want to."

"Share what?"

Cassie sounded annoyed with herself. "Never mind, it's not important. I'll call you tomorrow to find out how everything went."

"Cassie, are you going to let me die of curiosity?"

"You won't die. Besides, you'll figure it out soon enough."

"Cassie—" she began, but her friend hung up.

Eric came into the room soon after. Adriana briefly wondered if he had been listening by the door, but quickly remembered he wasn't the type.

She watched him walk to his desk, her mind brimming with curiosity. What was Cassie talking about? What wouldn't he want to share? There didn't seem to be anything different about him. "Are you feeling well?" she asked.

"I'm fine, thank you." It was a nice polite response that offered her nothing. She pushed her curiosity aside. Why Cassie had called him was none of her business. It was probably something dull anyway.

After another half hour of debating, they finally settled on a budget.

"It's going to be difficult at first," Eric said as he handed her the final plan. "But the end reward will be worth it."

Adriana folded it and pushed it in her handbag. She hated it already. She felt as if the fun and freedom that were an integral part of her life had been taken from her. Eric wouldn't understand. He wasn't the sort to indulge in simple pleasures. Unfortunately, he was to be her saving grace. She had come to him for help and she would do what was necessary to get out of debt. It was difficult to fly on the wings of fun and freedom with debt chained to your ankle.

"Thank you." Her voice came out muffled.

"Sometimes the word *budget* scares people."

Or makes them ill.

"Try to think of it as a spending plan. It is not set in stone and is flexible for your needs. It's just a guide to help you achieve your goals. For example, money for your parents' care."

She had given him that financial goal just to impress him. She knew that if she had told him the truth he would have scoffed at her.

He rested his arms on the desk and clasped his hands. "However, we still have one thing we need to address."

*Oh no.* "What?"

"I want you to write down everything you spend for an entire week."

"No."

"Either that or only use a checkbook."

No plastic? "Why?"

"Because even though you gave me a detailed list of your expenditures I know that money is running through your fingers. We need to know where it is going."

She swung her foot, annoyed. "You don't need to put it like that."

"I find honesty very helpful. You're an impulsive shop-per."

"I like to shop. I wouldn't call it impulsive."

"You could make shopping an Olympic sport."

She grinned bitterly. "Thank you. I always go for the gold."

"You would have a lot more in your savings or more to invest if you would use only cash in stores and wait a day before you purchase something that catches your eye. Es-pecially sales."

Time out. He'd overstepped the line. Sales restrictions were off-limits. "You've helped me with my budget. I don't need any more of your advice."

"If you buy it on sale and you don't need it, it's not a bar-gain."

She tapped her foot and blinked.

He leaned forward, his voice lowering to a coaxing tone. It had an unsettling effect on her. Only he could get excited over money like this. "Give me just a thousand to invest for you and I can show you how it will grow."

She grabbed her bag, ready to leave. "No, thank you."

"Listen, Adriana—"

He stopped when the door flew open. A young woman dressed in a dark winter coat with hood and blue knit scarf entered the room.

"Are you Eric Henson?" she asked in a high New York accent.

His reply was flat. "As it says on the door. Why?"

"Because I've got a message for you." She turned to Adriana. "Don't worry, this won't take long." She pulled a tape player from inside her jacket and place it on the desk. Suddenly, raw, raunchy strip music filled the tense air. A light flashed; the woman's clothes dropped to the floor. She began dancing in front of Eric, dressed in a red, sequined bikini that glittered and shook with each gyrating motion.

Adriana managed to pull her eyes away from the display

to stare at Eric. Her mood went from shock to amusement to dismay. The poor woman was wasting her time. Eric wasn't even impressed. He rested his elbow on the desk and watched her with the same interest as a scientist observing a research participant. Even as the woman wrapped a scarf around his neck and let her blond hair cascade around him he didn't even flinch.

Her dismay turned to disgust. Wouldn't he even smile at her? Cool the stone in his gaze or soften that hard mask on his face? He was completely inhuman. Any healthy male would at least show some interest in a beautiful woman dancing solely for his pleasure. Even she, as a female, was amazed by the woman's shapely form and awe-inspiring moves. She glanced at his granite profile, waiting for even the barest of emotions.

She was about to look away when he turned and winked at her. Adriana gasped, the soft sound drowned out by the music. In that one fleeting moment she knew that he was very male and could be very dangerous to any woman who underestimated him.

She pushed the thought away. Her flare for the dramatic was taking over her common sense. Eric was a dull, ordinary intellectual. She must have imagined his wink. She stared at him again. His impassive mask was firmly in place, confirming her suspicions.

When the music stopped, the woman kissed him, leaving bright red lipstick on his cheek. "Happy birthday," she whispered. She gathered her clothes and left.

Adriana stared at the closed door, then said, "I guess we all splurge once in a while."

He wiped his cheek and frowned at the red smudge on his fingers. "I didn't pay for that." He grabbed some tissues and wiped his hand. "My sister will, however."

"Jackie sent her?" She turned to him and laughed.

He began to clear up his desk.

"So today's your birthday, huh? How old are you?" She

held up a hand. "No, wait, let me guess. You're not a day over a hundred and four."

He disappeared behind the desk. "A hundred and ten." He peeked at her, his serious eyes teasing. "The lack of gray tends to fool people."

Adriana smiled. The guy was definitely quick. She wanted to see how he would respond to a few more harmless taunts. "So how are you going to celebrate? Dust off a couple of dictionaries, read the financial expenses of a nineteenth-century household, or organize the soup cans in your kitchen?"

She heard the sound of the bottom drawer closing. He straightened. "Actually, at the stroke of midnight I'm going to ask Lynda to marry me."

She dropped her handbag, spilling the contents on the floor. She didn't notice. "I don't believe you."

He came from behind the desk and began gathering her things. "It's true."

She kneeled down and stared at him as if he were a Gucci bag marked 85 percent off. Why was it just when she thought she had him figured out, he did or said something unexpected? "But that's so romantic."

He picked up her bag and flashed a wicked grin. "Surprised? Don't be. The reason is practical." He handed her the bag. "It has to do with midnight and when I was born."

She clutched the bag, her eyes never leaving his face. "What about it?"

He hesitated.

She shook his shoulder. "Go on. Tell me."

"I was born dead. They were going to bury me when my grandmother took me and dunked me in ice water. I let out a yell just as the clock struck midnight. So I always thought midnight on my birthday meant a special change." He suddenly frowned and bit his lip, annoyed with himself. "But don't let me bore you."

She grabbed his arm before he could stand. "You're not

boring me. It's absolutely fascinating and wonderful." The story was as beautiful and haunting as a myth. "I just never thought of you as romantic. It's hard to believe you're going to ask her to marry you tonight."

He looked down at her hand clutching his arm. She pulled away. "I told you I'm not being romantic. However, I do have proof that I'm going to ask her." He reached inside his jacket pocket, pulled out a small velvet box, and held it out to her. "Go ahead and open it."

She looked worried. "Shouldn't she be the first one to open this?"

"No. Why?"

"Something to do with luck."

"Don't worry." He sensed her hesitation and opened the box for her.

Adriana gazed at the diamond ring, gleaming against the blue interior of the box. "It's lovely."

He studied her face. "You're not impressed."

"Of course I'm impressed."

A smile played with the corners of his mouth. "It's a little too traditional for you, isn't it? You'd probably prefer a large sapphire surrounded by rubies or the brilliant blue of a lapis lazuli."

She offered him a small grin. "Perhaps. It is beautiful though."

Her ex-husband had given her one similar to it when he had proposed to her in their sophomore year of college. It was on the banks of the tidal basin. She had been so ready then to be what her family wanted. Stable, educated, married. Laurence had been the perfect traditional man for a young woman searching to be the perfect daughter. He knew the right things to say, do, be, and he eventually suffocated her. She remembered the sense of relief when she had taken his simple diamond ring off her finger. "My ex-husband gave me one like it."

He met her eyes. "I didn't know you had an ex-husband."

And a daughter, but he didn't need to know about that. "Yes, one of my many accomplishments in life."

"You didn't mention alimony."

"I'm not getting alimony. I don't deserve it. Poor Laurence."

"Why do you say that?"

"I tried, but I didn't make a very good wife. Actually, he was a lot like you, except . . ." She trailed off.

"Except what?"

Except that he was what he seemed while Eric, though undoubtedly cerebral, seemed to have a wild energy that he kept well tamed. Any time she was near him she felt somehow threatened by his controlled isolation in a purely feminine way. It both annoyed and intrigued her.

"Except that you're both different," she finished lamely. "So how are you going to do it?"

"Do what?"

"Ask her to marry you?"

He scratched his head, confused. "Isn't there just one way? The man holds out the ring and says, 'I think we should get married.'"

Her shoulders fell. She grasped the front of her shirt in dismay. "Oh no! Don't say it like that!"

"Why not?"

"Because that's horrible and boring. You must put some heart into it. Some passion. Say something like . . ." She glanced at the ceiling and tapped her cheek. She suddenly held out both hands. "I've got it! Listen to this." She lowered her voice and rested a hand on her chest. "Lynda, you make me the happiest man in the world. I can't imagine going on without you." She grabbed his hands and pulled them to her. "I love you with all my heart, mind, and soul. Will you be my wife?"

She looked at him. He looked at her. They burst into laughter.

He had a wonderful laugh. It wasn't awkward or forced, but deep and true, waking something within her.

"All right," she said, sobering. "I admit it's a little corny."

"Corny? I couldn't even imagine those words coming out of my mouth."

"But you have to have some romance, some words that will have lasting sentimental value."

"I think 'will you marry me?' is sentimental enough."

She nodded. "Simple and straight to the point. You can't go wrong there. Just don't get down on one knee. Or if you do, make sure to watch where you land. Laurence kneeled on a rock and it led to a few awkward moments. He ended up limping."

"I'll remember that," he said sincerely.

She wished his eyes weren't so intense. At such a close range their cool glow sent a shot of heat up her spine. How could something so cold be beautiful at the same time? To combat her wayward thoughts she began to ramble. "Are you going to pick her up at her apartment? Does she know you're coming? I hope so. There is nothing worse than having an unexpected visitor arrive when you have a mud mask hardening on your face."

"You speak from experience?"

"I was scarred for life when my high school crush arrived on my doorstep to sell Girl Scout cookies for his little sister. I think I bought thirty dollars' worth just to make up for my face."

"Caramel Delites and Thin Mints."

"How did you guess?"

"You seem the type."

"And I bet you're a shortbread cookies man."

He raised a brow, but said nothing.

She snapped the velvet box closed. For some reason the sight of the ring was beginning to annoy her. "So are you madly in love?" He looked blank. She had used the wrong words. Eric, she reminded herself. She was speaking to Eric. "I mean do you feel a warm affection for her?"

His brows furrowed. "I wouldn't be asking her to marry me if I didn't."

She smoothed out her skirt. "You'll fall violently in love eventually. It will come as a shock to you one day. You'll look up from your *Newsweek* and see her pounding away at the calculator with a pencil stuck lovingly behind her ear."

His eyes twinkled. "Are you an expert?"

"On love? No."

"How do you think it will be for you?"

She glanced out the window, no longer able to meet his gaze. "It will fall on me like a load of bricks."

"Sounds painful."

"Love is painful."

"Did you love your ex-husband?"

"I tried." She looked at him, ashamed. "Sounds awful, doesn't it, not loving your husband?"

He shrugged. "It sounds honest."

She abruptly stood. Kneeling on the floor together had become too intimate. He stared at her with such intensity her knees began to shake. She knew she was going to start babbling again. She went to his desk and stared at the picture there—a portrait of Lynda.

She had a pleasant, intelligent face. The type of face that spoke of belonging to the right family, going to the right schools, and having the right career. She imagined that's how she had looked on Laurence's desk in the early days.

"You don't like her," he said from behind.

She didn't move. If she stepped back she would touch him and her traitorous body would probably enjoy it. "I'm happy she's marrying you."

"Ouch. That means you really don't like her."

She turned and looked at him, her face earnest. "No, don't misunderstand me. I mean she's perfect for you.

She'll make you happy. You deserve to be happy. Everyone does and when you're lucky enough to find the right match you should snatch them up right away and not worry about what other people think or say." Oh God, she was babbling! "She seems like a nice woman, educated, attractive, almost perfect." Why wouldn't he move back? "You'll be happy. Very happy." Somehow she wanted that. He was obnoxious at times, but basically good, and deserved to be happy in the way she had never been able to make Laurence.

"I'm not looking for perfect, just suitable."

"Do you think she loves you? It is possible," she snapped at his disbelief. True, it was hard to imagine anyone falling in *love* with Eric. Although his brother and sister cared for him and Cassie adored him, Eric seemed like a hard man to love. She changed the subject, not wanting to hear the answer. "So does Drake know about your plans?"

Eric sat behind his desk, his mind still on the possibility that Lynda could love him. He would hate that kind of burden. Drake, his older brother, loved his wife. It was his marriage to Cassie and the birth of his niece that prompted him to seriously start thinking of having a family of his own. He had vaguely thought about it but the urgency rose when he had held Ericka in his arms.

He wanted someone with a similar temperament and a background far better than his own. Lynda fit those requirements. He had known her only six months but was sure they could build a promising future. He didn't expect to experience the great love his brother had for Cassie—he wasn't the type. He would settle for contented. That was a reasonable goal. Lynda was stable, sensible, and would fall into his life with ease.

"No," he said. "You're the only one who knows."

She sat on the edge of the desk. "I'm flattered."

He knew she wasn't mocking him and offered her a brief smile. "Now let's get back to your concerns about the budget."

She waved the topic away with an impatient gesture. "Forget about the budget. What do you plan to do before midnight? It's your birthday. You must celebrate."

"It's no big deal."

"You're one hundred and ten, of course it's a big deal." She swung her foot for a moment, then leaped off the desk. "I've got an idea. A few friends and I are seeing a play, then going for drinks afterward. Why don't you join us?"

"What's the title of the play?"

"Does it matter?"

"I want to know if it's something I've read about. Reviews can be a helpful gauge for how good or bad the show is."

"It's all a matter of opinion. Besides, this is a small play that hasn't received much notice yet. It's called *The Ink Spot*."

He adjusted his glasses. "Is that what we'll be staring at all evening?"

"Eric, it's your birthday." She leaned toward him. "I can't have you sitting around until midnight strikes. Think of me as your fairy godmother."

He reached out and touched one of her earrings, his knuckles brushing against her cheek. "Are these your magic wands?"

"Yes," she managed, surprised by the gesture. "Your life will soon change and you have to celebrate."

"We don't even know if she'll say yes."

"She'll say yes."

"How do you know?"

"I'm optimistic."

He rested his chin in his hand and stared out at the October sky. The wind had settled. Distant buildings lit the coming darkness.

She came behind the desk and grabbed his hands. "You're coming with me. I can't leave you on a cold autumn

day with nothing but your thoughts to keep you company."
She handed him a tissue.

He frowned at it. "What's this for?"

"You still have lipstick on your cheek."

He let her drag him to the door. He sensed his life would change tonight, but not in the way he expected.

# Two

"It was brilliant!" Tanya Leonard exclaimed, fanning her hand through the air. Eric ducked to avoid decapitation. The gold bracelets on her pale wrist clinked, as her brown eyes reflected her enthusiasm. "Did you ever see something so expertly executed?" The arm flew through the air again. Eric covered his beer before the loose sleeve of her peasant blouse dipped in it. "The lighting, the stage, the set."

He lifted his drink and frowned. What set? He only remembered seeing a chair and a large black rug—the ink spot presumably.

He was an unsuspecting traveler lost in the hummingbird's forest. Her friends hummed and buzzed like a various assortment of birds. Adriana somehow stood out from the dramatic crowd. She complemented them in dress, but in manner appeared much more subdued. Though even a hyperactive child would look sedate against this colorful group. Oddly enough, he liked seeing her there. He liked watching her in her domain. She truly enjoyed life and it was a rare person who did so. He had stared at her face through most of the play, watching an exhausting amount of emotions cross it: joy, despair, awe.

"The best part of course was Emily." The intimate group turned and applauded the small redhead dressed completely in black, sitting in the corner with a large piña colada. The star of the performance.

She blushed prettily, her freckles becoming more prominent. "You guys are biased. Your love for me clouds your view. We need a real opinion from an outsider." Her hazel eyes focused on Eric. "What did you think of the play?"

Eric stopped with his drink to his lips. An icy sense of dread descended.

"He doesn't know much about theater," he heard Adriana say.

"That doesn't mean he doesn't have an opinion. So give us your review."

He placed his drink on the table. "I was amazed by the sheer desolation the ink spot represented."

"Desolation?" Nanj said, toying with the leather choker around her neck, its metal spikes similar to a dog collar. Her dark eye shadow contrasted with the light gray of her eyes; her spiky black hair made her olive skin look chalky. She looked as fierce as a Doberman. "The ink spot represents the inevitability of death."

"But he does have a point," Emily allowed, her wide gaze still focused on him. "He comes from a different angle we haven't noticed before."

"Marvelous insight," muttered Hinton, an older man with shaggy white hair. A tie-dyed T-shirt covered his broad frame and three gold hoop earrings glinted in one ear.

"Hmm," Randan said, unconvinced, his attractive brown face fixed in a permanent scowl that promised a menace he sometimes delivered. He had his arm draped behind Tanya.

"And what did you think of my quill pen?" Emily asked.

Eric took another swallow. Hell, that's what she was? He glanced at Adriana, then said, "I haven't seen an inanimate object played so well since the brooms in *Fantasia*."

Emily smiled; Adriana pinched him.

Hinton rested two large forearms on the table, a small tattoo of a heart peeked from under his sleeve. He pinned

Eric with a skeptical green glare. "So how do you keep Uncle Sam rich?"

"He means what do you do for a living," Adriana said.

"I figured that." He met Hinton's gaze. "I'm a financial adviser."

Hinton grunted. "Hmm, a numbers man." He measured him in one quick assessment. "Yes, you look it."

Tanya shivered. "I hate numbers. I don't know a mutual fund from a CD. All that stuff is foreign to me."

"I say live now," piped Adriana. "Why save for a day that may never come?"

"Why not save for a day that may?" Eric countered.

Adriana softly groaned, sensing one of his lectures.

Eric ignored her. "Everyone should take control of their finances. You work hard for your money, why shouldn't you own it? Hinton, I notice you have a Harley outside. Would you calmly let anyone take it from you?"

He narrowed his eyes. "No."

Eric turned to Tanya. "I notice your purse is handmade. Would you give it away?"

She held the strap tighter as if he had just threatened to take it. "No, it means a lot to me."

He sat back and addressed the group. "Well, money should be treated in the same manner. It's something valuable. Society tries to trick you by giving you plastic— instant gratification with delayed consequences. Society says owning things is the ladder to achieving status, but that's the poor man's way of thinking." He pulled out his wallet and held out a ten-dollar bill. "This is not just a piece of paper. It's a ticket to dreams. You should gather some of these and invest them. Put your money somewhere and watch it gain interest."

Adriana turned to the group expecting to see them near catatonic, but their eyes were open, interested, and completely fixed on Eric.

"But understanding money is so confusing," Emily said. "I'm not smart enough to figure it all out."

Eric put his wallet away, his tone encouraging. "If I can understand it, so can you."

Hinton let a deep belly laugh escape him. "You're comparing yourself to us? Young man, I never even graduated from high school. How many degrees you got?"

Eric shrugged. "We all have the same capacity to learn. I'm not smart." The group stared at him in disbelief; he continued undaunted. "I just learned how the system worked in a way that made sense to me. Tanya, you said you didn't understand CDs."

She nodded.

He took out a pen and grabbed a napkin. "Let me explain them to you."

And he did. Soon the table discussion was more suited to an economics class than a club. They discussed the economics of population growth and the risks of 401Ks, Social Security, and retirement. Adriana watched amazed as Hinton argued his ideas, Tanya offered suggestions, and Nanj riddled Eric with questions—some laughable. However, he never laughed. Adriana waited for him to lean back in his chair, lift one of his sardonic brows, and use his condescending tone. He never did.

If she hadn't known him, she would have thought he was a different man. Yet he was still Eric, a man who had an uncanny knack to be interested in dull subjects. She rested her chin in her hand and watched him. Never had she seen him so animated. It wasn't noticeable to those who didn't know him, since his gestures were conservative, but his dark eyes glittered and his granite jaw hovered near a smile.

"So," Hinton said to Adriana once the discussion died down, "why didn't you mention this friend of yours to us?"

Eric lifted his drink and slanted her a quick glance. "Adriana doesn't consider me a friend."

"It's his birthday," she said.

The group turned to him and burst into congratulations. Emily began to sing "Happy Birthday" and Nanj bought him another drink.

"How young are you?" Tanya asked.

"One hundred and ten."

She gazed at him with teasing eyes. "You don't look a day over thirty-seven."

He raised his glass. "Thank you."

"He's going to propose to his girlfriend tonight," Adriana added. She instantly regretted the remark when he looked at her. It wasn't a look of censure or betrayal, just one of deep speculation. She didn't know why she had shared something that he hadn't even told his brother, but she felt restless, giddy, and was in the mood to celebrate.

The shouts of congratulations began again.

"Well, you're just full of surprises," Randan drawled.

Hinton frowned. "You're too young for prison. Live together."

"Don't listen to him, I think that's wonderful." Tanya stood and grabbed his hand. "Since you're soon to be shackled, why don't you enjoy this time and dance with me?"

Eric glanced toward the dance floor. He watched the array of lights strike the floor and felt the hard drumbeat pound in his chest. Perhaps it was just panic. He wasn't sure. "I don't know how to dance to this."

She grinned impishly. "I'll show you."

Eric looked at Adriana with resignation as Tanya led him away. Nanj and Emily followed.

Hinton grabbed Adriana's wrist before she could rise. "Oh, let them alone."

She watched Eric disappear into the crowd. "But he can't dance."

"Has that ever stopped Tanya before?"

"He's going to get married."

"She knows that." His eyes were assessing. "Why does it bother you?"

She turned to him and lifted her shoulders in a casual shrug, feeling agitated. "It doesn't bother me. Why would you think that?"

"By the way you look at him."

"Don't confuse that with any amount of interest in him as a man. I'm just trying to figure him out."

"Be careful, Adriana, curiosity can get you in trouble."

As if she needed to be told. "Don't worry."

Randan rested his other arm on the length of the seat and frowned toward the dance floor. "I don't know why you brought that old man here in the first place."

"Shut up," Hinton said. "You're just jealous that he's dancing with Tanya."

Adriana picked up her drink. "Besides, it's his birthday."

Randan tugged on his ear, his scowl increasing. "So? Doesn't he have his own friends?"

"I doubt it." She touched his sleeve, not wanting Eric to get on his bad side. He could make an unpleasant adversary. "Listen, Ran, he's not into the club scene and he can't dance. I bet you that Tanya brings him back in ten minutes."

Ten minutes turned into a half hour. Adriana watched the dance floor and waited but the small group didn't return. She grabbed her bag and stood. "I'm going to the bar."

Hinton sent her a knowing smile. "That's code for 'I'm going to look for him.'"

She shook her head, making light of the teasing, not wanting to admit to herself or him how close to the truth he was. She could not find Eric on the dance floor. Between the booming music and strobe lights it was like trying to find a needle during an air raid. She rejected a man's offer to dance and went to the bar, a sense of irritation making her throat dry. It wasn't fair for Tanya to monopolize Eric when she had been the one to bring him.

Not that she really missed him, she reminded herself as she ordered a Sprite. It was just that all this was a new experience for him and she wanted to be the one to guide him through it.

"It's my lucky day," a smug male voice said next to her. "A beautiful woman all alone at the bar. Let me buy you a drink."

"I'm fine, thank you."

Her cold tone did not deter him. He slid onto the seat next to her. She was hit by a wave of musky cologne. "The name's Brandon." He adjusted the lapel of his tailored dress shirt in an effort to impress her. The only thing Adriana noticed was the faded band impression on his ring finger. "If you're not going to let me buy you a drink, at least let me dance with you. The music's too good to pass up."

She drummed her nails against the glass. Even if he had not been married he wasn't her type. Tall, brown, and slick with enough oil to fill a bucket. "I'm really not in the mood." She hoped he'd get the hint and leave. She sighed when he called the bartender over and ordered a Sex on the Beach. He looked at her and winked. She groaned. She should have known better than to go to the bar alone.

"So what's your name, sugar?"

"Gloria."

"Then Gloria hallelujah I met you tonight." He smiled, impressed by his own wit. "Destiny must be working overtime." He narrowed his eyes. "Have we met before?"

"Yes."

"I thought so."

She sipped her drink, watching the condensation drops fall to the counter. "I believe I flushed you this morning."

She glanced up. His Adam's apple bobbed up and down in rage. He opened his mouth to reply, but was unable to meet the challenge in her eyes. He took his drink and left.

"Good aim," an amused male voice said behind her. "It's always successful to hit below the belt."

Adriana turned to see Eric taking the seat Brandon had abandoned. At least he looked like Eric. She wasn't sure. The voice was right, as were the glasses, but the top three buttons of his shirt were undone and he had a calm, magnetic presence about him that was dangerously enticing in this high-energy atmosphere. She looked at her drink and pushed it away. It was nonalcoholic, but one could never be too careful. Something was affecting her judgment.

"What happened to your tie?" she asked him.

He grabbed his shirt and glanced down where his tie should have been. He scowled. "I don't know." He turned to the dance floor. "I think some woman is currently using it as a lasso."

"Are you having a great time?"

He took the beer he had ordered and took a healthy swallow. "No, but I'm not having an awful time either," he quickly added to soothe the fleeting expression of dismay on her face.

"Tanya kept you busy."

"A simple warning would have helped."

She grinned wickedly. "I think experience is the best way to learn."

He spun the light brown liquid and watched it swirl. "What was I supposed to learn?"

"Always stick by your escort."

His eyes met hers. "Were you feeling neglected?"

An outraged scream interrupted her reply.

"You low-down dirty bastard!" a female voice shouted behind him. She would have been pretty if her features hadn't been marred by a rage that flushed her honey skin and loosened the coifed hair that now fell about her face. "How could you do this to me? You said you were working late." She sent Adriana a venomous look. "Now I see what you are working on, you pathetic imbecile. All those nights

I worried about you and here you are. I thought you loved me."

Eric turned around. The woman grabbed his beer and threw it in his face. "You jerk, I hate you."

Adriana jumped to her feet, outraged. "What is going on here?"

The woman pointed an accusatory finger at Eric, who was calmly wiping his face with a napkin. "This man is my husband!"

Adriana looked at Eric, then the woman. "That's impossible."

"I don't know what he told you, but he belongs to me. So you can get to walking, sister."

"I think you've made a mistake."

She poked Adriana in the chest with one manicured nail. "Do you think I'm stupid?" She punctuated each word with a poke. "I know what my husband looks like." She glared at Eric; her mouth fell open. "Oh my God. You're not Brandon."

His voice was quiet. "No."

She took a step back, shame turning her skin a new shade. "I could have sworn I saw him sitting here a few moments ago."

"You did," Adriana said. "But he left."

"I am so sorry," she stammered. "But from behind you look just like Brandon."

Eric tossed his napkin on the counter. "I wish I could take that as a compliment."

She dabbed at his wet shirt. "Please forgive me, but I was furious when I found lipstick on his striped Chap shirt—the one I bought for him on his birthday while we were dating. It was also the same one he wore on our second anniversary. I couldn't contain myself. I—" She suddenly balled up the wet napkin, then leaned across the counter to squint at a man with his arm around a woman. She looked poised for flight, rage heightening her color again. "Wait a minute," she said in a low voice. "I think I see the bastard now." She raced around the bar and created the same beer-tossing scene. This time hitting her intended target.

Adriana turned to Eric. "Sorry about that."

"Why?" He cleaned his glasses. "Did you make her do that?"

"No. But you've lost your tie and now you have beer running down the side of your face."

He wiped his cheek. "I thought I got it all."

She grabbed a napkin and wiped the side of his face. "Let me order you another drink."

"I'm all right."

Without the shield of his glasses his eyes seemed somehow magnified in their dark remoteness—she wondered what a woman would have to do to bring warmth to such an expression. She turned away. At least he was handling the situation calmly. Keith would have been furious to be so humiliated, but what else had she expected? Eric handled the club like he would any situation—practical and controlled. He probably would have done better to stay at his office or go home. It was obvious he didn't fit in here. She saw Tanya and Randan dancing intimately and Nanj hitting a guy with a string using the same skill of a dominatrix with a whip.

Adriana said, "I think I see your tie."

He shoved his glasses back on and watched Nanj wrap his tie around a man's wrist. "I'm glad to know it's in safe hands."

For the first time she felt a little embarrassed by her friends' behavior, though nothing in Eric's tone hinted of him judging them. She turned from the dance floor and stared at the array of glasses and liquor behind the bar. "Thanks for being nice to my friends."

"You sound surprised."

"I wasn't sure you would be."

He kept his gaze on the dance floor. "Why wouldn't I be nice to them?"

She ran her finger around the rim of the glass. "They're not exactly intellectual."

"I gathered that from the discussion on who's the father of Olive Oil's son, Sweet Pea, and whether or not Bugs Bunny is a cross-dresser. I still say it was merely for survival."

"You're not half bad when you're not annoying."

"I'm getting older, I must be mellowing."

"Too bad." She gave a world-weary sigh.

"Why?"

"This Christmas you won't be visited by three spirits."

He snapped his fingers in regret. "Damn, and I was looking forward to visitors this year."

They both fell quiet.

She spun in her chair and studied his profile. She shouldn't have dragged him here. He was a casualty of her impulsiveness. "I didn't mean for you to have a bad time."

"You worry too much." He took her hand with a boldness that surprised her, yet his grip felt strangely natural—almost familiar. "Let me show you what a poor dancer I am."

She allowed him to lead her onto the dance floor, her head telling her this was a bad idea, her heart cheering her on. Dancing with Eric would probably be an awkward experience, but at least he was trying. He could have stayed in the corner somewhere and cast his sardonic gaze over the crowd.

She was right. Dancing with Eric did turn out to be an experience, but it was anything but awkward. She expected him to be a stiff, gawky dancer. But the moment he pulled her into his arms, she felt as if she had been tricked into the arms of a charmer. One who knew he was underestimated and used that knowledge to his best abilities. He had the artless grace of a con man.

The music wasn't even conducive to the slow way they were moving, yet it worked. Their bodies swayed in rhythm to the electric beat. He wasn't an excellent dancer with lithe, graceful moves. He had bold, slow, powerful movements—unsettling and much too mesmerizing for a mathematical nerd.

"Why the frown?" Eric asked, his breath warm against her forehead. It was a surprise she could hear him in the crush of bodies and loud music, but she suddenly felt as if she could distinguish his voice anywhere.

"You smell like beer," she said, unable to share the truth.

"I knew I should have worn a different cologne."

She wrinkled her nose in teasing displeasure. "Yes." The truth was he smelled good—beer, sweat, and male. The type of guy that usually had her hopping on the back of his motorcycle or into his truck ready for a night of mischief. She glanced up at him, reminding herself that he was no bad boy. He was conservative, practical, and dull. Although he felt anything but dull right now. He felt good. He felt exciting and hummed with an inner energy she wished to unleash. She bit her lip, but she wouldn't be the one to do it. That was Lynda's job. The woman he planned to marry and settle down with.

Eric gave her a gentle squeeze. "Stop frowning. I realize I'm not the greatest dancer, but you're beginning to make me feel self-conscious."

"Oh, it's not you, I was just . . . thinking about the plan."

He nodded. "Interesting. I was just thinking about piercing my nose."

She stared at him; he grinned. A wicked grin that forced her heart to beat faster.

"See? I can lie too. Don't worry, you don't have to explain the frown as long as I know it's not my fault."

But it was his fault. Everything she was feeling was his fault. And it was all wrong. It was the night's fault and the Rusty Nail she'd consumed earlier. It was him telling her about his proposal and how he had been born dead and was saved. In one horrible, unbelievable night Eric had changed. He'd become interesting, intriguing, exciting, and totally off-limits.

"Is Lynda a good dancer?" she asked, trying to keep his near fiancée on the forefront of her mind.

"Good enough for me. Is Keith?"

"Keith's not my boyfriend."

"That wasn't my question."

"Yes. He's wonderful." That was partially true. He was wonderful to watch. However, slow-dancing with him was unpleasant because he was too busy showing off to pay attention to her.

An errant elbow jabbed into her ribs, replacing her thoughts with pain. The perpetrator threw a casual "I'm sorry" over her shoulder. Adriana softly swore, glaring at the back of the woman's head.

"Are you okay?" Eric asked, rubbing the side of her ribs. His large hands were indecently warm against her, seeping through her cotton shirt, creating a soothing motion that was distracting.

"It's nothing." She laughed, hoping he would stop. Fortunately, he did and she could feel her pulse returning to its normal rhythm.

She had to relax. It was just one night. Why not enjoy herself? Tomorrow she would look at him and see ordinary Eric again. Ordinary, *engaged* Eric. She smiled. Her smile faltered when her eyes fell on a passionate couple in one of the darkened corners. She felt like shouting, "Get a room." Suddenly, her throat tightened as a horrible realization emerged. She recognized the female half of the pair: Lynda. Dressed in a skintight black leather skirt and a red cashmere blouse so small it could be used as a napkin.

Adriana's eyes jerked to the man who, as she expected, was Eric's complete opposite. The type of bad boy she would have dated in her wilder days—coarse and dramatic. As large as a linebacker and just as fierce. A cross tattoo decorated his arm, the rest of him was possessively wrapped around his companion.

"What's wrong?" Eric asked, when she stopped dancing.

She returned her gaze to his face and tried to keep her tone light. "Nothing. I just don't feel like dancing anymore. I really need to sit down."

Something in her face must have confirmed this. He immediately secured a seat for her at the bar. He requested a glass of water.

She rubbed her palms against her skirt. "Does—"

"Drink first," he ordered. "Questions later."

In no mood to argue with him, she finished the water, then held her head in her hands. This was awful. Should she tell him what she saw? Perhaps she had made a mistake. She hoped she had. What could she say? Guess what, Eric? I saw your girlfriend making out with another man. Happy friggin' birthday?

Instead she asked, "Does Lynda have sisters?" A twin perhaps?

If he found the question strange, he didn't show it. "No." His intense eyes searched her face. "Are you feeling better?"

No, she felt sick. She managed a shaky smile. "A little, thanks."

"It's probably all the heat, noise, and lights. Let me take you home."

Great idea. She would get him out of here. Her smile became more genuine. It froze on her face when she saw Lynda and her companion sit down behind Eric. Could the night get any worse? He'd lost his tie, had beer tossed in his face, and now the woman he was going to ask to marry him was sitting on another man's lap. Adriana thought of the diamond ring in Eric's pocket. It was like him—traditional, honest, and true. As dull as he was, people like him were rare and special. She couldn't let his birthday be shattered by the fickleness of her sex. She had to do something.

She grabbed his arm before he could turn. "Wait."

He looked concerned. "What?"

"Umm . . ."

"Don't worry, I can drive."

She seized his arm again, hoping he couldn't feel the blood rushing through her veins. Praying that her voice wouldn't belie her panic. "It's not that. I—"

A rich feminine voice floated toward them. "Oh, Bruce, I have never had so much fun. I don't know what I'll do without you."

Eric's brows furrowed as he tried to place the voice. He began to look behind him.

"Don't," Adriana said.

He stared at her, waiting. "Don't what?"

She searched her thoughts for something to say, but could only think of two words. "Happy birthday." She threw her arms around his neck and kissed him. She realized her mistake once their lips touched. She had expected his lips to be cold and hard like his eyes, but the warm, sweet taste of his mouth melted her defenses. She forgot about why she had started the kiss and let herself indulge in this pleasing development. She felt no fear, no censure. Though his body remained ridged, his mouth was supple.

She drank in the essence of him with feminine enjoyment, softly moaning as she curved into him, inviting more exploration. She had expected him to be an easy, practiced kisser. However, his mouth showed a mastery based on instinctive male possession.

He abruptly pulled away. She took a step back. They stared at each other and softly swore.

She covered her mouth as if she'd been caught enjoying a forbidden dessert.

He swore again. "You didn't expect that, did you?" he

asked. His voice had deepened to a level that seemed to vibrate within her.

She could only shake her head. She dared not speak. If she moved, he might notice that she was trembling.

He held his forehead, ashamed. "I'm sorry. I got carried away. Perhaps I *have* had too much to drink . . ." His words trailed off as his gaze fixed on something in the distance.

# Three

Lynda and Bruce stood near the far wall under a flashing neon sign. Eric looked at Adriana, then back at them, a rueful smile briefly touching his mouth. His eyes fell to the counter and he nodded as if finally solving a puzzle. He glanced up and watched the pair. "Happy birthday to me," he murmured.

She stared at him, trying to witness any amount of distress in his cool brown eyes. She wanted to see his jaw tense, his fist clench, to capture some sign that displayed even a small amount of anger. He only looked pensive. "Well?" she demanded.

He returned his gaze to her. "Well what?"

"Aren't you angry?" She pounded the counter. "Aren't you going to do something?"

"Like what?"

"Go up to her and tell her that you're finished. That she's not worthy of you. That she can have her plaything and get out of your life."

He studied the couple, his face unreadable, his eyes dispassionate. The pair had returned to their previous activity—necking.

She tapped her foot impatiently against the rung on the stool. "What are you thinking?" She was ready to see action, but all he did was stand there.

"I'm thinking you're very sweet."

She opened her mouth, then closed it, unsure of how to respond.

His voice was soft, his eyes sharp. "You knew she was here and tried to redirect my attention."

"Well, I—"

He placed a finger against her lips. "If I hadn't been drinking, I would have figured it out sooner." He let his hand fall. "I'm not exactly your type. That should have been my first sign." He grinned, a little sheepish. "Thanks."

She wanted to tell him that only the first part of the kiss had been meant as a diversion, but the next had been pure animal lust. All she said was, "You're welcome."

He tapped his fingers against the inside pocket that held the ring. He wasn't looking anywhere in particular, his mind lost in thought.

Adriana sighed. "You're not still going to ask her to marry you, are you?"

"You can't expect people to be completely faithful nowadays," he said absently.

"Of course you can. Cassie and Drake are faithful to each other."

"They're a rarity."

"I can't believe you're excusing her."

He rubbed his chin. "I'm trying to be practical."

"This is one of those rare moments when even men like you are allowed to be impractical. Even irrational. How about what you feel?" She tapped her chest. "You must feel something. If I saw my man with another woman, I'd probably do worse than toss a drink in his face."

He adjusted his glasses. "What would you do?"

"Throw a chair, break a favorite statue, tear up pictures."

"You think that would solve the problem?"

"It would make me feel better."

He nodded thoughtfully. "The fact is, I'm here with you."

"But we're not doing that." She jerked her finger at the pair.

"We were close."

Her mouth fell open. "I can't believe you're defending her."

"I'm not. I'm trying to see this from all angles."

They watched Lynda dip her hands in Bruce's jeans. Adriana tilted her head. "I think there's just one."

He slanted her a cool glance.

"Do you want Nanj to do anything to her?"

He blinked, then looked at her and smiled. An evil smile she wouldn't have expected from him. One that had her nerves trembling. "No, thanks." He handed her some bills. "Get yourself something else. I'll be right back."

She glanced at Lynda; then her eyes focused on Bruce. He was a lot bulkier than Eric and might not welcome his interruption. She grabbed his arm. "Perhaps this isn't a good idea."

"What's not?"

"You approaching her."

He looked annoyed. "You thought it was a good idea a few moments ago."

"I changed my mind."

"Why?"

"Tomorrow you could tell her what you saw tonight."

His voice deepened. "Why did you change your mind?"

She licked her lips. She knew a man's pride was an important yet fragile thing. She had to be gentle. "Now don't take this the wrong way."

He waited.

"Her companion doesn't look too bright."

He folded his arms. "What does that have to do with anything?"

"It's been my experience that those types tend to use their brawn more than their brains."

He still looked blank.

She glanced upward. "Eric, the guy's got muscles the size of your head."

His eyes grew dark and distant. "You think he'll hurt me?"

She'd made him angry, but she didn't care if it would save him a couple of broken ribs. Cassie would kill her if he ended up in intensive care. "He's a lot stronger than you. You spend your day behind a desk, that's no match to a man who probably does manual labor. It's just not safe."

He let his arms fall. "I should be insulted, but the fact that you care is touching."

"You can tease me all you like. Actually you can do it on the way home."

"Adriana—"

"I don't want you to confront them."

"I've listened to your suggestion and weighed the risks. Thank you. Stay here."

"But he'll hurt you. I don't even have your insurance number."

His voice was soft; she had reached his limit. "As I've said, I hear you but I've weighed the options and think it's worth the risk. Let's consider this a closed deal."

She did, but she watched him with such worried eyes that he softened.

"I used to get picked on in high school. It stopped in my senior year." His tone implied a painful and just end to his tormentors. Adriana felt a little relieved. Who was she to fuss over him like a mother hen? Why did she care if he got a few bruises? He was a grown man and must have had a few encounters before.

"I'll be right back." He offered her a quick smile—the rose a knight would give before charging into battle. He slid off the stool and made his way to the unsuspecting couple like a stalking panther.

Adriana saw the shock on Lynda's face when she recognized Eric. She knew she would have had the same expression if she'd met Eric in a place like this. Lynda began to gesticulate wildly, probably offering an explanation. Her companion only listened, studying Eric in a manner of disgust, confident in his power to defend and win his woman. He made the thought known to Lynda, who shook her head and continued explaining. Eric listened, then took out the velvet box and opened it. Lynda promptly burst into tears. He snapped the box closed and said a few words. Bruce shoved him against the wall. Adriana didn't realize she had left her seat until she was halfway across the room and could hear Bruce's voice.

"You'd better apologize."

"I rarely say things I need to apologize for," Eric said.

The man lifted his fist and aimed it at Eric's head. Everyone was certain it would make contact until Eric moved at the last minute. The man's fist hit the cement wall. A sickening crack followed as fingers broke. Bruce cradled his hand and fell to the floor in agony.

"Take some deep breaths," Eric suggested.

Bruce couldn't reply, pain making speech impossible. Neither woman stared at the fallen giant. Their eyes were fixated on Eric in amazement.

"Eric—" Lynda began, her voice full of awe.

"Good-bye." His voice was polite but final.

She seized his arm. "You have to let me explain."

"I've already listened to your explanation."

"I just wanted to have a little fun. You're always so controlled and serious. If I'd known you had this side to you I—"

"You'd what? Decide to be faithful? You were right the first time. I'm serious and controlled. No fun at all. Goodbye."

He turned and halted when he saw Adriana standing there. His expression didn't change. His eyes were like ice though his voice was cordial. "Came to my rescue, huh? You don't care very much about a man's ego, do you?" He took her arm. "Come on." He stopped and stared at her. "Why are you shaking like that?"

"I—"

Lynda pushed Adriana aside. "So who's she?" she demanded, jerking her head in Adriana's direction.

"Adriana Travers, a client," he said.

Adriana studied Lynda and immediately knew Eric had been saved from a terrible mistake. Though her small stature made her look petite and helpless, there was a selfish sense of entitlement that hadn't shown in her picture. She was privileged, knew it, and expected to be treated accordingly. No doubt she would have used Eric's lower background as a weapon throughout their marriage.

Lynda rested her hands on her hips. "If she's a client, what are you two doing here?"

Eric looked bored. "Celebrating my birthday."

"Am I supposed to believe that?"

"No, I suppose not." He began to walk away with Adriana in tow.

Lynda followed. "I think you came here to have a little fun of your own. Eric, you and I could have fun together and you wouldn't even have to pay me for it."

He spun around so fast, Lynda let out a little cry of alarm. She withered under his biting glare. "Pay you for what?"

She swallowed.

"I am a man with integrity and expect the same from my wife. You've displayed not only that you're deceitful, but that your loyalty is as stable as the stock market. If I had been wounded fighting for your honor, would you have left me as you have him?" He nodded toward Bruce, who continued to cradle his hand. His voice lowered. "And for your information I've spent a lot less on Adriana's company than yours. Class is priceless."

His words brought fire to her eyes. "So you're trying to marry yourself out of the gutter?"

Adriana took a step forward. "What did you say?"

"You heard me."

Eric yanked her in the other direction. "Come on."

She resisted, her eyes on Lynda. "You're going to regret tonight for a long time. And I'm here to make sure you regret what you just said."

Eric grabbed her around the waist and pulled her back. "Bye, Lynda."

Lynda pointed a finger at him. "Nobody insults me, then dumps me, Eric. You'll regret it."

He turned and began to walk away.

Bruce stumbled up to them. "You're going to pay for this." His threat fell flat against Eric's hard glare. He let Adriana go, his eyes welcomed action.

Lynda took Bruce's arm and led him away; Adriana took Eric's arm and did the same.

"I can't believe you let her say that about your background," she said.

"I don't believe in hitting women."

She glanced over her shoulder. "Nanj will hit her for you."

"Why are you still shaking?" he asked.

"It's nothing," she said quickly. It was a mixture of rage and fear, but she couldn't tell him that in case she annoyed him by doubting his skills. Men had such gentle egos.

"Nothing, huh?" He held her hand, feeling the trembling she tried to control. He said nothing. He found a vacant table littered with an ashtray overflowing with cigarette butts, numerous glasses, and crumpled napkins. They sat.

"I'm not angry," he said. "Don't look surprised, your eyes are as clear as crystal." He looked at the dance floor. "No, I'm not angry, few people can make me." He turned to her. "So tell me why you're shaking." He still held her hand, but it was his eyes that kept her still.

"I think the thought of fighting is fine, but I hate actually seeing it," she admitted in a shameful rush. "I know it's silly. Growing up with two older brothers, I saw them fight all the time. They felt they had to be my protectors. Even some of the guys I dated got into fights, but I would be affected for days seeing blood spout from someone's nose or hear breaking bones." A shiver raced up her back as the sound of Bruce's hand breaking echoed in her ears.

Eric gently rubbed his thumb over her knuckles, which soon calmed her. "I didn't mean for that to happen, but better his hand than my face." He tapped his glasses. "Do you know how much these cost?"

She smiled. Only he would mention something like that. She didn't know whether it was his dry humor or caressing hand, but her tremors immediately stopped. She felt her body relax. She rested her arms on the table and leaned forward.

"So what did you say that made that guy so angry?"

He let her hand go and fell back in his chair, his voice marked with regret. "I'm afraid I let my temper get the best of me." He paused. "If you don't like fighting, why were you going to hit Lynda?"

"I wasn't going to hit her."

"You looked ready to do something."

"Character assassination. I'm not proud of it, but I'm pretty good. I wanted to strip her bare till she was raw and vulnerable, and then I would go in for the kill."

He shivered in mock fear. "You're scaring me."

"I'm sorry."

"No, I like it. It's nice to know women can be as vicious as men."

"Why did you show Lynda the ring?"

"I asked her to marry me."

She straightened. "What?"

"I said I'd do it and I did."

"What did she say?"

He let his shoulders rise and fall. "She didn't say anything, she just burst into tears."

"I don't understand you." She shook her head. "Why would you still ask her to marry you?"

"Pride. Let her know what she lost."

"I think you just sealed your fate. She was impressed by your display."

He frowned, pushing the assortment of glasses to the middle of the table.

"Your macho routine," she explained. "It gives most women a thrill to be fought over."

"I didn't fight over her."

"It's the general principle of being wanted by two men."

He rested his arms on the table. "I made it clear I no longer wanted her."

"She wants you back."

"Me and my gutter self?" He stood. "It's merely a pride issue. She'll get over it."

She stood as well. "Where are you going?"

"I'm leaving."

"The exit is in the other direction."

"I want to say good-bye to your friends first."

"You don't have to . . ."

He was already heading toward them.

She overheard the group convincing him to stay longer, but he declined. "Thank you for an enjoyable evening. If you have any questions about what we discussed, feel free to call me. Adriana has my number."

"Hey, good luck on your proposal tonight," Emily said.

Adriana inwardly winced, but his expression didn't give anything away. "Thank you," he said with sincerity. He waved, then disappeared into the crowd.


It took her ten minutes to find him. He was three blocks away from the club, blending easily with the night stream of people bundled in coats as they rushed past. Lights from restaurant windows spilled out onto the sidewalk.

"Are you following me?" he asked as she came up be-hind him.

"Yes, I'm your ride, remember?" she said, a little breath-less. The man could move fast.

"I can take the metro."

"I'll save you money."

He stopped. "It's dangerous for a woman to know a man's weakness. Where's the car?"

They were silent as she merged her blue Acura into traf-fic. Eric was a companionable passenger. Unlike most men, he didn't criticize her driving or silently hold on to the door handle like a martyr. He just stared out at the city lost in thought—it made her crazy.

She gripped the steering wheel. "Will you please tell me how you do it?"

"Do what?"

"How you can be so calm. I ruined your birthday, in case you've forgotten. If you had gone home or stayed at work as you had planned, you wouldn't have lost your tie, had beer thrown in your face, seen your girlfriend with another man, or nearly got your teeth knocked in."

He moved the heat vent. "You forgot the play."

"What?"

"You forgot that if I hadn't come with you, I wouldn't have had to suffer through the play."

"It wasn't that bad."

He slanted her a glance, doubtful.

She waved her hand, searching for words. "It was on a different level."

"Between infantile and psychotic." He moved another vent. "What are you trying to do, cook us?"

"It's cold outside. I like heat."

"It's not that cold. You act as if this were the Arctic."

She reached for the knob. "Fine. I'll turn it down. I forgot ice melts."

He ignored the barb.

"You didn't understand the play," she said.

"Don't get on that artistic pedestal with me, I had to nudge you awake twice."

"I wasn't falling asleep, I was being quiet."

"That's what you call snoring?"

"I didn't snore."

He thought for a moment. "No, you didn't. That was the guy next to me. If he had leaned any further I would have had to introduce myself."

Adriana grimaced, remembering what had started the argument—his ruined birthday. "I'm sorry." He didn't seem to hear her, his eyes fixated on the lights of the city. She suddenly felt a cold rush of air ambush the car.

"Why is your window down?" she demanded, raising it.

"It's still hot."

"Then take off your jacket."

"I'll have to take off a lot more than that to get cool in here," he mumbled, slipping out of his black blazer.

"Suit yourself." She turned up the heat.

"All right then." He began to unbutton his shirt. "But be warned, many a female has fainted at the sight of my chest."

She laughed.

He sent her a mocking look. "I'm not sure I appreciate your laughter."

"A man's ego is always a source of entertainment." She glanced at his unbuttoned shirt and saw a flash of bare brown skin that wasn't supposed to be there. "Where's your vest?"

"I don't wear one."

In one moment he would be sitting half naked in her

car with his bare chest exposed for review. She turned down the heat. It was definitely hot in here.

"Ahh, much better." He rested his head back and gazed out the window. His shirt was still unbuttoned, but she didn't feel like mentioning it.

"You worry me," she said.

He turned to her, amused. "Afraid I might be suicidal?"

"You never know. The quiet ones are tricky to figure out."

"Don't worry. Suicide is a bit too dramatic for me. I'd rather die of old age."

"You don't have to pretend it doesn't hurt."

"I've made mistakes before," he admitted easily. "She's not the first."

"You asked another woman to marry you?"

He lifted his head and began buttoning his shirt.

"How many?"

He ran a hand down his shirt, straightening his buttons. "Two."

She looked at him, surprised. "Lynda was the *third* woman you've asked to marry you?"

"Yes. Rochelle originally said yes, but returned the ring after a week."

"Why?"

"Said that I scared her because I had no warmth." He straightened his collar. "No typical human emotions." He shrugged. "Whatever that means."

"Oh." She could understand how Rochelle came to that conclusion. Being his wife would seem a lonely place. Yet there was something below the surface that urged her to dig deeper.

"Why are you stopping?" he asked as she parked the car.

"I want to pick something up. I've ruined your birthday and want to make it up to you."

"You're getting me a cake."

She unlatched her seat belt. "Do you like chocolate or vanilla?"

"Surprise me."

She grinned. "Okay, but before I do, tell me about the first one."

He rested his arm on the windowsill. "The first one what?"

"The first woman you asked to marry you." She knew she was being bold, asking him about his past, but she was curious.

Eric reached for his tie, then remembered he didn't have it. He sighed. The first time he had proposed seemed eons ago. A time when he'd been young and reckless, slowly making his place in the world and leaving his background in the dust. He'd become overconfident when Catherine came into his life. She was smart, attractive, came from a good home and family, and was everything he wasn't.

"I met her at one of the young black entrepreneur meetings Drake liked to drag me to. I was sort of floundering careerwise." He looked at her. "You like to be bored to death, don't you?"

"Just finish the story. So you were floundering. I would never have imagined that. You seem the type to always have known what you wanted."

There was a brief flicker of his wicked grin. "I knew what I wanted. I was just having a hard time getting there." He unlatched his seat belt and shifted in the seat, resting his back on the door. "Catherine was doing a presentation on investment. I'd never seen a young woman with such poise and elegance. I . . . I was impressed, I was in awe. I wanted her and sought out to get her. She said yes the first time I asked her out. I was almost grateful. I wasn't used to . . . We dated for a few months and then at midnight on my twenty-second birthday I asked her to marry me."

"And?" she demanded when he fell silent.

He glanced down, pulling off invisible lint from his

trousers. "And she raised her lovely eyes and said in a voice filled with pity: 'If you were Drake, I would say yes.'" He shook his head to mask the pain that still lingered. "It was only then that I realized she'd been dating me so that Drake would notice her. I had been so blind. I hadn't even seen the signs. It wouldn't have been the first time." He glanced up. Adriana's eyes swam with tears.

"Hey, hey, don't do that," he pleaded, opening her glove compartment to find tissues.

Her voice was a whisper. "That is a horrible story." She stared at the tissues Eric shoved in her hands. He could be nonchalant about it, but she felt for the young man who had proposed a lifetime of loyalty to a woman who had used him to get his brother. She knew it hurt because she had seen it happen before.

She crumbled the tissues in her hand. "I hate people like that," she said, anger overcoming tears. "Users. They did the same thing to Cassie, you know. Guys would go out with her just so that they could flirt with me." She could still remember her friend's face—the hurt when she found out and the shame that followed. Cassie never believed her, but Adriana knew her pain intimately. Knew what rejection felt like. How it felt to be judged and discarded. Hearing Eric's story had reminded her of that.

Adriana had been thrilled when Drake met Cassie. He took no notice of Adriana—his eyes and heart meant only for Cassie. Of course convincing Cassie of that had been hard at first. Her full-figured friend couldn't believe an attractive man like Drake would truly like her. Fortunately, Drake proved very persuasive.

"It's the past," Eric said.

"But aren't you angry? You and I have nothing in common, but I'd never say I wished you were Drake."

He raised a brow. "Even if you thought it? Come clean, Adriana. Haven't there been times when you wondered how Drake and I could be related?"

That was true. They didn't even look like brothers.
Drake was darker, broader, with an all-consuming quality
that attracted most women. He had the masculine virility
of a superhero. Eric didn't even look like a sidekick; he
was the sidekick's accountant. She watched a knowing
smile appear on his face as if he'd read her thoughts. She
quickly pushed away the comparison.

"Okay, so most people are impressed by Drake," she
conceded. "But perhaps you think about the differences
just as much as they do." His arrogant smile fell. "Perhaps
sometimes you even accentuate it. Perhaps you didn't think
you could compete so you completely dropped out of the
game, becoming everything Drake wasn't."

He shifted in his seat again, staring out the windshield.
"No." His voice was cool.

She could feel him pulling inside himself, creating a distance between them. She wouldn't allow that. She had seen
a part of Eric tonight that she knew could be just as tempting and dangerous as any man. She refused to let him
isolate himself in his iron wall of control.

"I admit that you're here with me because I couldn't
imagine you celebrating your birthday alone. I usually
spend my time with guys who think inflation has something to do with balloons and could crack nuts with their
toes, but I learned a few things about you that I can't figure out. I don't know where you learned it, but you're like
a con artist." She warmed to her subject as the overhead
lamplight reflected on his glasses, shielding his eyes.
"You're not what you seem. You show the world that you're
serious and dull, but the truth is, if you wanted to, you
could be as sexy as Drake and as dangerous as a viper. And
that is definitely irresistible."

He turned to her, his eyes remote. She stared back, her
heart pounding so hard she feared it was audible.

Where the hell had that come from? Definitely irresistible? She felt like crawling out the door. What had

possessed her to say such things? Okay, his two ruined birthdays and disastrous proposals had made her feel sorry for him. And tonight he had seemed anything but dull and ordinary. That didn't mean he could compete with Drake or any other man. She had made an idiot of herself. Yet she couldn't look away. His eyes held her with invisible chains while the air around them crackled with untamed energy.

She finally turned and opened the door, eager to escape. To her relief he let her go. He didn't grab her hand or say anything that would make the moment even more unbearable.

She began to relax when she was assaulted by the bright lights of the bakery. She pitied him, that was all. It didn't go deeper than that. It wasn't anything dangerous like desire. She suddenly felt better, that rationale made all her crazy feelings make sense.

She saw a simple chocolate swirl cheesecake. It looked serious next to the flowery vanilla cakes plush with icing. It was perfect. She felt calm as she returned to the car. Eric would probably forget all that she had said anyway.

She slid into her seat. She stopped when she realized he was gone.

# Four

He probably thought she was crazy, or worse—drunk. He had most likely left disgusted by her display of emotions. She had made him uncomfortable by talking about his relationship with his brother. Or maybe he was just sick of her company, sick of the disaster she had made of his birthday. She didn't really like him, she told herself, only pitied him, but his absence made her feel miserable.

The passenger door suddenly opened. "Relax, Adriana," Eric said in a quiet voice. "I just went to get a few things." He put the bag between his feet.

She was so happy to see him, her voice was harsh. "I could have left you."

"You didn't see my note?" He lifted a tissue off the dashboard. A brief message was scribbled across it.

"What does it say? Your handwriting is terrible."

"It says 'Won't be long.'" He pushed the note into his shirt pocket. "Do you often jump to conclusions?"

She put on her seat belt.

Eric settled back as she started the car. He could see how her brothers were protective of her. Her eyes were dangerous—open, honest, amazingly innocent in a way that made a man feel protective. When he'd seen her panicked gaze, thinking he had left her, he had the crazy urge to comfort and hold her. He smiled to himself. Tonight he planned to do much more.

* * *

The hummingbird was nervous, but Eric was too pre-occupied to soothe her. Her apartment held his attention. It was as he had expected, yet it wasn't. There were no bold contrasting colors—like a purple couch with brown pillows. No unidentifiable works of art spread about the place. Instead it was peaceful. Cream walls and drapery with brown accents gave the room a natural earthy feel. Her couch was full of various-sized pillows and covered with a velvet slipcover. An antique phone sat on a side table. Iron candle holders hung on the walls. A large glass coffee table faced the couch with a polished black base.

Everything in the apartment invited a guest to use the five senses. The scent of vanilla drifted from the candles, soft chenille pillows tempted you to touch them, and a bowl of tangelos and oranges on the dining table tantalized you to indulge.

"I suppose you would like to have a tour to see how recklessly I spend money," she said as she placed the cake in the kitchen.

He nodded.

They went into the bedroom. A place of exotic, tranquil beauty. An ornate embroidered duvet with a patchwork border of sari and jacquard covered the bed in the colors olive and raisin. Numerous pillows sat on top in burgundy and gold satin with beaded lace. A sheer red suspended canopy hung above, trimmed with red crystals. Moroccan-style lanterns hung near the windows close to a beaded ottoman.

Wordlessly, he entered the bathroom. A sanctuary. A handwoven woolen rug lay on the floor, while white billowy curtains moved gently from the air of the vent. Ivory candles of various shapes and sizes sat around the claw-footed tub. He noticed the detail of the feet.

She followed his gaze. "It was hell getting that thing in here, but I had to have it."

He nodded and returned to her bedroom. He went to touch the bed and saw a flash of orange and white leap from the windowsill and dash out the door.

"I think I just saw Elena."

"Elissa," she corrected, leaning against the bed. "She's shy of people, so don't take it personally."

"I didn't plan to."

She glanced around the bedroom, then looked at him. "Disappointed?"

He toyed with the crystals on the canopy. "By what?"

"Most men expect women like me to have leopard-print silk sheets, half-naked statues, and lingerie hanging behind the door."

He surveyed the room. No, it wasn't what he had expected, but he certainly wasn't disappointed. "I like it."

"I should be worried." She left the room.

Eric dropped his bag and followed. She showed him her office and guest room, then went to her balcony.

"My view isn't exquisite, but nice enough." She went to the railing and turned. Eric rested against the door frame. "Come on. Don't you want to see the view?" She looked out on her quiet street. A dog ambled past under a street lamp, becoming visible, then invisible.

"Not particularly," he said.

She looked at him, surprised. "Why not?"

His eyes slid away a moment, then returned to hers. "I'm not a fan of heights."

An involuntary smile formed on her lips. "You don't like heights?"

"No."

"I never would have guessed. I thought the only thing you would be afraid of is a tax audit or a late bill payment."

He pushed up his glasses.

She clicked her tongue in a tsk, tsk manner. "What a

shame. You'll be missing a great view." She sat on the railing and swung her legs.

Eric watched her, his face impassive.

"You know, there is really nothing to be afraid of as long as you're careful. As you can see I'm perfectly safe." She swung one leg over the side and folded her arms. "See?" His expression didn't change. She almost wondered if he was lying about his fear and had another reason for not wanting to come out. She decided to tease him further. "Right now I am perfectly balanced. It's like sitting on a tree branch. However, if I did this . . ." She swung both legs over the side and looked down at the distant street. "Then I'd—"

She never finished the statement or demonstration. Eric grabbed her in one swoop and swung her over his shoulder.

For a moment, Adriana was too stunned to reply. She stared upside down at his back.

Eric said, "That's enough."

Her tongue returned to her. "Put me down!"

"Did you have fun doing that?" He closed the balcony door. "Are you finished teasing me?"

"I wasn't teasing you. Okay, maybe a little." She let out a little laugh. "I couldn't help myself."

"I see."

"Eric, put me down."

"Why?" He playfully patted her on the bottom. "I think I like this side of you."

She hit him in the back with her fists. "Put me down!"

He shook his head. "Not yet. It's my turn to tease."

"This isn't teasing, this is manhandling."

"Am I hurting you?"

"That's not the point. If you don't put me down I'll scream."

He adjusted her weight. "You're not the screaming type."

"I might pass out."

"I doubt that."

"Eric!" She punched him in the back again. "Yes, you are hurting me."

He paused. "I'll let you go, if you promise me something."

"What?"

"Never do that stupid stunt again for me or anyone else. No matter how tempting."

She closed her eyes and sighed, exasperated. He *would* give her a lecture. "Eric, I wasn't going to fall."

"Promise."

"I'm a grown woman, I can—"

"Promise."

She groaned. "All right, I promise."

He unceremoniously dropped her on the couch. She glared up at him. "That was completely unnecessary."

"As was your childish display on the railing." He threw up his hands. "If I had said I hated fire, would you have run naked through it?"

She fixed her skirt. "You are too serious, I was just having fun."

"That could have gotten you killed."

She was silent. He usually wasn't so adamant. She bit her lip. "I really had you worried."

He rested his hands on his hips.

She jumped to her feet. "I'm not stupid. It's not even that high." She grabbed his hand and walked toward the balcony. "Come on." She jerked to a halt when he didn't move.

"No."

"I thought you were a logical man."

"I am very logical," he said softly.

"Then you can't let an illogical fear rule you. Think of all the sunsets you'll miss. You'll never have the feeling of being close to the stars."

"You can describe it for me."

She tugged on his arm; he remained still. She glared at him; he smiled.

She gave up. "You're as stubborn as a donkey."

"I return the compliment."

"Let's eat." She went to the kitchen and retrieved two plates.

He followed behind her. "Do you need any help?"

"No," she snapped.

"Mad at me?"

She fetched a large knife from the knife block and flashed it at him. "Do you want a big or little slice?"

He took a step back. "I'll be in the living room."

She cut two healthy slices of the cheesecake and set the knife down. Oddly she wasn't upset, though she had every right to be. She'd never been swung over a man's shoulder like a sack of potatoes. She had never entertained any Jane and Tarzan fantasies before. Tonight she might start. It was an exciting and terrifying experience to be at a man's mercy. Eric's mercy.

That was strange. She frowned. The fact that he had acted so uncharacteristically was unsettling. She had expected a few stern warnings, even a lecture about the hazards of heights, but he had grabbed her like some Neanderthal.

In that moment she felt his strength, his impatience, and it called to every feminine impulse in her. It dared her to respond in kind. She glanced toward the living room. She was making more out of it than necessary. He was just scared. Imagine a man being afraid of heights. How pathetic. No lunches on the balcony, no hotels peering over the ocean, mountain cliff hideaways. Like him everything would have to be grounded, solid, and safe. Dull, dull, dull.

Adriana returned to the living room with the two slices of cheesecake in hand. She saw Eric sitting on the couch with Elissa purring loudly behind his head. She didn't

comment on Elissa's unusual behavior. She figured her cat
had mistaken him for a statue.

She handed him a piece of cake and sat down on a chair.
She threw her legs over the arm with her back facing him.
It was best to just get the night over with. Why had she invited him home with her anyway? What would they talk
about? They had nothing in common. She felt sorry for
him, but she couldn't blame the other women for refusing
his practical proposals. He had no passion, no fire, no mys-
tique. He was serious. Ready to delve into a lecture on the
smallest issue. She should have left him in his office. She
took an angry bite of her cake. At least it tasted good and
made up for an evening that was quickly growing worse
and worse.

"Adriana . . ."

She glanced at him over her shoulder. He hadn't touched
his cake. She nodded to his plate. "Don't you like it?"

"I'm sure I will."

"You won't know until you taste it. Go on," she urged
when he hesitated.

He took a bite and swallowed. "It's delicious."

"I chose it. What did you expect?" She turned away
again and sighed. She couldn't wait to take him home.

She heard him lay the plate on the coffee table and lean
forward. "Adriana, I am sorry I hurt you." He cleared his
throat. "I guess for a moment I overreacted."

She swirled her head around and stared at him. His eyes
were solemn. He thought he had hurt her. Oh God, why did
he have to ruin everything by being so nice?

"You idiot." She swung her legs to the floor. "You didn't
hurt me."

His jaw tensed. "But you said—"

"I only said that so you'd put me down."

He rested back, doubtful. "Are you sure?"

"Eric, I know you could never hurt anyone." She briefly
thought of Bruce's broken hand and the ease in which he

had swung her over his shoulder. He was a big guy. Apparently, he could do damage if he wanted to, but probably wouldn't. "At least not on purpose," she added. "Now stop being so serious and finish your cake or you *will* hurt my feelings."

He stared at it. "It's very good."

"The best compliment is an empty plate."

He finished the slice and got another. She glanced up at the clock and grimaced. "Oh no, I've missed the first part." She turned on the TV. A man working on an injured dog appeared on the screen.

Eric settled in his seat. "Oh, hell. I forgot that was on."

She turned to him amazed. "You watch *Pentel MD?*"

"Every week."

"I don't believe you."

"That's not the first time." He stretched out his legs. "I like the mysteries. I bet you watch it for Michael Pentel." The hunky veterinarian.

"What woman wouldn't?" She held a hand to her chest and breathed deeply. "The man is gorgeous."

"Right. I, of course, only watch to see the animals solve crimes."

"And watch his assistant."

He shook his head. "She doesn't interest me. I like a woman with more substance."

"She doesn't need any more substance," she said, extending her hands in front of her chest.

He slanted her a glance. "Careful, your envy is showing."

She made a face and turned to the screen. It was a classic episode. One they had both seen before. They spent a majority of the time arguing why certain clues were overlooked. Why the killer could have been anyone and who really solved the crime.

"I say it was the dog," Eric said.

Adriana widened her eyes. "The dog?" she asked, outraged that her beloved doctor should be upstaged by a little beagle.

"He found the weapon. He alerted them to the arsonist."

"You just don't like Pentel."

"What's not to like? He's *gorgeous*." He drew out the last word in mockery.

"Be quiet. He's not only attractive, he's kind and good with animals."

Eric lifted Elissa from behind him and placed her on his lap. "Have you noticed what good taste she has?"

She frowned at her contented companion. "It is amazing. She hisses at Keith."

He kissed the top of the cat's head. "I think I like her even more."

"What do you have against Keith?"

"His lack of skill for one. His freeloading for another."

She rested her chin in her hand. "He does not freeload."

"You pay him for work he doesn't produce."

"Of course he produces."

He surveyed the room. "Why isn't any of his work around here?"

"Because I am wearing his art. I don't need to hang it."

He lowered his voice to a conspiratorial tone. "Admit it, it's ugly."

"It is not ugly. It's expressive, abstract."

He put Elissa on the floor. The cat protested, then accepted the dismissal. She ran under the couch. Eric stood and grabbed a pen and paper. He scribbled something, then put it in her lap.

"Behold, destiny!" It was a line surrounded by squiggles.

She crumpled it up. "Don't be ridiculous."

"You don't like my work?" He fell on the couch and covered his eyes. "I am mortally wounded. I don't know if I'll ever work again."

She threw the crumpled ball of paper at him. "You're being obnoxious."

He looked up. "I'm trying to make a point."

"Keith's work is a legitimate art form whether you believe it or not." She pushed him back into the couch before he could stand. "Stay there."

She went to her shelf and grabbed a large book. She sat down next to him and opened it to a picture by Jackson Pollock.

Eric leaned across her. She swallowed, ignoring his warmth and the scent of beer mingling with his own. "My painting from the second grade. How did it get in here?"

She nudged him. "It's called action painting. But Keith loves expressionism like Vassily Kandinsky." She turned the page. When he said nothing, she turned the page again. She did so until he stopped her.

"That's not too bad," he said, admiring the work of Piet Mondrian. "I see how someone could see a four-sided polygon as art."

"The other works are just as exquisite. Especially if you see them in a museum."

He turned the page, narrowing his eyes at another Mondrian. "Fine, it's a date."

She hesitated, unsure whether he was joking or not. He wasn't. She could now understand why Elissa had been purring. He had a heat that exuded from his large frame, conflicting with his cold eyes. She abruptly shut the book, ready to take him home, eager to escape the wicked temptation he presented. Puzzles always had a special allure.

Eric covered her hand before she could move. "Don't run."

"I wasn't going to," she lied.

"Good."

She bit her lower lip. "Eric?"

"Hmm?"

He hadn't moved, but somehow he felt closer, his

warmth creeping up the length of her skin, igniting all her
senses. She couldn't voice what she was feeling, yet she
couldn't move away.

She turned to him. He slowly smiled, without wicked-
ness, but as a sensual invitation. It was his secret weapon,
transforming his face. He rubbed her chin with gentleness.
"Don't look so worried."

He was going to kiss her; she wasn't going to stop him.
She felt the heat come closer, then imprint itself on her
mouth. How could a man who appeared so distant, so
aloof, bring forth such fire? Show such strength, but handle her so gently? Her mind told her to resist him, to stop
him, but her heart didn't allow her to break the delicious
hold. She let him explore the inside of her mouth, taking
in the potent taste of him. He was wild, but safe. The rivers
of contrast were staggering and brought forth an almost in-
satiable desire.

She felt his hand slip under her shirt. Impatient fingers
wrestled with the back of her bra.

"Eric," she breathed against his cheek.

He grunted in response.

"The fastener's in the front."

"Figures." He quickly unclasped the bra and kissed the
tip of her nipple through her shirt. Adriana wasn't in the
mood for such foreplay, she wanted to be naked. To feel his
hot flesh against hers, the softness of his lips creating a wet
path up her chest. She tried to unbutton his shirt, her fingers shaking so much she couldn't manage the simple task.
Growing impatient, she ripped it apart. Buttons bounced
onto the carpet and zipped across the room.

Eric swore.

"Don't worry, I'll buy you another one," she said.

"That's not—"

She captured his mouth, not interested in words. Tonight
her curiosity would be satisfied. Who was Eric? What was
he about? Even if it was the worst sex in the world, she had

to know the answer. She let her hands trail the expanse of his chest, awed by the muscles there. Hills and valleys of masculine strength painted the color of earth. Hot like clay from a furnace.

"When did you find the time to develop these?" she asked.

He didn't answer. He grabbed the rest of his cheesecake and smeared it on her chest in a smooth S pattern. "Now I'm an artist with you as my canvas."

Adriana arched toward him as he licked his way around her chest. A moan escaped her as she felt the creamy, cool sensation of cheesecake followed by a hot tongue. She could feel herself melting beneath him.

He lifted his head. His dark eyes smoldering yet distant. "Let's go."

"Go?" Her voice cracked. "You want to stop now?"

"No. I want to go to the bedroom."

"Why?" Her hand snaked to the bulge in his pants. "We're doing perfectly fine here."

"I'm a traditionalist."

She narrowed her eyes. "Don't give me that. You just ate cheesecake off my chest."

"I want you," he whispered against her mouth.

She let her tongue touch his lower lip. "You have me."

"In the bedroom."

She sighed, feeling the moment passing. Did she really want to find out what a bore he was? He was a great kisser, but perhaps this wasn't such a good idea. "Eric—"

"Save my name for the bedroom." He lifted her and headed there. He tossed her on the bed.

She glared at him. She gathered her shirt together. "I should be outraged."

He undid his trousers. "Whatever makes you happy."

"You are—"

"Compliments later." He took off his trousers and threw

them aside. They landed on the door handle. "Don't worry, you'll enjoy this."

She swallowed, gripping her shirt, unsure of his mood. "But I—"

He climbed onto the bed. "We'll do it on the couch another time, but tonight I have my supplies here." He reached over her into his bag and pulled out a box of condoms.

Her mouth fell open. "*That's* what you bought?"

He loosened her grip on the shirt. "No need to thank me."

"I won't. I feel insulted."

He pushed the shirt from her shoulders and kissed the bare skin. "You find it insulting to be wanted by a man?"

She closed her eyes as he inched up her neck. "You think I'm easy, don't you?"

"Let me show you what I think of you." He tugged off her skirt, her panties followed. He held them up and frowned. "Now *this* is a disappointment."

"They're comfortable."

He raised a brow. "Fruit of the Loom?"

"They could be support hose."

He tossed it aside. "Oh well."

He rolled on a condom. Soon his body covered hers with passion she'd never known. A fervor of desire that brought forth a sheen of sweat, his body eloquent and well versed in lovemaking. She was speechless, her body an eager, selfish form taking all that he offered. Outside, morning pushed in, slowly gathering the shadows. Their bodies moved to the rhythm of one.

In the distance the clock struck twelve.


Her body hummed like a finely tuned violin. It had never hummed before with such awe-inspiring pleasure, such self-satisfaction. Her lover had been a masterful player and the music created would echo through many memories. She glanced at the sleeping form beside her. She lifted the covers to stare at his naked body. She was used to guys with piercings and tattoos—his skin was as smooth and clean as the day he was born. Not even a nick from a knife or a bruise from a childhood accident marred the surface.

She dropped the blanket and looked at his face. Not even sleep could alter his grave expression. Short black lashes jutted from his lids and nothing could soften that granite jaw. She traced it with her fingers. It felt like stone, the metal edge of a robot. Suddenly, reality crashed into her fantasy.

She had slept with Eric! Dull, ordinary, irritating Eric! Eric Henson—her best friend's brother-in-law. Her financial adviser. Had she been drunk? She delicately shook her head, but there was no sign of a hangover. She had been perfectly sober the entire night. Every thought and emotion came rushing back. How had she let this happen? Was this how far her sense of pity had taken her?

The phone rang, jarring her out of her panicked thoughts. Before she could reach it, Eric's arm slipped from under the blanket and picked up the phone. His husky voice, heavy with sleep, triggered memories of the voice that had wooed her in the darkness.

"Hello? Hi, Cassie. Just wait a minute."

She kept her eyes closed, knowing he would be able to read her if he saw them. She felt his rough cheek against hers as he gently kissed her good morning. "Cassie's on the phone."

She muttered something unintelligible and took the receiver. He disappeared into the bathroom.

"Adriana, are you there?" Cassie asked.

There in body, not in mind. She lifted the phone to her ear and opened her eyes. "Yes, I'm here," she croaked.

"Was that Eric?"

She bit her lip. "Yes, I—"

Cassie groaned, dismayed. "I am so sorry. Did he keep you up all night going over your budget? He has a hard time stopping once he's gotten started with something."

*Uh-huh.* "Yes, I know."

"He keeps going and going until he's satisfied."

Adriana pinched the bridge of her nose. "That's about right."

"He tries really hard to make sure you're satisfied too, of course. He wants to make sure you're both happy with the results. He's very thorough. Adriana?"

"I'm still here."

"So did you get a lot accomplished?"

She heard the shower turn on. "It matters what you mean by accomplished."

"Did he help you with a budget or were you two at each other like wild dogs?"

Wild dogs, cats, horses. "Close."

She sighed. "Why can't you two get along?"

She rolled onto her back and stared up at the ceiling. "Cassie, I have made a terrible mistake."

"Never mind. You'll get another financial adviser."

"No, you don't understand." She lowered her voice to a whisper. "I think I seduced him."

"Stop whispering. You're not making any sense. You sounded like you said you seduced him."

"Yes, that's right. I seduced him."

"Adriana, that's ridiculous."

"I know and it scares me. Sure, I'm used to being impulsive. It's never really gotten me in this much trouble before. Well, perhaps a few times, but not like this. This is horrible. I don't know what to do."

"What happened?"

"I slept with him."

"Is that all? Stop making it sound worse than it is. So you fell asleep together and probably woke up with your arm around him or something. A few awkward moments followed, but that doesn't mean you're attracted to him on some unconscious level. He was just a warm body. I know you can barely stand the sight of him, but you'll live."

"Cassie, I mean I *slept* with him." She paused. "I guess sleeping is the wrong word. We . . . had sex."

Her friend sounded as though she were choking. "That's impossible."

"Not anymore."

Cassie burst into laughter.

"Cassie," Adriana warned. "I know where you live."

"I'm sorry, it's just the thought of you two . . ." She laughed harder.

"I'm going to hang up."

"No, wait! I'm sorry. Talk to me. How did that happen? How could you two of all people . . ." She coughed before a fit of giggles escaped her. "Start from the beginning."

Adriana heard the shower cut off. "I can't."

"Why not?"

"I'll call you back later." She hung up on Cassie's protests.

She brought her legs to her chest and covered her face. How could she look at him? She'd seen him naked. Now it would be like having X-ray vision. She would look at his shirt and see through to his chest; she would look at his trousers and see through to his . . . She had to relax. It was no big deal. Who cared that he'd given her an orgasm so wonderful it would vibrate in memory? It was over. Done. Many people had one-night stands and lived to tell about them, even brag about them. She would survive this, but she wouldn't brag about it. Last night would be relegated to her Wall of Shame.

"Do you have a headache?" he asked.

She peered between her fingers and nodded. She felt the mattress sink as he sat on the bed. She nearly jumped when he placed his hands on her shoulders. He smelt like lavender from her soap, the heat from the shower slipping into the room. "It's probably the phone waking you out of a deep sleep. You know—"

Oh God! Eight in the morning and he was giving her a lecture. She took a deep, steadying breath, feeling her heart pound. Perhaps someone could die of shame. Although right now only her mind felt shame, her body felt something else. His hands were turning it into Jell-O. "I'm okay now."

He sounded unconvinced. "Are you sure?"

"Positive. Let me get showered." She raced into the bathroom and rested against the door. She slid to the floor, realizing she was still naked when her bum hit the tile floor. She quickly stood and took a deep breath. She was acting like an idiot. She had to get a hold of herself. He didn't appear shocked and neither would she.

She took a shower, lathering herself until her skin felt numb. She went to her room, relieved to see it empty. She frantically searched through her closet for a good after-sex outfit—one that wasn't enticing (miniskirt with cashmere blouse), but not too ashamed (a sweatsuit). One that reflected a nonchalant attitude. She chose a maroon sweater and wool skirt.

When she walked into the kitchen, she was greeted by the smell of eggs and sausage. Eric was dressed in his clothes from yesterday. They were so pressed they looked like new. She frowned at the feat since he had no buttons on his shirt. She had stepped on one on her way to the kitchen.

"Safety pins," he said, reading her thoughts.

She set the table and then they sat down to eat. She tucked into her eggs as if they were in danger of scurrying off her plate. She couldn't look at the man in front of her who silently ate his breakfast. Soon the silence became unbearable. She would have to face him, face what they had done. She took a deep breath and raised her eyes.

His were closed. He was asleep with his fork piercing a sausage. She nudged him with her foot. "Eric."

He opened his eyes halfway. "Hmm?"

"Didn't your mother teach you not to fall asleep at the table?"

He scratched the night growth on his cheek. "Sorry. I usually don't do well if I don't get six hours of sleep."

"I'm sorry to have kept you up," she said dryly.

His sleep-heavy gaze cut across the table. "Trust me, I wasn't complaining."

He didn't exactly smile, but he had the pleased expression of a buccaneer who'd succeeded in stealing his share of treasure. In the morning light he even looked as dangerous with his lazy, dark gaze and stubbled jaw. His shirt wasn't completely buttoned, slipping to the V of his chest. She let her eyes fall. What was wrong with her? The evening was over; when would her overactive imagination cease?

She pushed herself away from the table. "Let me make some coffee."

She put on the coffeemaker, willing herself to stay in one place so she wouldn't pace. She wished she could think of something witty to say, since he was too busy trying to eat and keep his eyes open. The October morning was mellow with the soft rustling of leaves and the city beginning the morning rush. At last the sound of coffee drizzling into a pot filled the room. She handed him the coffee and watched him pour five spoonfuls of sugar in his mug.

"That's coffee, not lemonade," she said.

He stirred his drink. "Another weakness, I have a terrible sweet tooth." He took a sip, added a little more sugar, then took a long swallow. "Thanks, I think this might do it."

"Add some carbonated water, and you've made your own soda."

"Hmm."

She shifted in her seat, determined to eat in silence. She soon changed her mind. "Uh, Eric—"

"Yes, I know the eggs are bland, but I couldn't find any of your hot spices. Not even Tabasco."

"That's because I can't eat hot spices. They burn my gums."

He looked at her with pity. As if she had a debilitating affliction. A Caribbean American that couldn't eat hot spices? "Really?"

"Really."

He shook his head, amazed. "That's like a European allergic to beer, an Asian allergic to rice, a—"

"That's enough, Eric."

"I'm sorry."

"Not as much as me," she mumbled. "Aren't you going to say anything about last night?"

A wicked grin of pleasure spread on his face. "Best birthday I've had ever."

She frowned. A man with glasses shouldn't look so sexy in the morning. "That's not what I meant."

"Do you want me to expand on that?"

Good heaven, he could even lecture on sex. "No, I don't." She set her fork down. "Where between trigonometry and the economics of public issues did you learn to . . ." She waved her hand, unable to articulate it.

He shook his head. "A man never tells." He began typing in numbers on his watch. "Will you be free for dinner next week?"

"Yes." She shook her head, frustrated. "No. I—we can't see each other again."

He clasped his hands together and rested his chin on top. "Why not?"

"Because what happened last night shouldn't have."

He blinked.

"You're on the rebound and I'm—"

"A worrier."

"I'm not worrying." She was more on the verge of a panic attack. "I should have been the responsible party. You and I don't blend. And this is not about sex," she added when he opened his mouth.

He furrowed his brows. "You've lost me."

"Last night you asked a woman to marry you. A woman you were prepared to spend the rest of your life with. You were devastated by both her betrayal and rejection. Last night your masculine ego was wounded and I was a diversion for your broken heart and ego."

"You're not a diversion."

"You need time to heal."

He softly swore. "I was afraid of this." He stared into his coffee. "How long do you think it will take for me to heal?"

She felt herself relax. He wasn't going to argue. "Who knows? People heal at different rates."

He nodded. "I give myself two days."

"That's too short."

His eyes met hers. "Then how long?"

"I don't know," she stammered. "Don't get upset."

He leaned back. "Do I look upset?"

"No."

"But I should be. The woman I want says I have to wait until my imaginary broken heart has healed."

"Do you even have a heart to heal?" she asked, annoyed by his flippancy.

His eyes pierced hers. "I think I lost it when my parents died."

Shame heated her face. She hadn't fought fair. Yet her question was in earnest. She wondered if his response was too.

He suddenly stabbed his sausage and took a bite. "How long?"

"A month."

He nodded. "So are you free Saturday?"

"Eric, didn't you hear what I just said?"

"Yes, but what do you expect me to do? Eat Haagen Daz and watch soaps?"

"Don't be silly."

"I'll try not to sleep with you, but I still want to see you. Or is that against the rules too?"

"There are no rules. This is fact. You're on the rebound."

"I'm not expecting a relationship."

She hesitated. "You're not?"

"Just a nice fun-filled affair. I think we can handle that."

"I still think you need a month."

He raised his hands. "Fine, I surrender." He rested a hand on his chest. "I'll try and heal myself."

"Good."

"Next Saturday we'll got to the museum. The Hirshhorn."

"But that's a modern art museum."

"Yes, I know. I think I need to get used to being around interesting figures I can't touch."

# Five

Nothing could alter his good mood. Not even the cryptic call from his ex-business partner, Carter. No, he was going to enjoy today and the memory of last night. Eric whistled his way through the lunchtime rush at the Blue Mango Restaurant his brother owned. He passed by the waiters, through the low roar of voices, and the sound of clinking utensils that filled the elegant room. He headed toward the manager's office, but halted when he saw his brother smiling at a group enjoying the Blue Mango specialty—chocolate desserts. He shook his head in amazement. Marriage had really changed his brother. Until Cassie had come into Drake's life, Eric hadn't even been certain he knew how to smile.

"Did two buses stop by?" Eric asked as his brother approached him.

Drake glanced around the restaurant, satisfied. "It's been a great year. Our name's really getting around." He patted Eric on the back. "So how was your birthday?"

"Have you seen Jackie?"

He fought a smile and headed to a far wall out of view of the customers. He ran a hand through his graying hair. "No. What did she send you this time?"

"A stripper."

Drake raised a brow. "Not bad."

"She sent her to my office. I had a client."

He winced. "Ouch."

"Yes, that's exactly what she'll say when I'm through with her." Eric glanced around the restaurant again. If Jackie was there he would find her. She was definitely hiding from him. He'd checked his place and hers already. His brows furrowed when he spotted a young waiter with a black ponytail reading a letter.

Drake followed his gaze and frowned. "Cedric."

The young man looked up, guilty. The expression made him look younger than his nineteen years. He came toward them. "Yes, Mr. Henson?"

Drake snatched the note and carefully folded it. "Am I paying you to read?"

"No. I'm sorry, sir."

"How's Pamela doing?"

His face lit up at the mention of his girlfriend's name. "She misses me." He colored violently, a harsh contrast to his olive skin. "I mean she loves New York. She's fine."

"Tell her I said hello." Drake handed him the note. "On your own time."

"Yes, sir." He walked away.

"Amazing that relationship is still going," Eric said.

Drake shrugged. "They're young."

"You don't think it will last?"

"College changes things. She's going; he's not. We'll see." He folded his arms. "So aside from the unexpected striptease you had a good day?"

"I enjoyed the striptease, but Adriana was there."

Drake swore.

"She took it in good fun. We went to a play, then a club."

"You went to a club with *Adriana?*"

"Yes. It was educational."

"Educational?"

"I saw Lynda there with another man."

Drake narrowed his eyes. "I would say I'm sorry, but you don't look concerned."

He shrugged. "I'm not. It's always good to know when

you've made a mistake. I realized I was with the wrong woman." He leaned against the wall looking smug. " I changed that."

"How?"

"I went to Adriana's place last night—"

Drake's face changed. "Oh no, you don't."

"What?"

"You're not allowed to get involved with Adriana."

Eric took off his glasses and cleaned them.

Drake stared at him, amazed. "You've slept with her already?"

He put his glasses back on and grinned. "Last night was—"

Drake held up his hand. "I don't want any details."

"I wasn't offering any."

Drake pinched the bridge of his nose. "How?"

"My regular MO. She felt sorry for me."

"That doesn't bother you?"

"We had sex."

"But she felt sorry for you."

"Let me reiterate: we had sex. It doesn't matter the reason, just the outcome. It was great."

"How can pity sex be great?"

Eric raised a brow. "Get Cassie to pity you one day."

Drake waved his hand in disgust. "Pretend I didn't ask."

"We're talking about sex."

"No, we're talking about my wife's best friend. You two have nothing in common."

"When has that stopped me before?"

"Adriana is not like your others."

"I know."

"What does she think about this?"

"She's a little worried." Eric rubbed his chin. "She thinks I'm suffering from a broken heart, but I'll handle that."

Drake covered his eyes as everything came together.

"You slept with her *after* you found out your girlfriend was cheating?"

Eric paused, then nodded. "That's basically it."

Drake let his hand fall. "What are you going to do when the pity wears off?"

"I always leave before then. No worries, we're just having fun. She's sweet."

"A dangerous temptation for a man with a sweet tooth."

Eric grinned. "Exactly."

Jackie entered the restaurant. She ducked behind a wall when she saw Eric.

"Too late," he said.

She came out of hiding. The top of her head reached her brothers' shoulders. She had large brown eyes and straight black hair that swept her chin.

Eric folded his arms. "I'm waiting for a reason."

She pushed her hands in the back pockets of her jeans and swung from side to side. "I thought you would like it."

"You wouldn't be hiding from me if that was true."

Her hands fell to her side. "It was fun. You like women, right?"

"Yes, but not dancing half naked in my office. I had a client."

Jackie began to smile. "Didn't he enjoy it too?"

"It was a she."

Her face fell. "Oh no. I'm sorry."

He shook his head. "No, not yet."

"Oh, come on, Eric. I was trying to give you something special. You didn't want us to plan anything and I thought you should have a few festivities while you're alone in your office. I'm truly sorry you didn't enjoy it." Her big brown eyes gazed at him with sincerity.

He immediately forgave her. He always did. He turned away, disgusted with himself. "Spoiled brat."

She grinned at them. "A result of the two best brothers in the world."

Eric glanced at a lamp. "What do you want?"

Drake looked at him. "How do you know she wants something?"

"Practice."

Jackie looked appalled. "I don't want anything."

"See?" Drake said.

"Except—"

Eric flashed a superior grin. "Except what?"

She turned to Drake. "I want to borrow Marcus."

He frowned, suspicious. "For what?"

"A photographer is doing a hunger campaign and I thought he'd be the perfect model."

"No."

She kissed her teeth. "Hear me out."

He held up his hand. "No. I will not have my son's face plastered all over the city for a hunger campaign. Think of the hypocrisy. His father owns restaurants."

"No one needs to know he's your son."

His voice hardened. "The answer is no."

She sighed and held up her hands in surrender. "Okay, okay, withdraw the fangs. Could I borrow some money then?"

"Why? You going to bribe some parent to hand over their child?"

"No, it's for something else."

"What?"

Eric opened his wallet. "Why ask? The reason will just make you crazy." He handed her some bills. She gave him a quick kiss on the cheek, made a face at Drake, and raced out.

"You spoil her," Drake mumbled.

He shrugged, putting his wallet away. "I know. It's a weakness."


"What the heck is that?" Cassie demanded as Adriana dumped two bags from Nordstrom on her kitchen table.

The house was unusually quiet since her two kids were napping. The sun flooded the yellow kitchen, passing over the pine table and polishing the copper pots hanging above—baby bottles dried in the sink next to little plastic utensils. Adriana looked at her best friend since childhood. She wore jeans and a sweater with her hair pulled back in a braid. Her dark eyes reflected concern behind glasses.

Cassie glanced into the bags, then looked up. "What happened?"

She fell into a chair. "I'm not sure. I went into the mall to relax and the next thing I knew I'd left with these."

"I thought you were going on a budget."

She rested her arms on the table and held her head. "I know, I know. Don't remind me."

Cassie removed the bags from the table. "How did you end up with Eric?"

She stared down at the table. "I took him out for his birthday. He had a miserable time."

"How miserable?"

"He lost his tie, got confused for an adulterer, and found his girlfriend tongue-wrestling another man."

Cassie bit her lower lip, trying not to grin. "Yes, that would qualify as miserable."

"I tried to make it up to him. I bought him a cake and took him to my place. We watched TV, then . . ."

Cassie leaned forward. "Then . . ."

"It happened."

"We're not talking about the Big Bang. *How* did it happen? Did he suddenly jump on you? Did you rip your clothes off?"

"He kissed me."

"He kissed you first?" She sat back and shook her head, confused. "Then why are you blaming yourself?"

"Because I didn't move. A part of me wanted him to. I encouraged it. I was leaking pheromones and after being rejected he just fell for my trap." She sighed. "Our hormones got the best of us."

"What did he say this morning?"

"He said he'd had the best birthday of his life."

Cassie raised her brows, impressed. "Congratulations."

Adriana glared at her. "It's not funny."

"I'm not trying to be funny. He could have said nothing. That would have been worse."

"It shouldn't have happened."

"But it did. It was fate."

"It was hormones. He's on the rebound."

Cassie stood and got a drink. "That's not for you to decide."

"Someone has to think rationally. He wants to have an affair."

"Then don't worry." She pushed a glass toward her. "He's pretty good at those."

Adriana glanced at her glass, distracted. "This is gorgeous. Is it crystal?"

"Hand-cut. Kevin bought a set for us."

"Does Drake know?" she asked. Drake disliked Kevin.

"He pretends ignorance."

She ran her hand over the intricate design. "Do you know how expensive these are?"

"Who cares? To Kevin they're equal to the prize you find in a Cracker Jax box."

"It's so nice to have rich friends." She took a sip and sighed, her mind returning to their original topic. "You think this is funny, don't you? Eric and me."

"I think it's about time."

Adriana ignored the hint. "He is taking me to the Hirshhorn Museum."

"You love it there."

"I know," she said gloomily. "I just know we're headed for disaster. Nasty breakups are such a pain."

"We're talking about Eric. A nasty breakup would require some passion."

Of which he definitely had some.

"I think it will be a nice change for you. It will run its course, then end. It's no big deal unless . . ." Cassie's eyes widened. "Uh-oh."

Adriana stiffened. "Uh-oh what?"

She chewed her bottom lip. "I know what the problem is."

"You're only now figuring it out?"

"You like him."

She pounded the table. "I do not!"

"Shh!" The warning came too late. Ericka let out a wail from her crib.

Adriana swore. "I'm sorry."

Cassie stood, brushing away the apology. "It was time for her to get up anyway."

They entered the nursery with its raspberry wallpaper and the calming scent of baby powder and lotion. Cassie lifted the baby and quieted her, then looked at the bed where her two-year-old son slept. "That one could sleep through an earthquake."

Adriana looked at Cassie holding Ericka, whose tears had begun to dry. She touched her soft dark curls and then stared at Marcus, hugging his pillow of a giant ice cream cone. Cassie was everything she'd tried to be but couldn't—a good wife and mother.

"How's Cassandra doing?" Adriana asked.

Cassandra Graham was Cassie's alter ego, a celebrated speaker and self-help author.

"Fine. I'm the keynote speaker at a conference in April."

Adriana nodded. Cassie had found some balance between work and family. She knew she couldn't do the same. She folded her arms, feeling out of place in the domestic scene, a reminder of her private failures. "I'm not like you, and Eric isn't Drake."

Cassie sniffed. "Thank God, the world could only take

one pair of us." She stopped being flippant, sensing Adriana's unhappiness. "Laurence is still a ghost, isn't he?"

"I haven't thought about him for a long time."

"And Nina?"

"She's happy with her father. That's the way we planned it. Eric has nothing to do with them."

"You like him and you want this to work. That's why you're all nutty."

"I am not nutty."

"Adriana, if Eric didn't mean anything to you, you wouldn't be here. You would have let things take their course."

"I find him intriguing. I don't like him."

"He's a nice guy." She winked. "Even though his brother is cuter."

"He's cute," she defended. "In a mathematical nerd sort of way," she added when Cassie sent her a knowing look.

"I have a suggestion."

"What?"

"Indulge your curiosity. I think dating intelligent men is stimulating. You prefer life-size pincushions. Try and prove me wrong."

A challenge. That sounded good. A nice healthy excuse to indulge herself. "You've got yourself a deal." She glanced at her watch. "Let me go. I'll show myself out."

"I'll call you later." Cassie watched her friend leave the room and then smiled down at her daughter, who tried to eat her fist. "You know what, Ericka? I think Auntie Adriana is falling in love."


Adriana stared at the piece of string and cloth.

"What the hell is it?" Sya Chen, her store manager, asked. Her straight black hair was braided back and entwined in silver string. She wore a long turquoise skirt and a black and white swirl top.

They sat in the back office of Adriana's lingerie store Divine Notions. They looked over the work of a young designer seeking a place to sell her work. Right now the young woman was putting more money in her parking meter, giving them some time for an honest evaluation.

Adriana drummed her fingers. "It looks like a pastie."

"A what?"

"You know, those things you attach to your nipples."

Sya wrinkled her nose in distaste. "What kind of store does she think this is?"

They scanned the selection of full body garters and see-through pajamas.

"You have to admit she's creative," Adriana said.

Sya held up the item. "But *what* is it?"

"Heaven knows."

"Heaven would probably reject it."

They heard the bell from the front door. Soon the young woman came into the room. Her name was Mandy Wilton. She had deep-set eyes, dyed brown hair with black roots, and a heavyset build, drowning in a large muddy dress. Her mousy appearance contrasted dramatically with her designs.

Adriana smiled gently as the young woman took a seat. "You have worked hard."

Her face fell. "You hate them, don't you? I knew you would. Nobody can understand my vision. My freedom of form."

"I didn't say I didn't like them."

Sya held up the string and cloth. "How does someone wear this?"

Mandy demonstrated on a mannequin.

Adriana winced. Sya caught her eye and mouthed, "No."

"My idea is that a woman's body should be celebrated, not covered up," Mandy said. "Clothing should be fun and daring."

Adriana nodded. "Yes, but at Diving Notions we have a more conservative view of a woman's sexuality."

Sya crossed her legs. "You'd do better at a porn shop."

"They're not called porn shops," Adriana said quickly, shooting Sya a warning look. "More like specialty adult stores. I think you would have a more receptive audience there. Try Palace Pleasures. I know the owner there. Tell him you spoke to me."

Mandy looked hopeful. "So you do like them?"

"It doesn't matter what anyone else thinks, you must believe in your product. Believe it is something consumers need."

"I do."

"Then sell it."

"Thanks." She gathered up her things.

Sya smiled once Mandy closed the door. "I admire your tact. Think Limond will take her?"

"I don't know, but I don't want to be the one to give her the final no."

Sya pushed the mannequins against the wall. "Rita came by. She wants to discuss the details of the fashion show with you. We were so lucky to reserve the ballroom at the Montgomery Hotel for Valentine's Day weekend."

"It was destiny." The proceeds from the show helped a women's center.

"It's going to be a big night for you too. Are you really going to show your designs?"

She rested her chin in her hand. "I'm not sure."

"You're more talented than that weird little mouse that came in here. You have to be confident."

"I know. It's coming." However, exposing her dream of being a lingerie designer was scary. She felt ridiculous having such a dream. She came from a family in medicine. It was bad enough being in a business that marketed underwear.

Her love of design had begun on a college internship to

France where for four months she worked with a design firm. She was able to see how the company worked, which designs were used, and what ideas were launched. But then she came home and got married and began a proper career as a merchandiser at an upscale boutique.

She pushed her past out of her thoughts and entered the main store.

Two girls about fourteen entered. A girl with messy red curls and a short build gripped the arm of a gangly girl with dull blond hair and a quiet demeanor.

"She wants to buy some pretty things," Curls said.

Adriana came up to them. "You came to the right place."

"She has a date."

Adriana paused, looking at the young girl and wondering just what she meant by "date." "I hope you don't expect this young man to see your . . . pretty things."

"Oh no," Curls replied. "It's to give her confidence. That's what my mother taught me. Feel good underneath, feel good all over."

Adriana nodded. "That's true." She turned to the other girl. "So how would you like to feel?"

She shrugged, her eyes downcast.

Curls spoke up. "Something simple to begin with. She's going out with Nathan Cumbers. He's a real nobody, but at least he's a boy."

Adriana glanced at the other girl and saw a blush spread on her cheeks. Nathan was anything but a nobody to her. Adriana knew it was best to separate the two, in order to give the other girl a chance to speak. "Why don't you look around while I help your friend?"

"I'm here to help her too," she protested.

Sya came up to them. "Then let me show you some of our best-selling items."

Curls hesitated, then shrugged. "Okay."

Once Curls was gone, Adriana was able to discover the girl's name was Helen. Adriana noticed that she was getting the dreaded "four breasts" because she was wearing the wrong-sized bra—one of her mother's. She instructed her on how to figure out her size, then helped her select a comfortable and cute pink satin bra and panty set. Helen offered her a shy smile as she bought her purchase and then both girls left.

"God, I hope I wasn't that opinionated as a kid," Sya said.

"I think she's an original. I just hope they're not double-dating."

The rest of the day went smoothly. Adriana checked with her Web site manager, went to her other store and addressed the shoplifting issue, then researched advertising opportunities. She returned to Divine Notions at closing. She was locking the register while Sya checked the back when the front bell chimed. A black man dressed in a knit cap and ski sunglasses entered the store carrying a portfolio.

"Is it that cold outside?" Sya asked.

He pushed the glasses to his head. "I just like the look."

"Hi, Keith," Adriana said. They had tried the boyfriend, girlfriend thing but it had not worked out. They had met four months ago at a small gallery and instantly liked each other. He was a new artist and she saw him as a protégé. He rested his portfolio on the counter and unzipped it. He was medium height with quick, smooth movements, a goatee, and brown hair with blond highlights, complementing his fair skin.

"I've got some work. You'd be crazy not to love it," he said.

Sya frowned. "I thought artists were supposed to be self-effacing. Are arrogance and big egos the new trend?"

"It's not ego, it's genius. I can't wait around for people to recognize it."

Sya rolled her eyes; Adriana smiled.

She liked his freedom, his daring to do what he wanted

in the face of convention. She didn't understand most of his works and wouldn't hang them on the wall, but she could imagine with the right exposure he could make the living he desperately needed. She was glad he was moving away from expressionism to abstract. She liked his abstract the best—a story or vision she could understand. The side of a face, the impression of a sunset created with bold shades of red, yellow, and orange bursting from the page. She felt a sense of accomplishment that she had helped him to bring forth his talent.

"It's wonderful," she said. "You've been working hard."

"You're impressed?" It was more statement than question.

"Yes. I always am." She closed the portfolio.

He slipped his glasses to the end of his nose and gazed up at her. "So impressed that you'll loan me some money for new oils?"

Her enthusiasm faltered. "I'm on a budget."

He pushed the glasses up. "Just two hundred."

"I don't know."

"This is my chance. I'm getting really good reviews and comments about my work." He lowered his voice. "Sartan is definitely interested in looking at more work." He owned a small gallery. "You know that once I make it I'll pay you back twofold."

She picked up her handbag. She wanted to be the support she'd never had. "All right." She quickly wrote a check and handed it to him.

"Thanks." He kissed her on the cheek and left.

Sya put on her coat and pulled on a hat. "I don't trust him."

"Why not? All artists are a little off-the-wall."

"Maybe, but I thought his name was Keith Trenton."

"It is."

"Then why did he sign a painting KSY?"

"Are you sure?"

"Unless he can't write."

She hadn't noticed that. "I'm sure there's a reason."

Sya opened the door and glanced over her shoulder. "There's always a reason. Let's just hope it's a good one."


Sya's comment echoed in her thoughts on her way home. She didn't get the sense that Keith wasn't genuine, yet the fact he hadn't told her about his signature was worrying. She pushed the thought aside as she entered her building. Her home was her refuge. She'd leave the events of the day outside.

She dug into her handbag for her keys as she turned the corner to her apartment.

"Hello, Addie," a familiar male voice greeted.

She dropped her keys and stared at the man and child standing on her welcome mat.

# Six

Icy brown eyes pierced him like a stake. He had known Eric Henson for over fifteen years and still couldn't meet his gaze head-on. He glanced at him, then the wall behind him.

"Ten thousand," Henson repeated. "Are you in trouble?"

Carter felt drops of sweat gather on his upper lip. "How could I be in trouble with just ten thousand dollars? I thought I explained it to you. My business is going great, the investors are patting me on the back. I am just waiting for a deal to come through. My lawyer is negotiating the contract, so that's holding things up. I just need a loan."

"You try a bank?"

"I thought I would try a friend first." He inwardly winced. He knew Henson never bought sentimentality crap. He didn't now. His eyes hardened. Carter said quickly, "You can trust me and I can trust you. No hidden agendas, that's why I came."

"I see." He clasped his hands together. "How's Serena?"

His wife was blissfully ignorant and he meant to keep her that way. All he needed was Henson's money to buy him time, and then he could fix everything. And cover his lies with some truths. "Fine. She's doing well." Spending his money like it was a hobby. He hated catalogues and that damn Internet. He never said anything though—never could.

She felt she had married a loser anyway and he didn't

need to give her ammunition. He had taken money from the family fund, a savings her family had trusted her to look after, and used it on a high-risk investment. It had promised to make him rich. Unfortunately, the bottom fell out, crashing on his head.

Her family was going to check the fund in five months and the missing money would certainly be noticed. If only the investment had gone through. His ideas always seemed great in the beginning but failed in application. This risk had been his worst. He was a gambler with an addict's luck. Win big once, doomed for life.

He folded his arms to hide his trembling fingers. He was glad he didn't blush. As white as he was, that would be a definite handicap. He was fortunate he had honest green eyes and a handsome face that had kept him out of trouble for years. He looked at Henson, silently begging him for a check, his nerves as taut as a heroine addict's at the mercy of his dealer.

"I'm glad to hear that."

His stomach unclenched when Henson reached for his checkbook.

"When will I be reimbursed?"

He grasped for a number. "A month?"

"Fine." Henson wrote out the amount.

Carter took the check and folded it, making sure his expression was bland. He would have to work fast. First he'd put this money in the fund, then find a way to pay Henson.

Carter walked down the sidewalk as the city lights pushed the night darkness away. He felt free, hopeful. A check for ten thousand could do that to a man. He shoved his hands in his jacket pockets. What if he could make it more? Perhaps he could put seven thousand in the fund and use the rest on something he was sure would make a profit.

He stopped at a pay phone. He couldn't use his mobile since the number could be traced. Serena had a bad habit of checking up on him. He wasted some money making bogus calls, then dialed the number he wanted.

"Yeah?" The gravelly voice on the other end brought chills to his system. He'd been out of the game too long.

"It's me. I've got some money I need to triple."

There was a cold laugh. "Nice to hear your voice. What can I do for you?"

Adriana pasted on a smile as she opened the door for her ex-husband and daughter. "Well, isn't this a surprise?"

Her ex stepped in front of her with the unconscious arrogance of the elite. He looked like a life-size paper doll in gray trousers and sage dress shirt. His clipped mustache added a polish to his dark, striking features. A gift of his Ghanaian ancestors. "Addie, we have to talk," Laurence said. There was no urgency in his tone, it was stated as fact.

"So talk." She looked at her daughter. Nina hadn't changed since last Easter. She was a cute, reserved girl with black hair braided up to a bun on her head with serious brown eyes. She had her father's nose and chin. Adriana guessed she'd inherited her smile though she saw it rarely. She looked like an old woman rather than a seven-year-old girl in her wool coat and polished black shoes. "Would you like anything to eat?"

She shook her head.

"We need to talk in private," Laurence said.

"All right." She turned on the TV for Nina and then they went to the kitchen. She sat at the table and sent Laurence an expression of patient expectation.

"So what brings you far from the rolling hills of Maryland?"

He took off his coat and placed it carefully on the back of the chair. He sat. "I'm getting married."

She waited for the pain to hit, the sense of loss and finality. The man she had vowed to love and cherish forever was getting married. She felt relieved. Everything between them was over. "Congratulations," she said, sincere. "I'm very happy for you." She stood. "Let's celebrate."

"No, wait. That's not all."

"I figured as much." She retrieved two wineglasses. "Don't worry I'll look after Nina while you and your new bride enjoy your honeymoon." She grabbed a bottle of champagne.

"No, it's bigger than that." He tugged on his collar. "I need you to look after Nina permanently."

She popped the cork. Champagne bubbled to the top, spilling down the sides. "What?"

"You're dripping champagne on the floor."

She banged the bottle down on the counter, trying to keep her temper. "What did you say?"

"I want you to keep Nina."

She poured some champagne in a glass. "Why?"

"Irene doesn't like children."

She took a long swallow, then poured some more. "So?"

He stood, placing a hand on her shoulder. "Addie, she's the love of my life. I can't afford to lose her."

She shrugged his hand away. "Nina is your daughter."

"I know." He sighed wearily. "I've been thinking about this decision for days. It was hard to come to, but in the end I know it's the right one."

She pointed a finger at him. "Don't try to crawl out of your promise," she warned. "You said you wanted a child and I gave you one. You said you would take care of her for the rest of your life, giving her all that we both want for her—stability, education. And unless your time on this planet is nearing its end, which at this point it just might, you haven't finished your end of the bargain."

"Haven't you ever been this much in love?"

She glanced around her. "Where's my puke bucket?"

"Addie."

She took another long swallow and lifted the champagne

bottle again. She wanted to feel numb. He couldn't do this to her. He couldn't upset her life again the way he had all those years ago when he'd come home and said, "Let's get a divorce" as if it were a planned holiday. "You're not going to win this argument."

He took the glass and bottle from her. "You have to help me out."

"You are the best person for her. You're more steady, more financially secure. Let's face it, you're rich. You can give her everything she deserves."

"You're her mother."

The champagne was taking hold. She felt a strange tingly feeling. She grabbed a box of crackers. "Yes. I know that. Every time her birthday comes around I scream out in agony just to be sentimental."

He drummed his fingers on the counter. "Irene and Nina just don't get along."

"Make them."

"I'll visit, but ultimately this arrangement will be the best for everyone."

She bit into a salt cracker. "No."

"Either she moves in with you or I send her to a boarding school in Scotland."

She pushed the box away. "Scotland? Why Scotland?"

For a moment he looked smug. "Everyone sends their children to Swiss boarding schools, I want to be different. I've read about excellent ones there."

She rested her hip against the counter, glancing around her simple kitchen. It looked like a kiosk compared to Laurence's black and chrome one. "After a few days with me she'll probably choose boarding school," she mumbled.

Laurence clapped his hands, satisfied. "Perfect. Problem solved. She spends a couple of months with you. If she doesn't like it, off to the best boarding school in Scotland."

She stared at him, now knowing the dangers of arguing in the kitchen. So many tempting sharp objects to use. A long wooden butcher knife would look so nice in his chest. The bright red of his blood marring the perfect tint of his shirt. Her voice was cool. "Selfish bastard."

"No need for childish name-calling."

"Sorry. I thought they'd christened you that."

Unperturbed, he pulled out a paper from his pocket. "This is a listing of all her likes and dislikes, her classes, tutoring sessions, and music lessons. Don't worry, I'll still pay for everything."

"I can't do it, Laurence. I'm a single woman who runs a business. I don't have time to shuttle her around to tutoring and music lessons."

"I can pay you enough to stay at home. I'll provide your income."

"I said no over five years ago and I'm saying no now. I like my work."

"You'll be a single mother now. You'll need to make Nina your main focus."

"I'm not quitting my job and I don't need your money, except what you promised Nina."

He thought for a moment. "Maybe Scotland would be best. Boarding school is a wonderful experience."

"No."

"You just have the American aversion to it. It's nothing like the dramatized version you see in films. Remember, my sister went."

"Unfortunately, it didn't make her any wiser to the world."

His jaw tensed. He hated anything negative said about his older sister's failed marriage. "That wasn't Diedra's fault. Her husband was a conniving gold digger. However, that is beside the point. We both want what is best for our daughter."

She knew Nina would probably receive an excellent education, but something in her heart still rebelled at the idea of sending her to a boarding school in another country. She wanted her daughter to be with one of her parents. "No."

He sighed, resigned. "Then I suppose the argument is over. Nina stays with you on a trial basis. Make sure she goes to bed at the same time every night to keep her system balanced and she must have a full breakfast every morning."

"I'll make sure the cook handles that."

He placed the list on the table. "You'll have to change your priorities."

"As easily as you have?"

"A daughter needs a mother. All the money in the world can't change that."

"It helps. Trust me. I had a mother, remember?"

He wisely left the subject. "I'll call you to see how things are going."

She put the box of crackers away. "Have you told Nina why she's here?"

"Yes. She's a bright child, a true Shelton. Naturally, she took it all in a mature and dignified manner."

Adriana rolled her eyes. "Not even a little tantrum? How pathetic. When should I schedule her therapy sessions?"

He didn't smile. "You'll find Nina to be a very practical, unassuming young girl. You'll not have any trouble as long as you provide a stable environment."

She snapped her fingers. "Damn, there goes my orgy parties. Then again, as a *mother* it is my duty to educate her in—"

"I'm not kidding, Addie."

She stopped. That tone always sobered her, making her feel like a naughty child. "So do you have a picture of the love that's broken our happy arrangement?"

He took out a picture. Adriana expected to just glance at it, but ended up staring. "No wonder she doesn't like Nina. They're almost the same age."

He tried to snatch the picture. "She's twenty-two."

"You wish," she scoffed, gazing at the youthful round face, pouty mouth, and elaborate hairstyle. "But if her parents give their consent, then it's fine by me." She handed him the photo and patted him on the back. She wasn't completely surprised by his choice. His new wife would have to be young. Someone he could mold and shape into the woman he wanted.

He grabbed his jacket. "I'm glad everything is all set." He took out his mobile. "Hi, Marco? Yes. You can bring everything up."

"Who was that?" she asked once he put the mobile away.

"Mover. He's bringing some of Nina's things up."

Nina might as well have had her own suite. The movers brought up boxes, drapery, furniture, electronics, and an armoire.

Adriana stared when they brought up paintings. "This is obnoxious."

"She needs to feel at home."

"She's seven years old. She's not moving into her own apartment."

Once the movers had finished, Laurence tipped them and then went to Nina. She sat perfectly still, staring at the TV screen.

"Nina, it's time to say good-bye," he said as if addressing a business associate rather than his daughter. "I know this is a hard transition, but it's for the best. It's either this or boarding school."

Nina nodded.

"You'll be good? Remember Shelton pride."

She nodded again.

He kissed her on the cheek and left.

Adriana stared at the closed door feeling suddenly lost. She had been alone with her daughter before, but usually for short periods of time with every hour planned. Now she felt as helpless as a mother with a newborn. She didn't know the first thing to do.

She turned from the door and smiled at her. "I'm afraid you didn't hit the jackpot when it came to parents, sweetie."

"Daddy's in love," Nina said in a bored tone. "He always acts silly when he's like that. He'll come to his senses soon enough."

She didn't know how to reply to such a dour, practical statement. "Yes, perhaps."

Nina stood. "May I set up my room?"

"Sure. Call me if you need help."

She never did.

The next morning Adriana woke up feeling as if she were in a maraca. Someone kept shaking her.

"Not now, Elissa," she grumbled, trying to push her away.

"Mom."

She paused for a moment, then remembered her daughter was now with her. For a second she feared her cat had spoken. She sat up, wiping her eyes. "What is it?"

"You have to take me to school."

She lay back and pulled up the covers. "Take the day off."

She shook her again. "*Mom.*"

"All right, all right." She squinted at her clock. "What time is it?"

"Six-thirty."

"Ugh."

She dragged herself into the kitchen and searched for something to feed Nina for breakfast. She spotted a box of Special K. She added a banana, hearing Laurence's lecture in the back of her mind that she needed a balanced breakfast. "You look very nice," she said as her daughter sat at the table in her blue and white uniform.

"Ms. Johnson always has my uniforms pressed."

Adriana nodded. Of course. "Think she can work here part-time?" she joked.

Nina stared at her.

She sighed and pulled bread, ham, and cheese from the fridge.

"You don't need to make my lunch," Nina said. "I'm on the lunch program."

Adriana put the items away, relieved.

"Dad made sure I was on the plan. They have a great menu."

"I'm glad he's so thoughtful." A thoughtful bastard.


Brenton Girls' Academy loomed like a Victorian mansion as they approached the circular drive. Manicured bushes and brick stone steps led up to large glass doors. Adriana felt like a servant in her little Acura, driving behind Lexuses, Cadillacs, and Mercedeses filled with children and their drivers.

"Do I need to tell you when school ends?" Nina asked as she opened the door.

"No, I'll remember."

"Since this is bothersome, you can go to the main office and schedule the academy bus to pick me up. I don't mind."

"Thank you."

Nina hesitated. "Do you want me to kiss you?"

Adriana lifted her cheek; Nina kissed her. It was an awkward scene for both of them and fortunately short. Adriana watched her daughter walk up the stairs as the solitary little figure she was. She didn't greet other girls or find a group in which to belong. Even though all their uniforms were the same, Nina stood out like a disco suit in Bloomingdales. Adriana sighed and found a parking space. It would be better to have her driven to school; perhaps she could make friends on the bus.

Fortunately, ordering the academy bus wasn't as harrowing as she had feared. Another group of girls lived nearby, so the bus would remain on its route.

At home she quickly showered and changed, bemoaning her lost hours of sleep. After masking her puffy eyes with makeup, she went to work.

Sya said, "You look exhausted."

She walked past her. "I don't want to talk about it." She called Cassie for lunch and they scheduled to meet at the Golden Diner, a pricey restaurant with an easygoing atmosphere. A few hours later they sat in one of the booths.

"Fate hates me," Adriana said, pushing food around on her plate.

Cassie poured dressing on her chicken salad. "No, it doesn't."

"Laurence came by yesterday. He's getting married. His new love doesn't like kids. So now I have Nina permanently."

"She's a good kid."

"That's not the point. We're strangers. She thinks I'm a moron. Always has. She even frowned at me as a baby."

"She does not think you're a moron."

"She hardly talks to me."

"She's probably upset."

Adriana chewed her food, thoughtful. "I would actually be pleased to know that, but she doesn't give anything away. She just . . . she's not a normal kid. Never was. I swear the doctor had to whack her twice to make her cry."

"Stop exaggerating."

"Come with me to pick her up and I'll show you what I'm going on about."

"That's not necessary. I've met her before."

"Please? I need the support. She makes me feel like Edina on *Absolutely Fabulous*. Some selfish, incompetent tart."

"You can't be Edina, because that would make me Patsy

and you know that's impossible," she said, referring to Edina's svelte, alcoholic best friend.

"You know what I mean."

"I think you need to relax. But I will come with you."


Nina was not hard to spot on the red front steps, her clothes as perfect as that morning. She sat reading a book, while a few leaves blew past and students and teachers walked around her.

"I wonder if anyone knows she's there," Adriana said. "I'm surprised no one has stepped on her."

Cassie poked her. "She's just shy."

"No, grave. She'd be a nice addition to the Addams Family."

"Be nice. She's your daughter."

Adriana put down her visor and checked her makeup. "With her father's blood." She pushed the visor up. "He has some real kooks on his side." She pulled up to the curb.

Nina looked up, walked to the car, and climbed into the backseat.

"Hello, Nina," Cassie said.

She nodded politely. "Hello, Auntie Cassie."

"How was school?"

"Quite enjoyable."

Adriana shivered in disgust. Cassie nudged her. "That's wonderful. What did you learn?"

"The samurai of ancient Japan. Samurai warriors were skilled in all kinds of fighting. They didn't use shields, only two swords, a katana and wakisashi."

"How did they use them?"

Nina spent the rest of the drive explaining samurai fighting and their armor. At home she went straight to her room to complete her homework.

"Well?" Adriana asked once they heard the door close.

"She's delightful. I never knew the samurai . . . Oh, I forgot she's an intellectual."

"It's not just that."

"You'll just have to get used to each other."

"My daughter *likes* homework. I went down in history as having the best excuses of all time."

"Children are not meant to be our clones."

"Obviously."

"Then again she could have been your clone and driven you crazy. You'll eventually find things in common. She's your daughter, find ways to bond."

"Bond," she scoffed. "Neither of us bonded with our mothers. It's just some Western word to make us feel guilty."

"Whatever it is, you have to live together. You might as well get used to it."


Adriana opened her fridge trying to think of something for dinner. She usually lived on the single girl's diet: anything frozen or prepackaged. However, Nina would probably choke on a Lean Cuisine after living on gourmet meals. Tonight they'd go out for dinner. At least there they wouldn't be alone together.

They went to a Greek restaurant and settled in a booth amid low lights and blue vinyl cushions. In the corner of the restaurant they could hear a man alternatively whispering "moussaka" and "baklava" to himself.

She lifted the menu. "I'm not sure what pastitsio is, but it sounds interesting."

Nina spread her napkin on her lap. "It's a Greek lasagna. I usually prefer stuffed cabbage leaves."

Adriana stared. Her seven-year-old knew more about Greek food than she did. She'd probably seen and done more in her little life. She was knowledgeable and cosmopolitan. Wasn't that what Adriana had wanted for her?

At the price of making her a stranger? They attempted a stilted conversation, but ended up eating in silence.

The week progressed in the same manner. Eating out soon became costly and totally defeated her new budget. She would have to think of an alternative like . . . she shivered at the prospect: cooking.

Short awkward conversations became routine. They'd chat, then separate. Nina to her room and Adriana to her office, where she tried to focus on her designs.

She dreaded the weekend. What would she do with Nina all day? What would she feed her for lunch? Would she stay in her room the entire time? When Saturday arrived the day moved along slowly. By three Adriana was ready to tear out her hair. She wasn't used to staying in. She was used to shopping, hanging out at a friend's place, going to a club. Staying indoors was maddening.

Then the doorbell rang.

She checked through the peephole and groaned. Fate was making her life more complicated. She had forgotten her date with Eric.

# Seven

She opened the door. A part of her was glad to see him, grateful for the reprieve, another part relieved that she now had the perfect excuse never to see him again. "Eric, I am so sorry. I completely forgot about our date."

He stepped inside, his calm presence bringing serenity to her frantic nerves. She wanted to scream out, "Help me!" but refrained. Elissa came up to him in greeting, winding around his legs. He gave her a quick pat. The rough buccaneer of last weekend was gone. Dull, ordinary Eric with his dark, remote eyes was back. For a moment she wondered if it had all been a dream. "That's okay," he said.

"I'm afraid I'll have to cancel."

"Why?"

She closed the door behind him. "I've had a very crazy week."

He nodded. "You want to reschedule?"

"No, there's a lot going on right now and I don't think I can handle it all."

His eyes searched her face. "You're worrying again. Tell me what's wrong."

She tugged on the hem of her shirt. "Nothing is exactly wrong. I mean it shouldn't be wrong. It's something I should be able to handle. Any levelheaded adult with common sense could deal with it. It's just . . ." She trailed off. She was babbling and he knew it.

He glanced over her shoulder and saw Nina on the couch. "You have a visitor."

Adriana turned around, bewildered. Nina had been in her room. Perhaps she had heard the doorbell and thought it was her father. Adriana's heart sank in pity.

"Yes, my daughter," she admitted with both pride and shame. "She's come to stay with me."

He waited. There was no sign of surprise. "Are you going to introduce us?"

She walked toward the couch. "Nina, this is Mr. Henson. Eric, Nina."

The girl stood and held out her hand. "Nice to meet you, Mr. Henson."

He shook her hand. "The pleasure is mine." He glanced at them and then headed to the door. "Let's go then."

Adriana stared at him, appalled. "I can't leave her here."

He scowled. "I didn't expect you to. I'm sure they still allow children into the museum."

He was once again her savior. She would get out of the house and not be alone with Nina. She felt bad using him this way. Especially since she knew what he really wanted. "You don't have to do this."

He opened the closet and pulled out her coat. "I suggest you put some shoes on."

She wouldn't argue. At least she wouldn't have to worry about dinner and be annoyed that her child preferred her bedroom to her mother's company. She went to her room and grabbed sneakers. She came out and saw Eric helping Nina with her coat and asking her a few questions. Nina nodded solemnly.

Adriana watched the pair, her heart sinking. The evening would be a disaster. A night caught between two nerds. The bright side was they would keep each other company. The question was, what would she do? What could they all talk about? She briefly thought about her last disastrous evening with Eric. She sighed. It would be a long night.

\* \* \*

Eric would never have pictured himself as a knight in shining armor. Yet the relief with which Adriana had looked at him gave him the same feeling. Her anxious caramel eyes tugged at some protective instinct he hadn't had for anyone outside his family. He was glad to be here, recognizing how eager he was to see her again. He didn't analyze the feeling. He didn't deny that her vibrancy attracted him. Today she wore jeans and a purple, long-sleeve tunic with slit sleeves, large, silver earrings, and a pendant. His hummingbird looked ready to dart away from her cage.

When he'd figured out the situation, he couldn't understand her distress. Her daughter—a word that seemed strange when he looked at Nina's solemn face—was an amiable child who kept to her room except when her mother took her out to dinner, as she described it. They were awkward with each other. Tonight he would try to change that.

"So what do you think?" Eric asked Nina as they stood in front of a wall covered in various mutilated toys.

She said, "It's nice."

He patted her on the shoulder. "An obvious reflection of your mother's upbringing. Personally, I think a drunken elephant would have more talent."

"Keep your voice down," Adriana ordered.

"Sorry. Am I embarrassing you?" he asked without apology.

"You're being closed-minded and obnoxious."

"I have behaved myself for two floors." He glanced around him. "I find the design of the building very impressive in fact."

The Hirshhorn Museum was a four-story cylindrical

building that surrounded an inner courtyard. Sculptures stood proudly around the building as well as in the sunken garden across Jefferson Drive.

She rested a hand on her hip. "There are impressive figures inside also."

His eyes skimmed hers. "To that I agree."

She narrowed her eyes and went into the next room. She stood in front of a large wooden sculpture set under recessed lighting. "This was carved out of a tree trunk. It represents breaking away."

"From what?" Eric asked.

"Lots of things."

"I like it."

She frowned at him, doubtful. "No, you don't."

"Yes, I do. You've convinced me."

"You're making fun of me."

He sighed and pinched her chin. "Worry, worry, worry." He looked down at Nina. "Do you think I'm making fun of your mom?"

She hesitated, then nodded.

He grinned. "All right. I'm caught. Show me something else so I can tease you some more."

She endured his teasing good-naturedly after that. He knew a little about art and argued his points well. Their conversations occasionally dipped into harmless debates.

"Look at this Hans Hofmann," she said. "The lines, the colors."

"Actually it's a Rothko," Eric replied.

"It's a Hofmann. The brushstrokes and bleeding colors make it obvious. I'm the art expert. I can tell."

"It's a Rothko, miss," a woman gently corrected.

"Creatively called *Blue, Orange and Red*," Eric added in a dry tone.

"Oh." Heat burned her cheeks. Her ignorance bare for all to see. Even Eric knew more about art than she did. She had stepped out of her league, which wasn't unusual. Even in school she knew she was stupid when it came to academics. The only time she felt clever was in a store or in her office surrounded by her designs.

Despite Eric's teasing, she didn't say much after that, wanting to keep her ignorance to herself. She was glad when he turned his attention to Nina, leaving her to chastise herself. She wanted to go home and hide.

Instead, Eric took them to a Chinese restaurant. Peach walls, white tablecloths, a bubbling aquarium of goldfish, and watercolors of the sea and mountains created a sedate environment.

It was after they had ordered, Adriana noticed something missing from the table. "Where are the utensils?" she asked, picking up the chopsticks.

Eric looked at her. "Right in front of you."

She dropped them back on the table. "I can't eat with these."

"Sure you can."

Nina picked hers up to demonstrate. "It's really easy, Mom."

Of course *she* would know how to use them. Great, another humiliation. "I want a knife and fork."

"At least try," Eric said.

"Why don't you laugh at me now and get it over with? I don't feel like entertaining you." She caught a waiter's attention. "I'd like a knife and fork, please."

"She's mistaken," Eric said. "Thank you. She'll do fine without."

Sensing his authority, the waiter nodded and left.

Adriana glared at him. "You had no right—"

"At least try it. Why are you so afraid of trying?"

"Who are you to talk about fears? You can't even—" She met his eyes and stopped. No, she wouldn't throw his fear of heights in his face. Fine, he wanted to humiliate her, she'd do it and never see him again. This was why she never went out with intellectuals. She always had to prove herself, to perform.

When the food came, she sat and looked at it. She was prepared to starve until she was able to take it home and eat it properly.

Eric had other ideas. "Let's try this." He came around the table to stand behind her.

"Sit down," she ordered in a whisper. "People are looking."

"Nobody is looking. Now pay attention."

It was difficult to pay attention when her eyes kept noticing how huge his hands were as he tried to guide her movements. "Keep the bottom one still while you move the top one against it," he said.

Nina spoke up. "Like this." She picked up her rice.

Adriana tried and splashed herself; rice landed on her blouse and in her lap.

Eric said, "Try again."

She glared at him.

"Just do the movements first before trying to pick up anything. You'll be a little sloppy, but it's your first time."

He helped her through the movements until she seemed to capture them. He nodded, pleased. "Very good."

She looked to see if he was teasing but his praise was genuine. She amazed herself by how quickly she got the gist. The rest of the meal went well. Although there was one moment when she lost grip of her broccoli and it sailed across the table into Nina's plate. Another time a shrimp kept slipping from her grasp and she speared it instead. She glanced at Eric; he pretended not to notice.

Nina and Eric talked about their first experiences with chopsticks and the messes they'd made, and then they all discussed their favorite foods. The evening ended sooner than Adriana had expected. She took her chopsticks home as a souvenir, pleased Eric had forced her new skill. Though she would never tell him so.

\* \* \*

"Are you going to marry Mr. Henson?" Nina asked as she brushed her teeth.

Adriana stopped herself from bursting into hysterical laughter. "No, we're just . . . friends."

Nina rinsed her mouth. "He's nice."

"You get used to him."

Nina looked suddenly concerned. "Do you think he minded me having to come?"

"No. He likes kids."

"If . . . he comes again, do you think you could take me too?"

The end of their affair. "I'll ask him. I'm sure he won't mind."

Nina flashed one of her rare, brief smiles and went to bed.

Adriana went into the kitchen and saw Eric with two mugs. He held out one to her.

She frowned at it.

"It's tea," he said.

"Oh."

"Why are you so tense?"

"I'm not tense." She took a sip and gagged. "Did you melt an entire sugarcane in this?"

"Too sweet?"

She dumped the tea in the sink.

He came up behind her. "You haven't answered my question."

"I'm not tense."

He wrapped his arm around her waist.

Her body responded like a light switch. "Eric, you promised."

"I promised not to sleep with you. You said nothing against this." His lips brushed against her neck. She leaned against him, too tired and too comfortable to argue.

"Why does Nina make you nervous?"

She inwardly winced. It was that obvious? "I'm not a good mother."

He paused. "What do you mean?"

"Just what I said. I can't relate to her. I don't know what to do or say. She probably knows more than me anyway. She's traveled, she's socialized. Her father could give her everything. All I have is a three-bedroom apartment and Lean Cuisine."

He turned her around to face him. "You have more than that."

"Such as?"

"You have a home."

She sniffed. "A home is the smell of baked cookies, ironed clothes, clean carpets. My mother could do it all."

His eyes fell, his voice grew soft. "After our parents died, Drake found a place in an old drafty building, with rodents, old boards, broken windows, and trash outside. Winter was settling in and the cold slipped in through every crevice." He looked up at her. "But we called it home."

She looked at him, wishing she knew the right thing to say. She didn't know much about his past. Cassie had glossed over how Drake had taken care of his younger brother and sister when their parents had died, but in the face of their current success, she'd forgotten about the struggle they'd gone through.

"How old were you?"

There was a ghost of a smile. "In years or experience?"

"Years."

"Thirteen."

"Must have been awful."

"I survived."

For a moment she saw the man behind the shield, saw a glimpse of the young boy whose faith in the goodness of the universe was shattered. She knew he didn't share much, making his story a gift. "Why did you call it home?"

"Because a home is where the people you love live."

A simple concept, but she wasn't sure it was true. She loved her family, but could never call their grand English Tudor *home*. She thought about the rooms she could never enter, the dining table that was always set. Her mother happily cooking in the kitchen while her brothers studied or played football in the backyard. Her father's heavy footsteps and his scowl when he saw her dismal report card. She watched her mother fawn over her father and brothers while working part-time as a nurse. Always cheerful and happy with the many roles she played. Adriana watched her privately, knowing she could never be like that.

He lifted her chin, forcing her to look at him. "Stop worrying about how you think the relationship should be and let it be what it is." He kissed her briefly, tenderly. "I'd like to say the same about us. Are you willing to take the risk?"

She shook her head.

He pulled away, his voice deepened. "Why not?"

"Because I can't figure you out."

He held his arms out. "There's nothing to figure out. You date guys who could bend steel with their pinkies. What's so threatening about me?"

She shook her head, unable to put her thoughts into words.

"Let's not talk about this anymore."

"Yes."

At least she would have said yes, if his mouth hadn't reached hers first. His kiss was more persuasive than words. He was a definite threat, making her feel things he had no right to.

"I can't handle this," she admitted when he pulled away.

"You don't have to handle me." He headed for the closet. "Trust me." He opened it and glanced down.

Adriana softly swore.

He lifted a shopping bag. "What's this?"

She shrugged, feigning innocence.

He dug to the bottom of the bag and pulled out the receipt. He read the date, then looked at her. "Did you write down these purchases?"

"No. At least not yet."

He scanned the items and then dropped the receipt in the bag. "Take them back."

"What?"

"You don't need them. They haven't been worn and you haven't missed the return date."

"I can't return them."

"Why not?"

She held up her hands. "Listen, I know I ruined your birthday, but your constant humiliations have more than made up for it."

He looked at her, amazed. "Humiliations?"

"You made me look stupid at the Hirshhorn."

"How?"

"You said Hofmann was Rothko. You could have at least pretended not to know."

"I didn't know. I read the label."

"And you embarrassed me in front of Nina at the restaurant. Now you want me to add to my disgrace by returning these clothes."

"How can that be humiliating?"

"It will look like I can't afford them."

He sighed, exasperated. "But you can't. Do you have the money to cover these charges?"

"That's not the point."

He shut the closet. "We'll return them tomorrow."

She narrowed her eyes. "I'm not returning them."

He only smiled.

* * *

She hated him. With every ring on the register she hated him more. Each deduction echoing in the air added to her shame. Nina watched in the background. She'd probably never seen such a thing before. Each deduction said: *Your mother's pathetic. She has no money. She has no willpower*. And this latest humiliation was all his fault. She stared at the culprit.

Eric leaned against the counter studying the screen. She hated his face, his eyes, his voice. She hoped he fell through a manhole. She resisted the urge to stab him with the pen the clerk handed her. She signed the receipt and left the store, ignoring his presence for several blocks.

"Adriana," he said.

She sidestepped a wino.

"I'm proud of you."

She stopped and glared at him. "No, you're only proud of yourself. Congratulations, you made a complete fool out of me."

"Impossible."

She walked again. "You don't understand how it feels, the snickers, the whispers. The clerk sent me a knowing look. She *knew*."

"I know how you feel," he said quietly.

"How?" she asked, doubtful.

"I used to take a brown bag to lunch."

"So?"

"There was nothing in it. Everybody knew there was nothing in it, but I still carried the bag."

"Why?"

"Image. I didn't want people to know I didn't have lunch. I soon learned to stop pretending."

It wasn't the same. He had been a little boy. She was a grown woman, which made it that much worse. She was still pretending to be something she wasn't and her daughter had been there to witness it. The rush of an October wind stung her eyes.

"Why don't we all go to the movies?" Eric suggested.

"Yeah," Nina said.

Adriana wanted to go home. "You two have fun. I have things to do."

If Eric or Nina was disappointed, neither showed it.

"Next time," he said.

"Bye, Mom."

She watched them leave. It wasn't the first time in her life she'd felt the odd one out.

She didn't go home. She went to the mall. A shopaholic's ultimate high. She bought a brown, suede jacket and a red, silk blouse. Eric wanted to tame her. He lectured her as if she were a little girl, but she would remain free. From him and any man that tried to control her. She wrote down her purchases in large red ink.

Once home the euphoria wore off. She looked at her bag in disgust. No wonder Eric treated her like a child since she acted like one, hurting herself just to spite him. She wouldn't return the items though. She'd figure out a way to pay for them. She always did. She took off the tags and hung the things in her bedroom closet.

She was reading the Style section when they returned home. Nina told her about the movie like a trailer announcer, then went to her room. Adriana expected Eric to leave also, but he hung up his jacket and sat on the couch.

"So what did you buy?" he asked.

Heat stained her cheeks. She turned the page.

"I don't know why you act like I'm the enemy. It's your habit that's gotten you into trouble."

"I know that," she said in a tight voice. If he began to lecture her, she would hurt him.

"Then stop acting like a child and face it. Admit you have a problem and we can fix it."

She fluttered her eyelashes. "I'm in complete denial. Perhaps you could schedule an intervention."

He drummed his fingers on his knee, then said, "Open your palm."

"Why?"

"Just open it."

She did.

He placed a five-dollar bill in it. "This is called money."

She tore it in half. "And now it's called paper."

He stared at her, stunned. "You ripped it up."

"I know."

He fell on his knees and gazed down at the ruined dollar. "I can't believe you ripped it up."

"Just tape it. Sorry, but I've never felt the need to worship money."

He took the two halves of the bill and tried to align them on the coffee table. "I don't worship money. I respect it." He shook his head. "I can't believe she ripped it up," he mumbled to no one in particular.

She grabbed her purse and handed him five dollars. "There. Does that make you feel better?"

"No. Do you use fifty-dollar bills as confetti?"

"Eric. Stop making this a tragedy. It's no big deal." She fetched tape from her office and quickly repaired the damage. She held up the bill. "See? Good as new. Do you wish to bow or just salute?"

He didn't reply; she didn't expect him to. She returned to her paper.

He watched her. She could feel his eyes. After a few moments, her patience snapped. She threw her paper at him. "Stop studying me like a scientist! I'm not some mathematical equation that needs to be solved or a system that needs to be fixed. Your impenetrable dark eyes are irritating!"

He pushed up his glasses. "I'm trying to think of something to say."

"How about good-bye?"

He glanced away and muttered something under his

breath. "Nina and I had a great time," he said finally.
"We—"

Adriana grabbed a magazine, determined to ignore him.
"I'm not interested."

"Stop being afraid."

"Listen here, Mr. Courage. If you go out on my balcony
and touch the railing, then I'll have an affair."

His jaw twitched. "I don't do ultimatums."

"Then you know where the door is."

Eric stretched out his legs. *Calm,* he reminded himself.
He had to be calm. He wasn't upset. If he wasn't careful he
was going to lose her. He didn't plan to do that. He made
his voice casual. "You want me to go onto the balcony?"

"Yes."

"You think I'm a coward?"

"Yes."

He relaxed his grip on the couch. "You're right," he
agreed smoothly. "It's ridiculous for a grown man to have
such a fear, isn't it?"

"Yes."

"Do you want me to leave?"

"Yes."

"Free Friday?"

"Yes."

He stood.

She blinked as he opened the door. "Wait a minute!"

He placed a finger over her lips. "I'm saying good-bye.
Happy now?"


"Cassie told me," Drake said as Eric entered the Blue
Mango's back office. The gray, drizzly day seeped into
the austere finish of the room.

He hung up his jacket. "Told you what?"

Drake stood against the wall with his hands in his pockets. "About Nina."

Eric took a seat and opened a drawer.

"Quite a complication."

Eric pulled out a folder and shut the drawer. "She's not a complication."

"It's hard to have a relationship with a kid involved."

He glanced up. "You speak from experience?"

"Common knowledge."

"Nina will not be a problem."

"You're determined to make this work, aren't you?" Drake sat, crossing his legs at the ankles. "If I didn't know you better, I'd say this was serious."

"Fortunately, you do know me."

"Sometimes I wonder."

Eric began reviewing the expenses. He knew his brother couldn't figure him out. He preferred it that way. He had maintained a distance from people all his life. He knew a psychologist would say that his parents' deaths had traumatized him so much he was fearful to get close to anyone. It ran much deeper than that. There was a dark part of him no one would understand. At times it even scared him. He made sure to keep it well hidden.

"I still think this is a bad idea," Drake said.

"Since when is having fun a bad idea?"

Drake rubbed the back of his neck. "Adriana is not like you. She can't cut off from people like you do."

Eric pushed up his glasses. "Do you honestly see her getting attached to me? One thing I'm not is a heartbreaker."

"You deserve more than this. You can't keep on having affairs."

"I take what I can get."

"You can get better than this."

Eric tapped his pen against the desk. "Want to place some odds on that?"

Drake lit a cigarette; Eric tightened his grip on the pen.

His brother only smoked when he was worried or upset. He hated to see him do it. Hated to know he was the cause.

"I thought you were quitting," he said, watching the smoke drift to the ceiling.

Drake smiled without humor. "I'm always quitting."

"If it's an oral fixation, why don't you just suck your thumb? You'll look just as ridiculous."

Drake exhaled and studied him through the haze.

Eric sighed. "I like my freedom. I like trying new things, meeting new people. No one will get hurt."

"Jackie found an engagement ring in your room."

Nosy brat. He would have to get his spare key back from her. "I needed something to pawn." He hated lying to his brother, but it wouldn't be the first time.

Drake shook his head, not willing to probe further. "What about Nina?"

"She's not part of this equation."

Drake took a long drag and exhaled. "She will be. Don't be reckless."

"I'm never reckless."

Drake sent him a look.

"That was a long time ago."

Drake tapped his cigarette ashes in a tray, maintaining his gaze.

"I made money for us. Are you going to hold it against me?"

Drake took another long drag. "Are you?"

# Eight

Adriana watched Rita Detano walk into the ballroom of the Montgomery Hotel. She had the energy of a caffeine addict and a smoker's deep voice.

She ran her fingers through her short reddish brown hair as she sat. "Thank you for coming, Adriana." She set a small Coach bag on the table.

"I couldn't help it. You said it was an emergency."

"My life is an emergency, honey. I need help. You like the room?"

Adriana surveyed the space around her. The large gilt mirrors, chandeliers, wooden floor, and round tables would be transformed in a few months. "Of course."

"Good. Let's eat."

They went to the hotel restaurant. Adriana looked at the prices and silently swore. Eric would kill her.

"Don't worry, I'm paying," Rita said.

"I'll kiss your feet later."

"No need. I just had a pedicure."

They ordered and then talked about the fashion show. Rita said, "I got the Timmons modeling agency to provide six girls and four men."

"You mean women, not girls."

"It wasn't a slip of the tongue, honey. They specialize in twelve-year-olds that look twenty-five. I requested girls at least sixteen. You know how the industry is."

"Well, that's good."

"Mazur will handle the flowers and Praxton is handling the publicity."

"Will they be tasteful this time?"

Rita lit a cigarette and blew out the match. "People came."

"Yes, and were disappointed. Silhouette nudes give the wrong impression."

"They'll be tasteful this time." They paused when the food arrived. "So I hear you're going to show some of Divine Notions' new line."

"Yes."

"I'm sure it will be fabulous. Not like Vinton, who everyone talked about. He went to New York and fell flat on his face. There was nothing special about his work anyway." She tucked into her salmon. "So when can I see them?"

"Soon."

"You can't keep them hidden. You know I have to give a description to the announcer."

"I know."

Rita tapped a finger on the table, displaying her bright pink manicure. "You have until December, early January the latest, and then I have to see them."

Adriana smiled wearily and lifted her drink.


The thought of Rita reviewing her work was paralyzing. She couldn't work, her mind was blank, and her last date with Eric didn't help. They had gone to the National Air and Space Museum. She sighed. Would every date be an educational adventure? She bought Nina a necklace; she'd politely thanked her. Eric had offered to buy Adriana a small chain at the museum shop; she chose something else, offering to pay the difference. Adriana was glad to use him as a buffer with Nina but she needed stimulation—excitement.

She invited her friends over that week. She needed to bring back a semblance of what her life used to be before Nina and Eric. Nina politely introduced herself, then went to her room, whispering that they looked scary.

"So how's your friend doing?" Hinton asked, popping a beer can.

Adriana frowned. "Who?"

"The old man," Randan said.

"Oh, Eric, yes." She curled up her legs, grabbing a handful of pretzels from the coffee table. "My little mathematical nerd is becoming a nuisance."

"He seemed sweet to me," Tanya said.

"Then you try dating him. He actually schedules dates where we can bring Nina along. Not exactly a hot, passionate affair. You'd think he'd have passed the meaning of the word in the dictionary."

"You should be grateful he still wants to see you," Emily said. "Many men back off when a woman has a kid."

Tanya smiled. "I think men who like kids are sexy."

"I like kids," Randan said.

"Delinquents usually."

Hinton set his beer can down. "I don't think you're giving him a chance."

Adriana sighed. "But he's not like us."

"So what? We like him."

She made a face. "I don't know why."

He sent her a knowing glance. "For the same reasons you do."


She wasn't sure she liked him after he took them to a reading of funny poems and short stories. She fought to keep her eyes open. He was the bore she had suspected. He didn't even flirt with her or hint at sex. She might as well be going out with her brother.

"It's not going to work," Adriana told Cassie over the phone. She lay stretched out on the couch.

Cassie didn't argue. "Then tell him."

"Nina likes him."

"That's not a good reason to stay with someone who bores you."

Was it boredom or something else? She wasn't sure. All she knew was she was sick of museums, sick of seeing Nina and Eric together "discussing" things. She wanted her old life back. She wanted to be with a man who had a driving ambition to be something society rebelled against, someone raw and a little vulgar. She wanted to go to the salon, but couldn't for another week according to her budget. She was tired of signing school forms, ironing uniforms, and coming up with ideas for dinner. She didn't like the change in her life, and Eric was part of it.

"He's a nerd. A robotic geek."

"That's not fair."

"But it's true. Have you ever been out with him? I've got him programmed. If we got out to dinner I know what he's going to eat. If we go to a museum, I know which display he'll go to and what he's going to say."

Cassie sighed. "Fine, then break it off."

"I will tonight. He's taking us on a yawn fest. Driving around D.C. at night. Not clubbing—driving."

"It might be fun."

She moaned. "I'm sure he and Nina will have a great time."

The city showed off its finery as it sparkled in the dark night. They passed a memorial where a nineteen-foot marble statue of a tired, thoughtful Lincoln sat, his large hands leaning wearily on his armrests while he gazed toward the Washington Monument. The monument stood as a rigid granite and marble obelisk and loomed high above the city pale and gleaming.

She was supposed to be bored. She had been prepared, remembering her groan when Eric had offered to take them on a night time tour of the city. What was there to see? The shadow of buildings, homeless people gathered around a bin fire?

She didn't complain as she got into the car. She didn't sigh like a resigned prisoner as he pulled into the street. She gazed absently at the sights around her until he spoke. Suddenly, the city became a new and wondrous place. As if her eyes had been open for the first time. A city she had lived in for years became something new and wonderful like a relation one suddenly takes the time to know and discovers a life and history ignored.

They passed by the Vietnam Veteran Memorial, two V-shaped, polished black granite walls with the names of the dead inscribed on them. It stood half buried in the ground, the design as controversial as the war itself. She listened to him, no longer hearing a lecture but a history retold, coming to life in her mind.

She couldn't believe she was enjoying herself driving on a cold night through the city with a self-made tour guide and his seven-year-old fan. That's when she knew it wasn't Eric that bored her. It wasn't boredom at all. It was a restlessness, her resistance to change. A realization that there was another side of her she had chosen to ignore. A part that sought knowledge and culture. However, this wasn't the image of the woman she had created and it scared her. But she wouldn't analyze it tonight.

They warmed themselves with pastries and tea—milk for Nina—at a little café. Adriana went to order another cup. As she fixed her tea, a man in a dark suit came up to her.

"Hello," he said in a smooth, deep voice.

"Hi," she replied absently.

"Did you notice the moon?"

"No."

"I thought you would on your way down from heaven."

She turned to him, startled. He was flirting with her? "I'm sorry, but I'm not interested."

"I have my Mercedes out front, maybe I can persuade you."

"No, you can't."

"I've been watching you." His light eyes dipped to her chest, then back to her face. "I thought you needed a little rescuing. A beautiful, vivacious woman like you deserves more than listening to some guy talk all the time."

"I'm having a wonderful time," she said, defensive.

He looked unconvinced. "Uh-huh."

Eric reached behind her. "Excuse me."

She spun around, feeling guilty. "I'll be right there."

He sent her an odd look. "I'm just getting more sugar." He grabbed a few packets and left.

"He didn't seem overly concerned about us," her new companion said. He handed her his card. *Jared Moore— Architect* was written on it. "Just in case my offer interests you."

She wasn't impressed. Anyone could create a business card and become whatever they wished. She turned to him. "There is no 'us' and if you don't leave me alone, you won't have to go outside to see the stars."

He glanced at Eric and laughed as if she'd offered a Chihuahua as a guard dog. "Whatever you say, sister." He walked away.

She returned to her seat feeling foolish. Had she given off signals she hadn't been aware of? Did she really look so out of place with Eric? Why had she felt guilty when he came up behind her? She hadn't been doing anything. Was it because she had considered dumping him tonight?

Eric studied her. "Are you okay?"

"He gave me his card." She set it on the table.

He blinked. "Okay."

His calm was vexing. "Don't you care that another man was trying to hit on me?"

He raised a brow. "No, it's expected. I've seen you defend yourself, remember?"

"You trust me?"

"Why wouldn't I?"

Because no one else has. All her boyfriends would growl if a man even glanced in her direction. Then they would accuse her of flirting or trying to make them jealous. Laurence would have been on the man like a hound protecting his territory. Eric trusted her. She couldn't believe the freedom that came with that.

She tore up the card and lifted her tea. "Tell me about Union Station."


At home Nina said, "I had a nice time, Uncle Eric." On their third outing they'd decided Mr. Henson was too formal.

"I'm glad," he said.

She smiled briefly, then went to her room.

He turned to Adriana as she hung up her coat. "I'm healed."

She closed the closet door. "What?"

"My broken heart has been mended." He placed his hands on the wall behind her, trapping her in the circle of his arms. "And I want you."

She gazed up at him. "You don't know what you want."

"I want this." He kissed her mouth. "And this." He kissed her neck. "Especially this." He kissed her breast. She could feel the heat of his lips through her blouse.

"Eric." His name was a whisper.

"Am I beginning to convince you?"

Yes. "Nina could come out any moment."

"I hadn't planned on doing it out here."

"I hadn't planned on doing it at all."

His hand lowered to her blouse, he unhooked a button. "Fortunately, plans change."

"Not that fast."

"I've been patient. I haven't made any advances for two weeks."

Yes, she'd noticed that, but she hadn't been prepared for this. "True. However—"

"Do you want me to carry you or can you make it there yourself?"

"Eric—"

"Yes, that's what I thought." He swung her over his shoulder.

"Don't you dare!"

"Lower your voice," he ordered, heading down the hall. "Nina might hear you as well as half the building."

"Put me down," she ordered in a loud whisper.

"Don't worry, I plan to." He dropped her on the bed.

"You'll pay for this."

He tossed off his shirt and kneeled on the bed. "That's right, punish me. Make me beg for mercy. Blame me, if it makes you feel better."

It would be easy to do that. To be the helpless victim. Make him carry the responsibility of what they were about to do. But she wouldn't, because she wanted him too. She slipped out of her blouse. "No, I won't blame you." She pushed him onto his back and grabbed a condom from the side table. "But you will beg for mercy."

Neither knew who moved first. Their lips met as did their bodies, in a wild fervor of desire. Nothing was slow. Every movement was reckless, unheeding, almost violent as they grabbed each other, her hands roaming with audacious demand, her body thirsty for satisfaction, unrelenting of its quest. She didn't know why she always became impatient with him, forceful and commanding. Why she wanted to consume him or why he let her.

She kissed a path up his neck, the answer suddenly becoming clear. He kept part of himself hidden. He never asked for anything from her, no tenderness, no true intimacy, just sex. And as good as it was it suddenly wasn't enough. Their bodies were joined, but he was still a stranger.

She didn't want to sleep with a stranger, she wanted a man she could know and trust. She took a deep breath and then did something she never did during sex. She looked into his eyes and fell into their remote beauty. For a moment she saw a man there, hidden behind the ice. A man she could love. The thought frightened her. She turned away, knowing the image and memory would remain.

She wrapped herself in the covers when it was over, more a barrier to her feelings than from him. He didn't touch her or try to hold her. He just turned on his side. Adriana murmured softly to herself, staring into the darkness, then soon fell asleep.


Eric put a hand over his eyes. He had nearly lost it that time. He was an expert at being detached, but something about Adriana brought him close in a way that was dangerous. To him and definitely to her. When she had looked into his eyes, it took all his control not to envelop her, devour her in his need—the raw monster he kept hidden. He had to be careful, he knew where being reckless had gotten him before. Damn, he should end it now. End it clean. He grinned in spite of himself. The temptation was too sweet. He couldn't resist it until he had his fill.

It was just sex, he reminded himself, but damn, he didn't know a man could feel this good. This right. This real. He turned and reached out to touch her face, then pulled away.

They didn't have that type of relationship. They weren't supposed to fall asleep in each other's arms.

He rested on his elbows and watched her as the outside lamplight and moonlight slipped through the curtain, passing through the gauzy protection of the canopy, turning the pale light red. He wondered how it would feel to fall asleep with a woman in his arms. He would like to do that once. To know how it would feel to have someone belong to him. But he'd take what he could get. A man never found happiness by wishing for what he couldn't have.

He sat up, a restlessness nudging him out of bed. He changed and left the room.

He walked into the living room and stopped when cool air raised the hair on his arms. He saw the balcony door open. All his instincts became alert. The soft sound of crying changed it to concern. He saw Nina on the balcony wrapped in her coat with her purple nightgown peeking underneath the hem. She sat curled up, sitting in front of the railing.

He took a step forward, stopping when his bare feet hit the cold cement floor. A slow paralysis crept up his legs and torso. It was moments like these when he was most disgusted with himself. He tried another step toward her, but the paralysis reached up to his neck, threatening to choke him. He clenched his fists. He could run and grab her, but that would scare her. She would have to come to him.

"Did you have a nightmare?" he asked gently.

She glanced up and shook her head.

"It's cold out here. Why don't I make you some cocoa tea?"

She tilted her head. "What's that?"

"Hot chocolate." He held out his hand. "Come on. Tell me about the nightmare you didn't have." Relief filled him

when she stood and took his hand, his large one swallowing hers.

In the kitchen, he checked the cupboards. "I'm afraid
your mother doesn't have any hot chocolate. Why don't I
heat up apple juice and we can pretend it's apple cider?"

"You like to pretend things?"

"Sometimes." He poured the drinks and put them in the
microwave. "So tell me about your nightmare."

She made little circles on the table. "I didn't have one."

"But something made you cry."

She continued to make her invisible circles. Eric retrieved their mugs from the microwave. He placed one in
front of her and sat down. "Moving is always hard."

"I hate it here," she said in an angry, little whisper.

"Why?"

"Everything is made of stone, cement, and metal. It's
ugly and cold and gray. At my dad's house I had trees and
grass and bushes and flowers. Here even the trees have
cages."

"I know how you feel. When I left Jamaica I missed
trees bursting with fruits, the sound of coconuts dropping to the ground, the blue of the Caribbean Sea, the
feel of sand and pebbles beneath your feet and slipping
through your fingers, and the smell of water. To come
here to this concrete jungle was a shock." A place where
your poverty stared at you like a cracked mirror—
distorting your image, showing you a truth you'd never
seen. There were no neighbors to talk with whose quick
wit and easy laughter could lessen the struggles of the
day. There were no trees or bushes with which to pluck
fruit to ease the pain of hunger. Cold forced you to find
shelter.

"What did you do?" she asked.

He'd begged his parents to go back. Then they'd died and
he'd struggled to make the city a place he didn't despise,
not succeeding until he was grown. He didn't wish to re-

veal the destitute nature of his childhood. "I bought plants, lots of them. I learned to find the beauty that was here. There's plenty to see in the museums and there's the tidal basin, and the blossoms in the spring, the Mall. I also read lots of books and made up stories."

She wiggled in her seat with childlike eagerness. "What books? What stories?"

He thought for a moment. "Well, I'm sure you've heard the stories of Anansi."

Her brow furrowed. "Anansi?"

"In some stories he is a boy, but most often he is a spider. An arrogant trickster. Let's go into the living room and I'll start from the beginning."

They settled in the couch. Nina held her mug in both hands, her eyes fixed on him, expectant.

He slipped into patois. "Anansi, him neva did have nutten himself. Den a famine came in de land."

Nina began to giggle. "You sound funny."

He looked at her with mock severity. "You want me fi finish?"

She giggled some more but nodded.

He then told the tale of Anansi in Fish Country and two other tales of trickery until her eyes drifted closed.


Adriana woke to an empty bed. She hated the bereft feelings that filled her as her hand swept over the space Eric had lain. She hadn't expected him to stay till morning, but that fact didn't lift her spirits. She sat up when she heard footsteps down the hall. She grabbed her robe, opened the door, and turned on the hall lights. Eric squinted at the glare. Nina lay asleep in his arms.

"What are you doing?" she asked.

"She couldn't go to sleep." He looked at the two doors. "Which one is her room?"

Adriana went in front of him and opened the door. She

hadn't been inside since Nina arrived, feeling there was an invisible Keep Out sign. It was a typical child's room kept suitably messy and ten times smaller than her old room. The armoire and paintings emphasizing that fact. She watched Eric rest Nina on the bed and draw up the blankets. The scene was a little too natural for her liking. She turned away and walked into the hall.

He closed the door behind him. "I guess I should be going."

"You can stay till morning."

He glanced at his watch. "It is morning."

She went into her room. "Until daylight. I know how you need your sleep. I'd hate for you to fall asleep while driving."

"Hmm." He watched her in his intense way. Strangely the gaze didn't feel intimidating or cold. It was just him.

She touched his face, the stubble on his chin tickled her fingers. "You know you could grow a full beard in a week."

"I guess I should start bringing a razor."

They stared at each other, knowing what was happening between them was much more than an affair, but unable to admit it aloud.

She dropped her robe and slipped into bed. He took off his shirt and did the same.

She shivered. "I'm cold." It was an invitation more than a statement. She held her breath, preparing herself for rejection. Preparing that he would turn up the heater or offer to get her a blanket.

He drew her close instead, her back resting against his chest, his leg over hers. She moved her cheek against his arm. In moments they fell asleep.


Two days later Nina came down with a cold. Miserable and cranky, she stayed home and caused her mother anxiety, while she instructed her in what her housekeeper at her father's house used to do. Adriana bought every cold medicine she could find, turning her place into a sanitarium with windows drawn, utensils boiled, and rushing to Nina's room every half hour. Soon the chaos subsided when Nina's cold eased and she became her solemn self again.

Carter looked at his Visa bill and swore. He wished someone had warned him how expensive it was to keep a wife. Especially one that continued to glance over the fence to see what others had that she didn't. Their Chevy Chase home was never enough. The location alone cost him thousands, but that didn't matter to her.

Serena had a curveous figure, long, dark hair that tended to curl, and blue eyes. She was an attractive woman. He usually forgot that fact when she bitched at him. He glanced at her as she bent over to pick lint off the carpet, her Rock and Republic jeans showing off their price tags like dollars signs tattooed to her butt.

"The neighbors are getting a gazebo," she said.

"We have a pool."

She sat and grabbed a *Home and Gardens* magazine. "But a gazebo would be nice too."

"We don't need it."

She sat on the couch. "If you made more money—"

"What? You'd spend it faster?"

She ignored him. She had turned the activity into an art form, especially in the bedroom. Most nights he felt he should have married his right hand instead. When he made money, he'd probably get rid of her and get someone young, desperate, and grateful. A grateful wife would be a nice change. He looked at Serena as she folded down a page. No, he would not go young. He would get someone older. There were plenty of older women who wanted to get married and their biological clocks were ticking to the eleventh hour.

"What are you smiling about?" she asked.

"Nothing." Yes, a woman who wanted a baby would be good. He'd be there to help her out and finally get some action. Plus he wouldn't mind being a dad. It would be a nice change to have someone look up to him. He glanced at his wife again. She could ignore him now. He wondered if he'd get her attention if he hit her with divorce papers.

# Nine

The man was obviously lost, the clerk concluded. She toyed with her strawberry-blond hair as she watched him make his way through the aisles. Men like him usually didn't end up in a used bookstore like Papertrail Books where stacks of hardcovers and paperbacks lined the shelves. He was an incongruous shape, standing in the dusty children's section surrounded by old dolls and used toys. Yet something about him made it seem all right. He didn't have the hurried impatient look of most business-men, but she couldn't picture him with a family. He had a distant, isolated quality about him. Perhaps he was looking for a family member. Maybe he'd forgotten someone's birthday, but that still didn't explain what brought him here when there were plenty of stores to buy things new.

"Can I help you?" she asked, unable to curb her curios-ity.

He barely offered her a glance. "No, I'm just looking."

"If you need anything in particular, I'm right up front."

He picked up a picture book, then set it back. "Thanks, I will." It was a clear but polite dismissal.

She shrugged and turned to a woman in the reference section.

Eric lifted a hardcover book, running his hands over the cloth cover. He remembered Drake getting him books when he was sick. They usually were the ones the library or high school was giving away. They were cheap magical gifts that gave him a reprieve from life. He entered worlds where people weren't always hungry, weren't always cold, weren't always sick. The characters were strong and preserved—winning out in the end.

He wished he had brought Nina with him so that he could point out books he'd used to read and let her make her own selections. He would do that next time. Right now she was recovering from a cold and was probably feeling awful and depressed. He planned to make her feel better. He gathered a few books and headed for the counter.


"We haven't seen you in a while," Ana said as she did Adriana's nails.

She felt glad to be back in a salon. She smiled serenely. "I've been busy." *Trying to keep my life from going down the toilet*. Thankfully, Nina was recovering and back at school, but that wasn't her real concern. It was Eric. She shouldn't have made him hold her the last night they were together. Now every time she lay in bed she longed for his arms, his hands, him. It was a longing that had dipped into a haunting ache. An ache she hadn't felt since her divorce.

He had angered her when he'd made her return the clothes. She had wanted to strangle him but days later it had been a relief. She didn't have to look at her purchases with guilt and shame. Yes, she had to scheme how to pay for her childish revenge, but it wasn't nearly as much as she would have paid if she'd kept the other items. Plus seeing him with Nina that night continued to tug at her heart, his gentleness, his strength. She had felt glad he hadn't left her to wake in the morning without him.

They had gone to lunch and had a wonderful time. He was beginning to play a large role in her life. Too much like her father, a dominant bully who loved his children while he suffocated them. It was unsettling. She liked to keep her men on the sideline. Unfortunately, she knew Eric wouldn't last very long there. If they were going to have any kind of relationship, short or long, she would have to draw some limits.

Eric called later that day to say he had something for Nina. He arrived at the house soon after. Adriana opened the door and folded her arms at his package, peeking out of his jacket. "My birthday, and my daughter gets the gifts."

He looked startled. "It's your birthday?"

"Joke." She pulled him in and closed the door. "It's a joke."

He took off his coat. "When is your birthday?"

"If we last that long, I'll tell you." She disappeared into the kitchen.

He frowned. Recently she seemed to be doing that a lot, reminding him that their time together was limited. He brushed away the annoyance that always followed her hints.

He went to the living room where he found Nina on the couch wrapped in a blanket of a cartoon character he couldn't identify. "Feeling better?"

She sniffed and nodded. "I went to school."

He sat next to her. "I bought you something." He handed her the package. The wrapping looked like something someone had dropped and broken, but she didn't notice.

She said, "It's not my birthday."

"I know."

"And it's not a holiday."

"I know."

She carefully unwrapped the paper and sighed in awe. "Books and a garden." She hugged him. "Thanks, Uncle Eric."

"You're welcome." He lifted a long box. "This is your own herbal garden kit so you can start something on your windowsill." He shuffled through the books. "This is *When We Are Six* by the author of *Winnie the Pooh*. It's a little young but has some funny poems, then *The Little Princess* and one of my favorites, *The Secret Garden*."

She sighed again. "It's wonderful." She handed him *The Secret Garden*. "Read this one first, please."

He hesitated. "But it's for you to read yourself."

"I know I can read it, but it's much more fun to be read to." She looked anxious. "You don't mind, do you?"

"Not at all." He settled into the couch. Nina scooted next to him. Elissa sneaked onto her lap.

Eric opened the book and began, "*When Mary Lennox was sent to Misselthwaite Manor to live with her uncle everybody said she was the most disagreeable-looking child ever seen. . . .*"

A half hour later Adriana came into the room. Eric and Nina looked up. Nina leapt to her feet with an enthusiasm Adriana had never seen before.

"Look at the beautiful books Uncle Eric bought me."

Adriana stared down at the worn hardcovers and a paperback lying on the coffee table with bent covers and creased spines. One had the jacket missing. She picked it up, disgusted by the musky smell that seeped from it. "But they're used." She tossed it back on the table. "Couldn't you have gotten her new ones? I know you like to save money, but who knows what germs these are crawling with?" She looked at them. Her stomach dropped at the impact of her callous words. She had hurt him. She didn't see it in his face, but felt it in her heart.

He quickly gathered the books as he spoke. "You're right. I'll get her some new ones. I'll bring them by tomorrow." He stood and headed for the door.

Adriana followed. "Eric, wait."

His tone was casual, conversational. "Don't worry, there's a bookstore I know of. I'm sure it carries great children's books." He opened the door.

"No!" Nina cried, stunning both adults. "No! No! No!" She stomped her foot for emphasis. "No!"

Adriana turned to her, appalled. "Nina, keep your voice down!"

"No!"

Eric shut the door. "Stop that."

She tossed her blanket on the floor. "You said those books were mine!"

"They are, love, but—"

"Then why are you taking them back!"

"I'm going to get some new books exactly like these."

"No. You gave those to me and said they were mine. I don't care if they're used, I don't care if they're old. Library books are old and I read them all the time. They're mine and I want them back."

Eric glanced at Adriana and sighed, resigned. He looked at Nina. "You're right." He handed them to her. "They're your books and I had no right to take them."

She held them close as if someone would try to take them again. She glared at him.

"I'm sorry. Do you forgive me?"

Her expression didn't change, but she nodded.

He looked at his watch. "I'd better get going. I have some errands."

Adriana stepped toward him. "Eric—"

"I'll call you," he tossed over his shoulder before he left.

*I'll call you,* the kiss of death. He'd dumped her and closed the door. She didn't blame him. She stared at his exit until she felt an awareness, a warning, a sense of impending doom behind her. She spun around and saw two dark, burning eyes.

Nina trembled with rage. "You hurt his feelings."

"I didn't mean to," she said helplessly, feeling as though she had failed both of them. "I was just pointing out that these books are old. He can afford to get new ones. Besides, you already have *The Little Princess.* A new version with lovely watercolor pictures."

Nina shook her head, not sure how to put her feelings

into words. These books meant more. "The only friend I
have and you hurt his feelings. I bet he won't ever come
back now and then you'll be stuck with me and I know you
don't like me."

"That's not true."

"It is true and you don't like him either. You're always
calling him names. I hear you talk to Aunt Cassie. You
laugh at him." Tears spilled down her cheeks. "You think
he's dull and a nerd just like me. But he isn't. He's nice.
He's my friend. All your friends are stupid like you and
they dress weird and I don't like them. They're dumb and
scary.

"Now Uncle Eric is gone and it's all your fault. I hate
you. I hate you more than anyone in the whole world
'cause you're mean and selfish. I wish you'd send me to
boarding school." She raced to her room.

Adriana fell into the couch. She didn't realize she was
crying until she tasted her tears.


Nina slammed the door and dropped her books and garden kit on the bed. She pounded the pillows, then threw
them across the room. She sat on the bed and ran her hand
over the worn book covers, and smelled them. They had a
woodsy smell like Uncle Eric because he'd kept them in his
jacket. She tossed them down. Now he was gone and they'd
never finish *The Secret Garden* or any book. He would
never help her start a garden on the windowsill. She was
all alone again. She climbed under the covers and cried.


He should have known better, Eric told himself for the
tenth time that day. He should have known that Nina deserved more than a bunch of used books. Adriana's disgust
continued to ring in his ears. She had probably never
bought something used in her life. She'd never had to. The

difference in their backgrounds was a gaping hole between them. Instead of hiding their differences he had accentuated them and hurt a little girl. He wanted to apologize, but Adriana wouldn't return his calls. A loud snap cut into his thoughts. He looked at the broken pencil in his hands.

Drake pushed his chair from the dining table and held his hands up in surrender. "That does it." His hands fell to his lap. "Is your mind gone? What's wrong with you? Three days you've broken pencils and cursed under your breath."

Eric dropped the broken pencil and picked up a pen. "Would you rather I curse aloud?"

"What's wrong?"

He kept his gaze focused on the sheet in front of him. "Nothing."

"I may not be as brilliant as you, but I'm not stupid."

He scribbled down a few numbers. "It's nothing."

Drake folded his arms. "You have a fight with Adriana?"

He glanced up, twirling the pen in his fingers. "My relationship with Adriana is none of your business."

Drake's eyes hardened. "It is my business when you can't do your job."

"I'm doing my job," he said quietly.

Drake picked up a sheet of paper and tossed it on the table. "These numbers are wrong and I know the calculators aren't broken."

Anger propelled Eric to his feet. "Get off my back."

Drake rose as well. "Is it Nina?"

He grabbed Drake's shirt by the lapels. "Drop it," he said, his voice as cold as his eyes.

Drake stiffened, his gaze like polished amber. "You wanna fight me, little man?"

It was a name he'd used to taunt him when they were younger. It had the same effect now. He punched him in the face; Drake hit in the stomach. A war was waged as they sought to do as much damage to each other as possible. They fell over the couch and landed on the coffee table, shattering a porcelain vase and glass bowl. Suddenly, a splash of cold water soaked them. They turned and saw Cassie holding a large pot.

She rested the pot against her hips. "What the hell is going on here?" Her voice dropped dangerously. "And since you have destroyed my property, the answer better be good."

Eric shoved Drake away and stood. "I'm leaving."

"Sit down."

He grabbed his glasses from the floor and headed for the door.

She blocked his path. "Eric—"

He made a move around her. "I'm not in the mood—"

Drake's deep voice cut through his words. "Disrespect my wife and I'll make the mood worse."

Eric spun around and cracked his fist. "Perhaps I should have aimed for your mouth instead."

Cassie darted between them before another battle began. "That's enough! Sit down and don't argue with me."

Both men sat on opposite sides of the couch.

"What happened?" she demanded.

Drake leaned back; Eric glanced at a painting.

"Eric?"

He turned to her.

"You're not leaving until your temper cools. Then you're going to apologize to me for your behavior. Then you're going to apologize to Drake, who's kept me up two nights smoking like a chimney because he's worried about you—"

"I'm—"

"*Then* you're going to apologize to your nephew, who is crying in his room because his daddy and uncle are fighting."

Eric swore; Drake stood. "I'll go to him."

"Not looking like that." She turned to Eric. "You know

where the bathroom is. Take a shower, cool off, and clean up."

He took the towels she handed him and left the room, humbled. Cassie watched him go, then turned to her husband, who was wiping blood from his nose. His left eye was swollen shut and blood drops stained his shirt. A long tear threatened to detach his sleeve. She handed him a box of tissues.

"It's stopped," he said.

She sighed and sat down next to him, gently touching his face to check the bruising. "What am I going to do with you?"

He tried to smile but winced instead.

"Should I even ask what you said to him?"

"I handled it all wrong, as usual. He's never been one to confide in me. I don't know why I thought he would start now."

"Because he's your little brother and you love him."

"Right now that's debatable." He sighed. "For some reason he hates me."

She looked stunned. "No, he doesn't."

"Maybe it's not hate, but deep down there's something about me that gets to him. I don't know what it is."

"He loves you, he's just . . . I don't know." She shook her head. "I've never seen him like that. He's always so . . . cool."

"He has his moments. Something's gone wrong. He hates when things get out of control or he's made a mistake. I bet you it has something to do with Adriana."

"I'll have to agree. She won't return my calls. I'll go by and visit soon." She disappeared into the kitchen and came back with an ice pack.

Drake tightened his jaw as she placed it against his bruise. "I knew he and Adriana shouldn't have gotten involved," he grumbled.

"You couldn't have stopped it. Besides, I think they're good for each other."

"Unfortunately, it's not good for us." He stood. "I'm going to check on Marcus."

"Change your shirt first and take the scowl off your face."

Drake changed, then met Eric as he came out of the bathroom.

"Come on," Drake said as he walked to the nursery. "Let's pretend we like each other."

They entered the room. Marcus's cries were now whimpers as he lay on the bed, his face buried in a pillow. Drake sat on the bed. Eric stood near the window.

"Marcus," Drake said gently, rubbing his son's back.

He turned, looked at them, and began to cry again.

Eric moved toward the door. "We probably scare him."

Drake sent him a look. "Stay."

He scowled but returned to the window.

Drake stroked Marcus's back. "It's all right."

"You fighting," Marcus said.

"We didn't mean it."

Marcus turned to him. "Your faces is bwoken."

Drake nodded. "You know how you get in trouble when you play rough with your friends?"

He nodded.

"We did that and got in trouble. We won't do it again."

"In the house," Eric added.

Drake glared at him.

Marcus wiped his eyes. "Was Mommy mad?"

"Very," Drake said.

His eyes widened. "You have to sit in corner?"

Drake shook his head in regret. "No, it's worse than that."

"What?" he whispered, intrigued.

"No dessert."

His mouth fell open at the harsh punishment. "Oh."

"We want you to know we're sorry."

"I'm okay. Mommy's making coco cake. You won't get none."

"Any," Drake corrected.

Eric knelt. "If you give me a hug I will feel better."

Marcus ran and hugged him, kissing him on the cheek. "All better?"

He smiled. "All better."

Drake spoke up. "Mommy's in the kitchen now. Tell her we said we were sorry."

"Okay." Marcus ran out of the room.

Eric headed for the door. "I'll go now."

Drake seized his shoulder. "You're staying for dinner. I'll have to insist."

Eric hadn't called and Nina still wouldn't speak to her. Adriana stared at the phone. No one had called her. She was invisible. She picked up the phone to call Cassie, then put it down again. Cassie was probably busy. She had no right to disturb her with trivial affairs. She had created her own trouble. She stared at the phone again and then noticed the ringer had been turned off and the answering machine had been disconnected. She checked her mobile. The ringer was off too.

She stormed into her daughter's room. Nina sat at her desk coloring. "Did you turn the ringer off the phone?"

She didn't look up. "Yes."

"Why?"

"Because I felt like it."

"Nina, look at me."

She picked up another crayon.

Adriana took a deep breath. "I run a business. Phone calls are important. You can't just turn off the ringer."

Nina turned to her. "Why don't you just send me to boarding school?"

"Because I want you here."

*Dara Girard*

"No, you don't. You never wanted me. That's why you gave me to Dad after the divorce and visited twice a year."

"That's not true."

"It is true. You didn't want me then and you don't want me now."

"I did want you. I wanted you to have everything your dad could provide. You know I'm not as wealthy as he is."

Nina began coloring again.

To Adriana's own ears her reasoning sounded ridiculous, abdicating her role of mother so that Nina could have the wealth Laurence offered. How could a seven-year-old—no matter how bright—understand that? All Nina understood was that she had been abandoned. That she had a mother she would see a couple of times a year who asked her about school and gave her gifts.

"You might not understand this now," Adriana said slowly. "But I do love you and I wanted you to have the best. Unfortunately, I also made a mistake. I wasn't always there for you and that's a mother's job. I'm sorry."

Nina turned the page and started coloring a new picture.

Adriana didn't know what else to say, hoping that time would be a healer. "I'm going to see Uncle Eric tomorrow."

Nina looked up, excited. "Can I come?"

"No, you'll be in school. Is there anything you want me to tell him?" Adriana asked when her face fell.

"Give him this." She handed her a piece of paper.

Adriana looked down at a drawing—a picture of a man and a girl in a garden. Her absence from the picture was worse than Nina's silence.


Adriana gasped when Eric opened the door, looking like a mugging victim. "My God! No wonder you weren't at work. Did Bruce find you?"

He rested his arms on the door frame. "No. A little brotherly love. How can I help you?"

She tugged on the strap of her handbag. "I just wanted to see you."

He coughed. "You never returned my calls."

"Nina turned the ringer off. I'm not very popular right now."

Silence fell.

"I'm sorry about the books," she said.

He shrugged. "It's okay."

"Let's not start lying to each other now. I hurt you and I'm sorry."

He lowered his eyes. "You were right though."

"No, I wasn't. They were beautiful. I just couldn't see that at first. I guess I was jealous that she prefers your gifts to mine. That you can make her happy while I can't."

He coughed.

"You have a cold."

"Nothing to worry about."

She stared at the floor, then looked at him. "Please don't shut her out because of me. It's not fair. She really likes you, you're her only friend. She drew you a picture." She took it from her purse and handed it to him. "You and her in a secret garden."

Eric stared down at the picture. His voice was low. "Are you here for her or for you?"

"Both."

He didn't look up, but he held open his arms. She fell into them, burying her face in his chest. "I'm sorry."

"So your ringer was off?" he asked.

"Seven-year-olds are tricky creatures."

"She's angry."

She looked up at him. "You'll make her feel better."

"I can't fix your relationship with Nina. It's between the both of you."

"I know, but you make her happy." She touched his cheek. "Now what happened to your face?"

"Drake found it offensive and tried to rearrange it."

She hit him playfully in the chest. "The truth."

He winced.

She frowned. "He hit you in the chest too?"

"He hit me everywhere. Don't worry, I lived by the motto it is better to give than to receive."

"What happened?"

"We had a disagreement."

"About what?"

His eyes swept her face. "Doesn't matter anymore."

Eric sighed as his lips brushed her forehead. The scent of her shampoo came to him in a tantalizing aroma of strawberries. This was becoming a bad habit. He liked holding her and there was nothing sexual about it. That wasn't like him. It came from more than a primitive need. It was like a homecoming, a sense of safety, of belonging to someone. It was dangerous territory, but he couldn't resist the allure, the precipice that promised either success or failure.

Adriana rested her cheek against his chest. Safe, solid, secure. Those weren't the words she would have used to describe the men in her life, but Eric was all three. Words she used to scoff at, words she felt were confining and provincial were now like nuggets of gold. But it was still just an affair and whatever feelings she had were her secrets to keep.

"Nina really cares about you," she said, masking her own feelings with those of her daughter. "I bet she can't wait to see you. Why don't you pick her up tomorrow at the bus stop?"

"Shouldn't I wait until the bruises go?"

She rubbed her chin and studied him. "How do you feel about makeup?"

He saw her first—wrapped in her winter coat and gloves as if she were trekking across Alaska, her face a mask of composure as she stepped from the bus. She looked up and saw him. Her face lit up with such joy his heart lurched. He wanted to attribute it to his cold, but knew that wasn't the case. He had missed her. She ran up to him, then skidded to a stop, not sure whether to hug him or shake his hand. He lifted her up in his arms. "How are you doing?"

She wrapped her arms around his neck and squeezed tight. "I'm so glad you're back." She pulled away and stared at him. "Did you get my picture?"

He set her down and took her hand. "Yes, I put it in my office."

This pleased her. She began to skip beside him.

"Why didn't you let your mother in the secret garden too?"

"She's different than us." She looked up at him, curious. "You know that."

"Different doesn't mean bad."

She shrugged, unconcerned. "I know." She suddenly clapped her hands. "Now that you're here we can finish *The Secret Garden*!" She raced ahead of him into the building.

He tried to read, but could only manage ten minutes before a fit of coughing interrupted the story flow. He ignored Adriana's worried look as he closed the book and suggested something else to do. Nina was too happy to care. They started the herb garden in the kitchen. Eric helped her pronounce the different names and together they drew pictures of what the herbs would look like grown. Then they set the little greenhouse on the windowsill.

Later, Nina showed him her school projects and the pumpkin—a small one the size of a grapefruit— she'd picked out on the school trip to a pumpkin patch in Maryland. He lifted it up and glanced at Adriana hanging near the window. She had been keeping a distance since he had arrived.

"I think your little pumpkin needs a mother," he said. "Let's all go out and buy a big pumpkin that we can carve. Your mother could cook the seeds or make a pie."

Adriana looked horrified; Nina didn't notice. "That sounds like fun." They made a date for the weekend.

"I don't know how to cook pumpkin seeds," Adriana said in a low whisper once Nina had left the room. "I don't know how to cook a pie either. And I've never carved a pumpkin."

He looked at her, amazed. "Never?"

"No, my brothers always did it."

He patted her on the shoulder. "Then I'll let you take all the guts out."


Nina made her way through the pumpkin patch with a childish enthusiasm that was catching. Big, bright, orange pumpkins lay about like sleeping chariots waiting for the fairy godmother's wand. Tall trees changing colors sighed in the warm day against a gentle breeze.

Eric nudged Adriana forward. "Why don't you go help her pick one?"

She shoved her hands in her jacket pockets. "I don't think so."

"Try." He coughed.

"You should be wearing a scarf."

"A cough elixir?"

"Don't be facety. That cough should have gone by now. You probably picked it up when you visited Nina."

"Relax. When I cough up a kidney, I'll see a physician." She rolled her eyes. "Men."

"Women," he countered. "You'd rather scold me than talk to your daughter."

"I didn't make that choice. She won't talk to me."

"How old are you? Six?"

She glared at him, then sighed. "Point taken."

"Good." He turned. "I'm going to ask this guy about his squashes."

She approached her daughter with trepidation. She forced a smile. "This is fun, isn't it?"

Nina nodded.

She pointed to a pumpkin. "I think that would make a great witch."

Nina looked confused. "What?"

"Don't you look at the pumpkins and pretend to see what faces they have?"

"No, I just make sure they're round."

"They're round but they have personalities too." She walked up to one. "Like this one is sad. See how its stem is drooping?" She glanced at another. "And this one is sneering. It's more like an oval than a circle."

Nina giggled. "That's silly," she said, but was eager to play along. They searched the patch looking for a pumpkin with the perfect expression. They both stopped at one with a lot of personality. A pumpkin with an extra little growth.

Nina wrung her hands, unsure. "Uncle Eric wanted a big one."

Adriana tilted her head to the side, measuring it. "It's sort of big."

Eric came up to them. He saw what they were considering and groaned. "Oh no."

"It's cute," Adriana said.

"It's deformed."

Nina nodded. "Just like Quasimodo." Adriana stared at her, then realized she meant the cartoon, not the novel. "He's got his own hunchback and everything," she continued.

Eric picked it up. "Since you two have already made your decision, I'll keep my thoughts to myself. Come on. Let's give it a face."

* * *

"It's a shame there's no lightning," Eric said as they all stood in the kitchen. The pumpkins sat on newspapers on the table and they stood around it.

Nina looked at him, puzzled. "Why?"

"Because," he replied in a deep, slow voice, "there's nothing like bringing a pumpkin to life while there's a storm. The sound of a cold, harsh wind beating against the window, lightning slashing through the sky, tearing through the darkness as you raise your knife and sink it into the tough flesh." He stabbed the pumpkin. Adriana and Nina jumped. He grinned and pulled out the knife. "Oh well." He handed it to Adriana.

She took a step back. "I said I'll take the insides out. I'm not cutting it."

"Fine." He quickly cut the top and placed it aside. "There you are." He gestured to the seeds and stringy membrane. "Do you have your tools?"

Adriana held up a large spoon, Nina an ice cream scoop. "Then begin."

Adriana tried to maintain a cool expression as she sank her hand inside the pumpkin, her knuckles brushing against the slimy side. Nina kneeled on a chair and scooped out the smaller pumpkin.

Once all the guts were out, Eric checked to make sure they'd scraped the bottoms flat so the candles would sit level. Then they debated on the faces. They finally agreed on one smiling and one scary face. Adriana used a crayon to draw a scary face, Nina a happy one. Eric carved them. Later, he carefully pushed out the pieces, displaying the final product. He then coated the cut surfaces with Vaseline to seal in the pumpkin's internal moisture and help slow down the dehydration process. Nina and Adriana placed the candles inside and headed to the balcony.

"Come on, Uncle Eric," Nina called when she noticed him standing by the door.

"That's okay," he replied. "I can see from here."

"But it's nice out."

"I know." He nodded. "Nice breeze."

Adriana said, "He's making sure everything looks nice from the house." She caught Eric's eye and saw him relax. Nina shrugged and they went back inside. They sat on the couch, Nina sitting between the adults, and watched "It's the Great Pumpkin, Charlie Brown."

"So what do you want to be for Halloween?" Eric asked Nina as a Garfield special came on.

She thought. "An anthropologist."

Eric and Adriana shared a look. How typical of her. Not a fairy or a gypsy or even a superhero—an anthropologist.

"But I don't have a costume," she said sadly.

Adriana said, "I can make you one."

"Really?"

"I love creating costumes." She grabbed a sketch pad. "How do you want to look?"

Nina began to describe her costume and Adriana sketched an outfit that had Nina bouncing up and down with excitement. Eric said he would come to see her and take her trick-or-treating.

Nina went to bed and whispered to herself, "This is going to be the best Halloween ever."

Eric squinted at the words in front of him. His headache seemed to make everything double and wouldn't cease. He could barely raise his head when he heard his office door open.

"You look awful," Drake greeted, coming into the room. "What are you still doing here?"

"I think it's called working."

"Nice to see your disposition has improved."

Eric rubbed his forehead.

Drake sat in the seat in front of him. "Take the day."

He had too much to do. He had deadlines to meet and he wanted to be free for Halloween. "Why did you stop by?"

"Cassie wants to invite you for Halloween. Marcus's first trick-or-treating adventure. We're going to have a small party with his best friend and then go out."

"What is he going to be?"

"A tomato. I'm going to be taking lots of pictures."

Eric nodded. "Blackmail."

"Exactly."

He smiled faintly at the image. "Sorry, I can't make it. I'm taking Nina trick-or-treating."

Drake hesitated. "Are you sure you'll be up to it?"

Eric blinked. Damn, even his brother was beginning to double. "Yes."

"You should rest. I think I can hear your lungs expanding."

"That's what happens when your brother punctures them."

"Hey, I've only recently begun to blink my left eye."

"I think purple's a pretty color on you."

Drake stood. "Well, happy Halloween."

"You could have just called."

He opened the door. "I know."

Eric allowed a small grin. "Thanks."

Drake nodded and left.


"Mom! You're walking in the swamp again."

"Sorry," Adriana said, stepping out of the imaginary swamp. Nina had turned her living room into a jungle. She loved her costume so much that once she reached home, she changed and pretended to explore the deep jungles of the living room. It had been a gradual change—cushions moved, candles missing, Elissa wearing a blue handkerchief— until Adriana had caught Nina hiding behind a lamp.

# An Important Message From The ARABESQUE Publisher

## *Dear Arabesque Reader,*

Arabesque is celebrating 10 years of award-winning African-American romance. This year look for our specially marked 10th Anniversary titles.

Plus, we are offering *Special Collection Editions* and a *Summer Reading Series*—all part of our 10th Anniversary celebration.

Why not be a part of the celebration and let us send you four more specially selected books FREE! These exceptional romances will be sent right to your front door!

Please enjoy them with our compliments, and thank you for continuing to enjoy Arabesque.... the soul of romance bringing you ten years of love, passion and extraordinary romance.

Linda Gill
PUBLISHER, ARABESQUE ROMANCE NOVELS

***P.S. Don't forget to nominate someone special in the Arabesque Man Contest! For more details visit us at www.BET.com***

SPECIAL OFFER!
4 BOOKS FREE!

ARABESQUE

BET BOOKS

# A SPECIAL "THANK YOU"
# FROM ARABESQUE JUST FOR YOU!

Send this card back and you'll receive 4 FREE Arabesque Novels—a $25.96 value—absolutely FREE!

The introductory 4 Arabesque Romance books are yours FREE (plus $1.99 shipping & handling). If you wish to continue to receive 4 books every month, do nothing. Each month, we will send you 4 New Arabesque Romance Novels for your free examination. If you wish to keep them, pay just $18* (plus, $1.99 shipping & handling). If you decide not to continue, you owe nothing!

- Send no money now.
- Never an obligation.
- Books delivered to your door!

We hope that after receiving your FREE books you'll want to remain an Arabesque subscriber, but the choice is yours! So why not take advantage of this Arabesque offer, with no risk of any kind. You'll be glad you did!

In fact, we're so sure you will love your Arabesque novels, that we will send you an Arabesque Tote Bag FREE with your first paid shipment.

* Prices subject to change

# THE "THANK YOU" GIFT INCLUDES:

- 4 books absolutely FREE (plus $1.99 for shipping and handling).
- A FREE newsletter, *Arabesque Romance News*, filled with author interviews, book previews, special offers, and more!
- No risks or obligations. You're free to cancel whenever you wish with no questions asked.

## INTRODUCTORY OFFER CERTIFICATE

*Yes!* Please send me 4 FREE Arabesque novels (plus $1.99 for shipping & handling). I understand I am under no obligation to purchase any books, as explained on the back of this card. Send my free tote bag after my first regular paid shipment.

NAME _____

ADDRESS _____ APT. _____

CITY _____ STATE _____ ZIP _____

TELEPHONE ( ) _____

E-MAIL _____

SIGNATURE _____

Offer limited to one per household and not valid to current subscribers. All orders subject to approval. Terms, offer, & price subject to change. Tote bags available while supplies last.

*Thank You!*

AN054A

Accepting the four introductory books for FREE (plus $1.99 to offset the cost of shipping & handling) places you under no obligation to buy anything. You may keep the books and return the shipping statement marked "cancelled". If you do not cancel, about a month later we will send 4 additional Arabesque novels, and you will be billed the preferred subscriber's price of just $4.50 per title. That's $18.00* for all 4 books for a savings of almost 40% off the cover price (Plus $1.99 for shipping and handling). You may cancel at any time, but if you choose to continue, every month we'll send you 4 more books, which you may either purchase at the preferred discount price. . . or return to us and cancel your subscription.

\* PRICES SUBJECT TO CHANGE

THE ARABESQUE ROMANCE CLUB: HERE'S HOW IT WORKS

THE ARABESQUE ROMANCE BOOK CLUB
P.O. BOX 5214
CLIFTON NJ 07015-5214

PLACE
STAMP
HERE

They stared at each other, Nina gazing up at her, waiting for punishment. Adriana just tipped an imaginary hat, warned her to wear bug spray, and walked away. At that moment their relationship changed. As did her living room. At first Adriana was going to protest her pillows being scattered across the floor and her silk throw being used as a mosquito net. But it was so delightful seeing Nina out of her room and acting like a child, she said nothing.

"You're still in it, near the quicksand," Nina warned. "Here, let me save you." She got into her imaginary canoe and paddled toward her. "Get in."

She did.

Nina whispered, "You have to be quiet."

Adriana nodded, then gasped.

"What is it?"

"I see a crocodile rising out of the water."

"Where?"

She pointed. "See that moving log? Now its eyes are coming above the water."

"That's an alligator, Mommy. See the long, rounded snout?"

Adriana resisted rolling her eyes. Even in play, her daughter had to correct her. "Now it's opening its mouth."

Nina visibly shivered. "Let's get out of here." She paddled to firm ground. "Do you know how to get back to camp?"

"Yes. Dinner will be ready in two hours. We'll have snake."

Nina scrunched up her nose. "But we had snake last time."

"Then we'll have barbecued lizard with chocolate ants for dessert."

Nina licked her lips. "That sounds good."

* * *

At dinner Nina was quiet.

"You have to take your hat off," Adriana said after grace.

She put her hat aside. She picked at her brownie in her kid's frozen dinner.

"Your chocolate ants are not crunchy enough?" Adriana asked, noticing her lack of appetite.

"I don't want to go to boarding school," she said in a quiet voice.

"I wasn't planning to send you."

Her eyes watered. "But I said really bad things."

"They were hurtful, but I forgive you . . . like you forgive me." It was a question rather than a statement.

Nina nodded.

"Then all's well."

She shook her head, tears falling. "I didn't mean what I said. You're not stupid, you're fun. I wish . . . I wish . . ."

Adriana held her hand. "All is in the past. That was eons ago when we visited the Galapagos Islands and saw the golden rays. Now we're in the jungle and we're . . ." She faltered.

Nina gave her a watery smile. "Now we're friends."


He was late. Adriana checked her watch again, then looked at Nina, who waited on the couch. Her anthropologist hat sat low on her forehead while she swung her legs shielded in tall boots. "He may not be coming, sweetie. Why don't we get started?"

"He'll be here," Nina said, confident.

The doorbell rang. Adriana answered the door, relieved. Relief turned to worry when she saw his face. He looked exhausted.

He pushed up his glasses. "Sorry I'm late. I had to get things done."

His voice was deeper than usual with a raspy quality. "Can you do this?"

He didn't meet her eyes. "Of course."

Nina came up to him. "Do you like my costume?"

"And just who are you, madam?"

She giggled. "It's me, Nina."

He rubbed his chin. "Yes, I see the resemblance." He held out his arm. "Let's go."

Adriana hesitated, then grabbed her keys.


"Wow! Look at all that I got!" Nina said, dumping her candy on the living room floor. Adriana helped her separate the unwrapped candy as Eric sat on the couch watching TV. He'd become unusually quiet since they'd returned. Nina sent Adriana a worried glance.

"It's time to get ready for bed," she said.

She was about to argue, but thought otherwise. "Good night, Uncle Eric."

He managed a smile. "Good night."

"He's probably tired from a long day," Adriana said, walking with Nina down the hall.

Nina looked at her, anxious. "He has a bad cough."

"He'll be okay." Once Nina was settled in her room, Adriana returned to the living room. She saw Eric resting his head to the side, his eyes closed. She turned off the TV and nudged him. "It's time you went to bed as well."

He glanced at his watch. "No, there's something I need to get done."

"You can get to it later." She pulled him to his feet. "You need to sleep."

"I won't argue." He followed her to the bedroom, stumbling twice but quickly catching himself. Adriana's anxiety grew. That wasn't like him.

"How long have you had this cough?" she asked, unbuttoning his shirt.

"Don't know."

She took off his shoes and socks and helped him into bed.

He grabbed her wrist as she pulled up the covers. "I'm just tired. No worries." He rested his head back and immediately fell asleep.

Adriana went to sleep three hours later. Just as she was slipping into a wonderful dream, Elissa jumped on her side.

"Not now," she muttered. She gently pushed her aside and rolled over. Elissa meowed and jumped on her head and climbed down to her legs. Adriana moaned and raised herself on her elbows. She turned on the light, squinting in the glare.

"Come on, Elissa. It's too early to eat. And you know where your litter box is. Do you hear a noise?" She reached for her robe and headed for the hallway. She expected Elissa to follow but the cat jumped on top of Eric instead.

"Get down," she ordered.

Elissa meowed.

"What is it?"

She climbed on top of Eric's back and meowed again.

Adriana lifted her off. "Bad girl." The cat let out a disgruntled sound and jumped on the bed again. She climbed on Eric's back. Adriana knew there was a reason for her cat's unusual behavior. "You want him up too? This had better be good."

He was sleeping so peacefully she hated to wake him. Most of the covers had been pushed away, leaving his back bare. He was sleeping soundly. Too soundly. She touched his shoulder and snatched her hand back. He was burning with fever. She placed a hand on his forehead. Beads of sweat gathered under her fingertips. He lay so still she feared he'd stopped breathing. She hit the middle of his back with the flat of her palm. He took a deep breath and began coughing violently.

"Eric, wake up."

He continued coughing.

"Eric?"

The coughing soon subsided. He looked up at her, narrowing his eyes against the light. "What's wrong?" he asked, his voice hoarse.

She sat next to him. "You have a fever. Let me take your temperature."

He rolled on his back and wiped his forehead with the side of his hand. "Don't worry, it will go away. I'll be—" A fit of coughs interrupted.

She stood and headed for the door.

"Where are you going?"

"I'll be right back." She raced to the kitchen and called her brother Winston.

He answered after the third ring. "Do you know what time it is?"

"I need you to bring over your doctor's bag."

"Adriana—" he warned.

"Please, this is important." She hung up before he could argue.

She grabbed a towel and dipped it in cold water. She placed it on Eric's chest.

He sat up and swore, grabbing his head. "What the hell was that?"

She picked up the towel. It had slipped to his lap. She placed it on his chest again. "It's to help your fever."

He tried to push it away. "It's just dripping cold water on my trousers."

"Don't be stubborn. I don't have a large ice bucket to drop you in. Lie down." She held up her hand. "And don't say you're okay."

He lay back.

She fetched a rag and rested it on his forehead. "Now be still."

He closed his eyes and soon fell asleep again.

Adriana couldn't be still. She went to the living room

and organized things in her cupboard, started a word find, looked at a *Vogue* magazine, and flipped through TV channels until someone knocked on the door.

"So who is it this time?" Winston asked by way of greeting. "A trapeze artist with no health insurance? A musician who forgets his yearly checkups?"

"This is serious." She took his bag and pulled him toward the bedroom.

He released her hold and took off his coat. He tossed it over the back of the couch. He was a tall, neat man of medium build and impatient brown eyes. "Adriana, I told you, no more charity cases."

"When he's well, he'll be able to pay you. I promise."

He shook his head and went to the bedroom. He stopped in the doorway and studied the man in bed.

"What are you doing?" she demanded.

"Observing him."

"But—"

"Shh. Let me do my job." He went to the bed and let his eyes gaze over the man then turned to Adriana. "He's not going to like this, is he?"

"He's sick."

"Mm-hmm. I'll make sure to send the bill to you." He narrowed his eyes. "He looks familiar. What's his name?"

"Eric." She said his name quickly, hoping he wouldn't make the connection to Cassie and Drake. He'd been at their wedding and probably had met Eric at some point. She didn't wish to discuss their relationship right now. Thankfully, Winston was in his professional mode and didn't recognize him.

He nudged Eric awake. "Hello, Eric. I'm Dr. Travers. Adriana told me you have a fever."

Eric sat up, then held his head. He glared at him. "Who the hell are you?"

"I just explained it to you."

His voice was a low grumble. "Explain it again."

Winston sighed. He hated belligerent patients. "I'm Dr. Travers, Adriana's brother. She called me because she's worried about your fever."

"I'm fine."

"Let me do a quick analysis." He reached to feel Eric's lymph nodes.

Eric seized his wrist. "I said I'm fine."

Winston loosened the grip and folded his arms. "Do you have any sisters?"

He blinked. "Yes, one."

"A younger one?"

He nodded.

Winston's lips thinned as he glanced at Adriana. "Then humor me."

Winston checked for swollen glands, asked how long he'd had the cough, asked what medicines he was taking, and took his temperature. He later warmed the stethoscope on his palm, then placed it on Eric's chest and back. He finally folded the instrument.

Eric waited for the diagnosis. The silent examination was maddening. Seeing a doctor was like admitting weakness, admitting that you're sick, that you're helpless.

He said, "I'm not going to the hospital."

Winston lifted his shoulders in a casual shrug. "Then I guess I'll have to treat you myself or at least Adriana will."

They both began to protest.

He held up his hand. "With rest and the right medication you'll be fine."

"But—" Eric began.

"Are you allergic to penicillin?"

"No."

He searched through his bag. "Do you have any needle phobias?"

"No."

"Good. This will get the medicine into your system

faster." He looked at Adriana. "But I also suggest tea to loosen up what's in his chest."

"What's wrong with him?" she asked after he had administered the shot.

"My guess is bronchial pneumonia. I can't know for sure without an X ray, but I see little chance of that happening. If the penicillin works we won't worry about it, but if it doesn't, I'll have to insist."

"Doesn't pneumonia kill people?" Adriana whispered to him.

"He'll be fine, if he rests."

"How long will it take to work?"

"With his luck, probably two days."

Eric shook her head. "I don't have two days."

Winston lifted a brow. "Planning on expiring on us?" He smiled. "You don't have a choice if you want to get better."

"But—"

He closed his bag. "I'll be back in a few days. In the interim, my nurse . . ." He pushed Adriana forward. "Will look after you. Good night."

Adriana followed him to the front door. "He can't stay here."

He slipped into his jacket. "Why not?"

"I've never taken care of a sick person before."

"You'll be fine. He's so exhausted he'll probably sleep the two days away and only eat toast when he wakes. Make sure he rests, eats, and drinks."

"But what if he gets worse?"

"Then take him to the hospital."

She grabbed his arm as he opened the door. "Please, don't leave him here."

"Adriana, you can do this. You're a Travers, remember?"

"I'm the dumb Travers."

His face became serious. "Never say that again. You're one of us and that means nothing's too complicated." He kissed her on the cheek and left.

She rested her forehead against the door. Pneumonia. Not a cough or a cold or even the flu. Eric had pneumonia—an inflammatory disease of the lungs. What if he stopped breathing or started gasping for air and she could do nothing? She shook her head, she would not overdramatize this. Winston didn't seem too concerned and neither would she. Eric would stay with her and she would have to take care of him. Too bad she didn't know how.

He was asleep again when she returned to the bedroom. Her anxiety quickly turned to anger as she stared at him. A large male consuming her room with his sickness. So far an affair with him had been anything but casual and fun-filled. He was sweating on her sheets, taking up most of the bed, even the smell of illness permeated the room. Why hadn't he just stayed home? Why had he put her in this position? Did he expect her to take off days of work to take care of him?

She opened the window and sighed. No, he had come because he hadn't wanted to disappoint a little girl on Halloween. She sat on the ottoman and rested her chin in her hands. She wondered how much of a nuisance he would be. Whenever Laurence got sick he reverted to infancy, or acted as though the shadow of death was a new bedfellow. How would Eric behave?

Quite unexpectedly, she discovered. As her brother had predicted he slept all the next day. He woke briefly to grumble something before slipping off again. His exhaustion held him prisoner. The second day she tried to get him to eat but he refused, and she finally convinced him to drink some tea by threatening to choke him with it. He drank his tea on the ottoman as she changed the sweat-soaked sheets. That afternoon he still refused to eat, but had tea. His cough had subsided, but his fever remained and he kept quiet. She called Cassie. She and Drake came to visit that evening.

Drake headed straight to the bedroom, leaving Cassie

and Adriana to chat in the living room. He opened the door and saw Eric gazing out the window. He sighed, relieved. His brother usually had massive flus in the winter and would disappear for days, later emerging when he was better. He was glad that this time Eric hadn't been able to. His skin was sallow, his eyes heavy, his jaw tense, making his shame evident. Eric hated illness and Drake knew why. He hoped to make light of the situation. He closed the door. Eric turned to him. He managed a grin. "So you caught a cold from Nina. Why didn't you warn Adriana that you could catch a disease in a sterilized room?"

Eric pushed the blankets aside and grabbed his shoes. "About time."

"What are you doing?"

"Getting ready to leave."

"Why?"

"You're here to take me home, right?" He put on one shoe, then the other.

"No, I'm here to check on you."

"I'm fine."

"You're staying here."

"No, I'm not." He stared at Drake, envious of his strength, his health. He stood by the door large and looming. His vitality sucking the energy from the room. Eric felt his illness strap his body down, stripping him, making him helpless. His weakened body lay bare, ready for mockery. Drake didn't understand. He'd never been truly sick. His body never betrayed him. Eric rested against the headboard and studied him. "Remember how much fun it was taking care of Dad?"

Drake's jaw twitched. Their dad's illness and ultimate death still filled him with a mixture of anger and sadness. "It's not the same."

It was. Like their father he was consuming Adriana's life, taking her freedom from her. He couldn't—wouldn't—do that. "I'll pay you."

"You know I'm immune to bribery."

"I don't want them to see me like this."

"It's too late."

Eric's voice was harsh. "No, it's not."

"She doesn't mind you here."

"I'm a burden." He saw all he'd struggled to build—namely his affair with her—slowly collapsing. "She has a life of her own. She's already missed days of work. I won't be like Dad . . . please." The last word was forced from his lips.

Silence descended as they were transported back in memory to the small room where their father had died. They remembered the weeks before his death, changing the sheets under his skeletal form, feeding him, wiping his chin when food would seep out from the sides of his mouth.

They recalled the love that brought them to do it and the anger that kept them from looking into his eyes. The anger of knowing he was leaving them, as their mother had, in a country that was supposed to give them riches. In a country that, in tales, had promised a bright future.

Eric knew the burden of being a caretaker. He didn't want Adriana in that role—to ultimately despise not the illness, but him.

Drake sighed, empathy overcoming sense in the silent language of brothers. "Promise me you'll rest at home." He helped him to his feet.

Eric sagged against him, grateful. He just needed a week and then he'd see Adriana and fix the damage his illness had caused. Drake helped him into his shirt and opened the door. Cassie stood there. Both men recoiled.

"Get back," Drake demanded. "A new mother can't enter the room of a sick man."

Cassie frowned at him. "Of course she can."

His voice was firm. "No, she can't."

She rested a hand on the door frame. "I won't come in, if you put Eric back."

Eric spoke up. "Cassie, wait."

She stared at her husband. Drake put Eric on the bed. She rested her hands on her hips. "I should have known I couldn't trust you two."

Eric pushed up his glasses. "Cassie, listen—"

She shook her head. "I don't care how you were able to convince your brother, you're not convincing me. It's cold outside and you're going to stay here until you get better. Your behavior is ridiculous."

Drake coughed delicately. "Excuse me, but I remember a certain young woman crawling out of a man's apartment when she was sick."

She folded her arms, flashing a sheepish grin. "All right. I sympathize, but he's still staying here."

Eric's spirits fell. "You don't understand."

"I do understand," she said softly. "More than you know." She blew him a kiss. Then dragged her husband out of the room. "Now rest." She gently shut the door.

How could he rest when he felt imprisoned? Eric waited until the house was quiet to slip away. Adriana was in her office and Nina in her room. He grabbed his shoes and trod softly to the front door. The living room lights were dim. He carefully took his coat from the closet, and then a beam of light struck him. He turned. Nina and Adriana glared at him. Nina turned off the flashlight. Adriana turned on the lights.

"You're becoming a nuisance," she said.

"I know. That's why I'm leaving."

Nina tapped her foot. "You're supposed to stay in bed."

"I have things to get done."

Adriana took his coat. "Yes, getting better being a top priority. You're making it worse. You won't rest, you won't eat." She tossed his coat over her shoulder. "At least eat something."

"Please," Nina said.

He rested against the closet, his legs feeling heavy. "Fine."

He followed them into the kitchen. He sat and waited as Adriana cooked. A few moments later, Adriana placed a plate of runny eggs in front of him. The sight of the yolk bursting through the white and seeping onto the plate like yellow blood didn't agree with his system. He closed his eyes.

Nina moved the plate and whispered, "She's better with toast."

He managed a cup of tea—sweetened to perfection— and two slices of toast.

He set his empty cup down. "There. Can I leave now?"

"No!" they chorused.

He fell forward, holding his head. "But they're dying."

Adriana stared at him, wondering if his fever had reached his mind.

"Who's dying?" she asked.

"I'm sure Margarite and Charlotte are withering away," he mumbled, his thoughts distant. "Louis will hang on."

Adriana frowned. "Who are you talking about?"

"His plants," Nina said.

He continued to mumble. "I didn't water them. I should have watered them."

"Such drama," Adriana scoffed. "I'm sure they'll be fine."

He shook his head. "No. They—"

"All right, all right. I'll check on them," she said before he argued. "While I'm there, what else do you need?"


They went to his apartment after Nina returned from school. Adriana checked on him before they left, taking an extra precaution to prevent his escape.

His apartment was a jungle. A lush labyrinth of plants—

crouching, standing, climbing, and sitting as welcome oc-
cupants to the apartment. An ivy climbed a far wall,
tapering off into flowering blossoms near the window, a
hanging plant had its leaves crawling out of the pot like
an octopus, a large palm towered over the room as a waiting soldier, the air was fresh and vibrant. So alive with
energy that she half expected a large cat to pounce. She
grinned to herself. No, the cat was away, sleeping in her
bed.

"Wow," Nina said.

Wow was right. The type of man who kept these plants
alive was no ordinary, dull mathematician. Branches
weren't broken, limbs hadn't been chopped. In his limited
space life grew wild. She couldn't understand it.

Nina suddenly ran forward, waking Adriana out of her
thoughts. She closed the door behind her. She heard the
water running and found Nina in the kitchen, filling the
water pot and dropping in plant food.

Adriana nodded in approval. "You don't seem to need
any help."

Nina tried to lift the pot. "I could use help taking it out
of the sink."

She obliged.

As Nina watered the plants, leaving tiny puddles in her
wake, Adriana looked around. Except for the plants, the
place held no other luxuries—paintings were absent, there
were a few account manuals and a TV set, but nothing to
give the place a feeling of home. In his bedroom, the bed
was stark with tight brown sheets pulled military style, his
refrigerator was filled with leftovers from Drake's restaurant. The only thing he had in abundance was sugar,
pineapple soda, and vanilla sandwiches.

Something about the place bothered her. He seemed to
give all the luxuries to the plants—dressing them in handsome terra-cotta pots and porcelain vases but gave nothing

to himself. He didn't splurge on clothing, shoes, music, or videos. Not even a subscription to a business magazine.

She packed a few items. She found his drawer to be extremely tidy—socks properly rolled and sorted by type and color, shirts pressed and organized by sleeve length and style. She went to his desk and grabbed some papers he was working on, then zipped up the bag. As she slung it over her shoulder, the front door opened.

# Ten

"You don't need to worry, Gerta, I'm sure he's fine," a male voice said with tired patience and laden with a Norwegian accent.

A woman's voice replied, "When I see, I will know."

An older couple dressed in heavy gray coats, long scarves, and wool hats entered the room. For one panicked instant Adriana feared she had entered the wrong apartment. The couple turned and stared. Shrewd green eyes studied her. They looked vaguely familiar.

"Who are you?" the woman asked.

"I'm Adriana Travers. I'm sorry, I thought this was Eric's place."

The woman came forward, seeming to shrink as she came closer. "It is. Is he not here? Why are you here?"

Adriana blinked, looking down at the woman, wondering why she had to submit to such an inquisition if this was the right place. "No, he's not here," she said in the same brusque manner. "He's at my place. He's sick."

The woman turned to her husband, self-satisfied. "Did I not tell you that something was wrong?" She turned back to Adriana. "What is your address?"

"Why?"

"Because we plan to visit him."

"She has been worried," the man said.

"Who are you?"

"Mr. and Mrs. Larsen. We have known Eric since he was a boy."

Adriana smiled at the thought of Eric ever being a boy.

"Has he not told you about us?" Mrs. Larsen asked, hurt.

"He's a private man," Mr. Larsen said. "He won't tell everyone things."

Adriana clutched the bag and nodded. "Yes, we've only become friends recently."

Mr. Larsen looked behind her. "And who is this?"

Nina came forward. "Hi."

"My daughter, Nina," Adriana said.

They both nodded. "Nice to meet you."

Mrs. Larsen narrowed her eyes at Adriana. "I am sure I have seen you somewhere before."

"Perhaps since you know Eric you probably know Drake—"

"The wedding, of course! And the babies' baptism." She clapped her hands in delight. "Such joy, such joy! Are we to hear wedding bells again?"

"Oh no," Adriana stammered, feeling flushed under the intense stare. "Uh, we're just friends. Why don't I take you to my place to see Eric? He's very grumpy."

"He is always grumpy when he is sick. Poor boy has always been sickly."

"Really?"

"He stayed with us many times because Drake could not watch him," Mr. Larsen said.

His wife added, "I did not like where they lived. I would have let them stay with us but our place was so small. So we watched Eric when he was ill, usually in winter like now, and he would read whatever we gave him and watch the kids playing outside, knowing he could not join."

Adriana's heart constricted, imagining a sickly little boy who developed his mind because he couldn't develop his body. She imagined the shame he must have felt having his brother, who was already overworked, hovering over him when certainly he wanted to help too. No wonder he had such a hard time accepting her assistance. He would have to learn.

Again he woke to silence. Eric sighed, relieved. They were gone. Freedom. He reached for his trousers. They weren't there. His shoes, socks, and shirt were missing as well. He swore. Adriana hadn't trusted him. Evidently with reason. He drummed his fingers on the bed. That wouldn't stop him from looking. He searched the place—her closet, the hall, the bathroom, in her office—his clothes were gone. He was trapped.

He rested against the wall, defeated. He would make the best of it. However, that did not include staying in bed. And he wasn't going to walk around half naked either. He grabbed her robe. It barely reached his knees and wouldn't completely close, but it was better than nothing.

He went into the living room and flipped through the channels, then turned it off. He had to do something. He turned to the kitchen and had an idea.

The smell of frying fish greeted Adriana as she opened the door. The heavenly scent pleased her until she saw Eric hunched over the stove, his eyes half closed and his face flushed. She stormed up to him, halting at the image he created: a large black man wearing a red silk robe with flaired sleeves.

She leaned against the counter as if she were in a bar. "Hey there, sexy."

He spun around, his eyes accusing. "You took my clothes."

Nina came into the room. She spotted Eric and began to smile.

Adriana glanced at her. "Go into the living room until I call you."

Her smile grew, she left the room giggling.

Eric scowled. "See what you've done?"

"Serves you right. What are you doing up?" It was a rhetorical question. She did not give him a chance to reply. "I told you to rest, Cassie told you to rest, Drake told you to rest. Are you too stubborn to listen to anyone?"

"You don't have to shout."

She took the spatula from him. "Your fever has gone up again."

"It's the kitchen heat."

She glared at him and motioned to the table.

He carefully sat. "I was only trying to start dinner."

"I could have bought something."

"That's not in the budget."

"I haven't had a chance to splurge because of you. Trust me, I have money."

She saw him clench his fist.

"I've missed days of work, had to reschedule a meeting with my leasing agent. I can't take time for a facial or walk by any stores for window shopping. I'm stuck in this place all because of you."

His jaw twitched.

"I've had to pay for the cost of your medicine, you've sweated through two of my favorite sheets, and I've had to make sure the temperature isn't too hot even though we're freezing. My nails are chipping and my hair is a mess because I spend all my time worrying about you. And you can't even stay in bed!" She tossed the spatula in the sink. "I've broken up with guys who've given me less hassle than you. And I'm sorry that I'm the type that strikes you as altruistic, but let me assure you that I'm not." She rested her hands on the table and leaned toward him. "I don't do anything I don't want to. If I didn't want you here, once Winston had gone, I would have taken your fevered behind home. And the way you've been behaving I'm wondering if that's a good idea."

His eyes clung to hers.

"But I won't and you know why."

He lowered his eyes.

She looked up and saw Mr. and Mrs. Larsen staring. She had forgotten about them. "You have visitors."

His eyes flew up. "Cassie and Drake?"

"No, Eric," Mrs. Larsen said, entering the kitchen. "Sit, sit."

"She was worried about you," Mr. Larsen said.

He stood. "I'm fine."

"You call this fine?" She tugged on the robe. "Come. Let's go to bed." She took his arm and left the kitchen.

Adriana laughed. "That doesn't bother you?" she asked, referring to the double meaning.

Mr. Larsen only smiled and followed.

Nina came into the kitchen still giggling. "Uncle Eric looked really funny."

"Yes." Adriana tapped her chin. "But he's given me an idea."

Mrs. Larsen helped Eric into bed. "Quite a woman you have here."

"You shouldn't have come." He rested against the head-board.

They both ignored this. They told him about their son, Sven, and his wife. Mrs. Larsen talked of her garden group, Mr. Larsen of his recent chess game. Eric was soothed by the smell of caraway, reminding him of their home and the stews she would make. He remembered how good it felt to climb into their guest bed—a cot, which to him was like a chaise—with all the covers to himself. Not having to share with his brother and sister. Having a warm meal served on dishes free of any stains or cracks. Having a mother's gentle hand on his forehead and the rough fussing that followed.

But he was a grown man now, not a boy free to selfishly indulge the kindness of others. As an adult it haunted him how hard his brother had struggled. How his constant illnesses had been a burden even though Drake never said so. He remembered Drake staring at him with resignation in his eyes, wondering how he could afford the cough medicine. He had forced him to make a difficult choice: dinner or cough medicine?

Drake usually went without dinner. Eric would watch him sit by the window and smoke until the hunger pangs went away, giving what little food they had to Jackie and him. He'd developed the nicotine habit for them, a habit that might ultimately cost him his life. If only he'd been stronger, more—

"Relax," Mrs. Larsen said gently.

He looked at her. "Take me home."

"You are home."

He looked at Mr. Larsen, who was studying a lamp. "She worries too much."

"You have a fine woman here," he said.

"She's not mine."

"Quiet. Just sleep." She hummed and soon his tired eyes closed.

Adriana did not ask the Larsens to stay to dinner; it was understood. They ate and chatted in the dining room, Adriana feeling Mrs. Larsen's shrewd gaze on her.

She didn't eat much. She felt bad eating a meal Eric couldn't enjoy, and having spoken so harshly to him. She wondered if his fever would go down and what damage his activity had done to his recovery.

Mrs. Larsen suddenly laughed. "He is right. You do worry too much. I can see it in your eyes."

Adriana lowered her gaze, ashamed. "I'm sorry."

Mrs. Larsen shrugged and turned to her husband. They

shared a secret glance. Later they begged off dessert, checked Eric once more, then left.

Winston came over the next day to see Eric's progress.

"You haven't been resting," he said, putting his stethoscope away. There was no judgment in his tone. His words were stated as fact. "Your pneumonia is as stubborn as you are."

"My fever's gone."

"Barely and your voice still sounds as if your cords have been savaged." He sat back. "So, Henson, don't look surprised. I remember you." He grinned. "How did you find yourself in the clutches of Adriana? She usually chooses people she can help. Started when she brought home that little fat friend of hers."

"I'm sure Drake would like to hear your description of his wife," he said, sarcastic.

"Drake's not here and I love Cassie like a sister. As does Adriana. You're an odd choice for her, however. She likes people she can help or fix."

"I'm here," he said, referring to his sickness.

"True, but I wonder if it's something else. Have you made a bad business deal? Suffered a broken heart?"

Eric looked at him, his face impassive.

Winston shrugged. "Just a warning. I'm sure you don't want to be another project of hers. Now I want you to rest. Find the word in the dictionary if it is foreign to you. It's a verb, something you do." He gathered his bag.

Eric kicked the blankets away once Winston left. He didn't want to be a project. He didn't want to be fixed. He stood up too quickly and fell back on the bed when the room began to spin. Why did he have to be so weak, so pathetic? How could he ever make this up to her?

He scratched his cheek, feeling the roughness of his beard. He needed to shave. He probably looked like a wino. He lay back on the bed and stared up at the canopy. He felt like a hermit in the bed of a princess. A princess who pitied him. For once the word made his gut clench. He didn't want to be pitied. He wanted her to desire him as she would any other man. But that wasn't how their affair had started. She had felt sorry for him. He squeezed his eyes shut, knowing his illness had only made it worse.

He woke to the sweet smell of coconut hair oil. He opened his eyes and saw Nina standing beside the bed. He could tell by the shadows on the floor that it was the afternoon.

"Mom wanted me to look in on you. I'm sorry you're sick," she said. "Do you want anything to eat or drink?"

He shook his head.

"Do you want me to read to you?"

"That'd be nice," he said in a raw whisper.

She climbed onto the bed and read *A Little Princess,* her soft voice soothing his restless mind.


Adriana went into the bedroom and undid the sheets, which had become twisted around his waist. He was a violent sleeper when he was ill. Even now his brow was furrowed and his whole body was tense. One of his pillows lay on the floor. She picked it up and placed it under his head and then stroked his back. Soon the muscles relaxed and he sighed like a contented child. She knelt next to him.

She wasn't sure what she felt for him then. It wasn't anger, it wasn't pity, it wasn't exasperation. She just wanted him well and had no desire to leave him until he was. His illness forced her to be still—it was a scary prospect. She was used to buzzing about, not staying still so that her mind could come up with thoughts or reflections.

For years she had rebelled against staying put. Afraid of the ideas that would sink into her mind: She wasn't always happy with herself or the men that she chose. At times she wanted to stay home rather than go out. That was too much like her childhood, forced solitude when other kids were allowed to play. She was free now and could play all she wanted. Yet the prospect no longer appealed to her as much. Hinton had called to tell her the group was going to a club and she refused them without regret. Keith had invited her to lunch. She told him another time. She didn't feel the need to escape as she once had.

Eric opened his eyes. She wondered what he saw when he looked at her, wondered why he still seemed so far away.

Her voice was barely a whisper. "Hi."

"Hi."

"Do you need anything?"

He shook his head.

"Asking is hard, isn't it?"

He blinked.

She lay next to him suddenly exhausted. "Well, giving isn't any easier."

Darkness filled the room when she opened her eyes. She sat up when she realized Eric wasn't in bed. She heard splashing in the bathroom and relaxed. She found him in the tub.

She looked at him, pleased that his color was back and his eyes were clear. "You're looking much better. Nice to see you relaxing. Why didn't you ask me to join you?"

"Because—"

She stripped out of her clothes. "I know it's the middle of the night, but this looks like fun."

He held out his hand to stop her. "No, wait!"

The warning came too late. She stepped in and shrieked. She jumped back out. "It's freezing!"

"I know."

She quickly dressed. "I thought men took those to . . . you know."

"That's a cold shower."

She felt his forehead. "Do you have a fever again?"

"No. I like it. Your body gets used to the cold eventually." He glanced at a candle. "It's invigorating."

She sat on the rim of the tub. "I'll never understand you. I can't believe you wear your glasses in the tub." She pulled them off. "There, that's better."

"No, it's not. I can't see you."

She shrugged. "One must suffer for vanity."

"Where are my clothes?"

She stood. "You'll have them in the morning."

"Adriana?" he called as she opened the door.

She turned to him. "Yes?"

He gripped the rim of the tub. *Don't pity me.* "I'll make this up to you."

"You don't have to."

"But I will." He said the words so softly she didn't hear.


Thank God he felt like a human again, Eric thought. He sat in the dining room amid papers and office paraphernalia. Unfortunately, he was a human with deadlines. He had completed his article for *Investment*, a monthly newsletter. It had taken him days to complete it, his foggy brain having rebelled against thinking. But now it was finished and he only had to type it.

"Lunchtime," Nina said, carrying a bowl of chicken noodle soup. It slopped precariously from side to side.

He pushed himself from the table. "Let me help you."

"No, I've got it." She set the bowl down. The soup finally made its escape, landing on his article, blurring his handwriting into illegible blobs.

He swore fiercely. He quickly glanced up, remembering

her presence. Stark dismay covered her little features and something even more threatening.

He pointed his pen at her. "Don't cry."

She pulled in her lips and nodded solemnly, her chocolate eyes melting into tears.

He sighed, resigned. His request was ridiculous. "Come here."

Her chin trembled. She shook her head and took a step back, poised for flight.

He picked her up, his voice gentle. "I'm sorry. Go ahead and cry."

She did. Deep heaving sobs that shook her entire body.

"Seems you're more like your mother than we'd both like to admit." He made light of it, but something about her crying worried him. It wasn't a simple childish sadness, there was deep sorrow, deep pain. She clung to him tight as if he would leave her.

He patted her on the back. "I'm not mad at you. You mustn't cry like that. Save your tears."

Adriana came into the room and quickly assessed the situation. She sent him a silent question.

"I think we need to go for a walk," he said.

"There's a track on the roof."

He frowned. "Not helpful."

"Oh, I'd forgotten." She had forgotten his fear of heights. Watching him hold her daughter as if he'd protect her from any known or unknown danger had caused her to forget his fears. He looked like a man without them. "There's a courtyard."

"Okay."

She quickly bundled Nina in her coat and then helped Eric with his. Only after she had tied a scarf around his neck and kissed him on the cheek did she realized what she'd done. She backed away, embarrassed.

"Sorry, it's become a habit."

His eyes laughed, but he said nothing.

"I only want you out for ten minutes."

He nodded and she turned to clear the table.

It was a regular November day. The city had decided to welcome fall, so the air was chill, trees blazing with colors, leaves swirling on the ground and dancing in the wind.

"Are you sad your dad's getting married?" Eric asked as they walked in the courtyard.

For once he wished he wasn't so blunt. She burst into tears again. He sat on a bench and pulled her onto his lap.

"He still loves you, you know."

She shook her head, her eyes lowered. "I was bad. Very, very bad. That's why he gave me to Mom."

He tweaked her chin. "You could never be so bad that he doesn't love you."

"I can. I didn't like Irene and I ignored her and moved things and played tricks. I thought if she didn't like me, then Dad would get rid of her." Her voice dropped. "But he got rid of me instead."

"He didn't get rid of you. He just didn't want to see you hurt."

She swung her legs. "I'm sorry about your work," she said finally.

"It's okay."

She met his eyes. "But you were so angry."

"I was annoyed."

"You swore."

"Not at you." He adjusted his glasses and watched a squirrel scurry past. "It's a bad habit of mine. I didn't mean to make you unhappy."

She shrugged. "It's not you."

"It's not you either. You didn't cause your parents' divorce. They both love you very much, but adults aren't as smart as they seem and sometimes they show how much they love you in funny ways. Your father saw Irene mistreat you and he wanted to protect you. He thought you deserved a mother that loves you, not a stepmother that didn't."

"Then why can't he marry Mom again? Why does he have to love Irene?"

"Love just happens, you can't force it. It just is."

She frowned as she considered this. "I won't mind if you marry Mom. I'll be good all the time if you want."

"You're always good."

She suddenly grinned. "No, not always."

He stood, recognizing the look of mischief, glad her sadness had passed. He changed the subject. "Let's go look at the plants in your garden."

Eric tried to finish his article, but he couldn't ignore the loud pumping sound coming from Adriana's office. He opened the door and stumbled back as if struck by a sonic boom. Drums pounded and guitars screeched, throwing out a hazard of sound from the stereo. He covered his ears and turned down the volume.

Adriana turned to him, surprised. "Did you need something?"

"How can you work in that noise?"

"I like to work to music."

He massaged one ear as if in pain. "Music?"

"I once dated the guitarist of that group."

He lifted the CD case. "Corrosion of Sanity." He set it down and came up behind her as she sat at the drafting table. "Yes, I remember now." He peered over her shoulder. "What are you doing?"

She moved to block his view. "Oh, just some sketches." She looked at him with expectation. "Did you need anything?"

He picked up a sketch of a man in briefs. "No." He

looked closer and furrowed his brows. "That looks like me."

"You gave me an idea."

He grabbed another sketch. "Why am I wearing high heels and a pink boa?"

She snatched it from him. "I was mad at you at the time."

He laughed. "So you turned me into a diva?"

She shrugged, guilty, relieved that he took no offense.

He lifted another sketch. "I'm impressed. Looks like a male version of your robe."

"It is."

"Don't make it yellow. Try more masculine colors."

"Yellow can be masculine."

"Not this color yellow. No man wants to end up looking like a daisy."

She looked at him.

"Straight man," he corrected.

"You have an unhealthy aversion to bright colors."

"That's not true."

"I have yet to see you in red."

He lifted a brow.

"Besides my robe."

"It's cold. I tend to wear dark colors in the winter." He moved her chair aside and bent over the table. "What else do you have here?"

"Nothing. I—"

He placed a finger against his lips. "Shh, I'm trying to appreciate the artwork."

"It's hardly artwork. I—"

He sent her a look; she closed her mouth. He liked the style and colors of her designs and the exquisite attention to detail. He didn't know much about lingerie but he wouldn't mind seeing her in any of them. He pointed at a sketch. "Are these tassels?"

"Yes."

"Hmm. I'm going to dream well tonight." He put the papers down. "Why didn't you tell me you have your own collection?"

"I don't," she lied. "I just do these for fun."

"Why? These look marketable. If you invested half of what you invest in others, you'd be a success."

"But it's costly. I'd need money for materials and to hire a seamstress. I know I need financial advice to pull it off, that's why I came to . . ." She broke off, shamefaced. Her secret was out.

He rested his hand on the back of her chair. "Let me guess. There's no parent fund."

"I didn't want you to laugh at me."

"I never laugh at good business sense. Actually, I think I'd like to invest in this."

She looked at him, alarmed. "No, you can't."

"Why not?"

"I'm not good enough yet."

He picked up a garter hanging off the drafting lamp. "This looks good enough for me."

She snatched it away and bunched it up. "It's just a prototype."

"Why are you turning me down?"

"Because you don't know anything about lingerie."

"I know you wear it. Do I need a degree?"

"You don't know the risk factors. It's a competitive field."

"Then let me visit your store and see the competition."

"I'm not sure—"

He turned and headed out the door. "I'm glad you agree."

She threw the garter belt as he closed the door.


The smell of lavender curled a sensuous finger, drawing him into the shop. Divine Notions' velvet drapery and various shades of red—from the carpet to the window display— demonstrated a confidence that it could fulfill the most jaded woman's deepest fantasies. He approached a rack of bras, their circular shapes maintained by sufficient padding. He cupped a satin bra, liking the feel.

Adriana slapped his hand away. "That's not how you handle the merchandise."

"You would really look good in this."

"What? You don't think I have enough?"

His eyes dipped to the curve of her blouse. "Actually—"

She lifted his chin. "That was a rhetorical question. Come on."

She was showing him some of her name-brand best-sellers, when the front doorbell was violently agitated. A cold rush of air dashed into the room along with a woman in a long coat holding a Divine Notions bag and a young girl whose head was bowed. Adriana recognized the girl: Helen.

"I would like to speak to the manager!" the woman demanded.

Adriana took a deep breath and approached the pair. "May I help you?"

"Are you the manager? I don't wish to deal with some useless clerk who can't possibly handle the situation."

"I believe I can help you."

The woman measured her in one long look. "And who are you?"

"I am the owner."

This admission ignited the woman with more energy. "Well, then I have plenty to say! I have half a mind to write a petition to get this . . ." Her eyes scanned the shop with scorn. "Place shut down."

"I'm sorry you feel that way. How has this shop offended you?"

"How?" She shook the bag. "By peddling these indecent wares to children. My daughter bought these items from here." She dug in the bag and waved a pink bra and panty. "These are outrageous."

"Mom, please." Helen glanced at Adriana, then Eric, and blushed furiously.

"How can you encourage such lascivious behavior in a young girl?"

"Lascivious?"

"Yes, I said lascivious. I saw my daughter prancing around like a prostitute because of these things. You surround yourself with filth and you are no more than a madam, luring innocent girls into this awful den of sin. My daughter should not be encouraged to stare at her body in such a way because she's wearing clothing that advocates that."

"I doubt that a healthy appreciation of your body is—"

"I don't want my daughter getting ideas. Soon she'll be like those girls. Wearing jeans so low their thongs show. "

Adriana sighed, choosing her words carefully. "I am sorry you find the concept of wearing underwear offensive."

The woman gasped; Adriana continued. "However, if you wish to return the items—"

"Forget it. Just stay away from my daughter." She dragged her offspring and raced out the door.

Adriana watched them. A blast of cold air touched the perspiration on her skin and stung her eyes.

"Prude bitch," Sya said.

Adriana shook her head. She turned and jumped back when she saw Eric standing there. She had forgotten about him.

His eyes were as hard as stone. "Does that happen a lot?"

She blinked quickly, waiting for the stinging in her eyes to subside. "Thank goodness, no. Unfortunately, there are enough people with such thoughts to make your days difficult." The woman was similar to her mother, who was embarrassed to tell her friends what her daughter did. Her grandmother, who wished she had a proper career. And her father, who thought she could put her talents to better use.

Eric draped a brotherly arm on her shoulders. "It's a shame how one person can ruin a perfectly good day."

She nodded.

"I once had this client, an attractive woman, I might add."

"Would you have mentioned her looks if she was ugly?"

"Of course not. May I continue?"

She rolled her eyes. "Yes, you may."

"As I was saying, she came into my office and told me all my ideas were illogical and poorly thought out."

She was about to express her sympathies until she realized he was talking about her. She smiled, chagrined. "And you slept with her out of revenge, right?"

His eyes darkened. "No. Do you want to know why?"

No. She turned away from his gaze. "Well, now you see the competition."

"And I'm still interested in investing."

"Then you have to be at the fashion show," Sya said. "She's going to show her designs."

Adriana looked at her and made a face in warning. "I don't think that's necessary."

Sya ignored her. "It's going to be a great show."

"When is it?" he asked.

Sya gave him all the details. Adriana pretended to straighten a rack. She wished he hadn't shown interest, because she would be disappointed if he didn't show up.

Eric sat on the edge of the bed, staring at Elissa as she groomed herself. He listened to water rushing in the bathroom sink as Adriana prepared for bed. He was getting too comfortable here. He was over his illness. He should have left by now, but he was still here. Still sleeping in Adriana's bed, eating her food, walking her daughter to the bus stop. He glanced around the room. Every night he spent here felt like a dream. The luxurious colors, the vibrancy shimmering under the surface, and the tranquil energy that calmed it—calmed him. It made him feel as though this was where he belonged. He couldn't keep up this illusion. He would have to leave.

He turned when the bathroom door opened.

"Close your eyes," Adriana said. "I have a surprise for you."

He shut one eye. "Okay, they're closed."

She peeked around the corner and glared at him. "Both eyes."

He shut the other one. "Now they're both closed."

He heard her move in front of him. "Okay, open them," she said.

He stared at her, his pulse quickening. She was dressed in a tight, white nurse's uniform.

She struck a pose. "Ta da!"

"What's this?"

Her hands fell to her sides. "What does it look like?"

"Like you're about to make rounds at Washington Hospital and get thrown out."

She adjusted her skirt. It was an inch higher than decent. "Don't tell me you've never had nurse fantasies."

He scratched his head. "Nurse fantasies?" He glanced up at the ceiling, pensive. "I've had waitress fantasies, stewardess fantasies."

"You mean flight attendants."

"Yes, those too and teacher fantasies." He shook his head and looked at her. "Nope. No nurse fantasies."

She removed his glasses, bending over just enough so he could have a peek at her cleavage. "Then you're going to start."

He touched the corners of his mouth in hopes he wasn't drooling. "And I'm willing to learn." He paused and frowned. "Wait, that's my teacher fantasy."

"Shut up." She opened his legs and stood between them. "Let's start with introductions."

"Just call me a happy d—"

She covered his mouth. "Behave."

"I thought we were supposed to be naughty."

She folded her arms and tapped her foot. "I'm going to leave."

He tightened his legs, trapping her. "Sorry to tell you this, but you look extra sexy when you do that. There's nothing like a woman who looks like she wants to punish you."

"Eric," she warned.

He held up his hands. "Fine, fine. I'll behave. Let's start again."

"First you have to open your legs and let me go."

He grinned. "Just think of it as part of my condition."

She sighed. "Okay. Hello, my name is Nurse Travers and I'm here to take care of you."

He reached for her. "Be gentle."

She pushed his hands away and wagged her finger. "I'm afraid, Mr. Henson, that kind of behavior is not allowed." She felt his forehead. "Yes, you do have a temperature." She unbuttoned his shirt. "Let me check your lymph nodes." She pushed his shirt away, her hands roaming his chest, falling to his trousers. "Hmm, just as I suspected, you are a little swollen here. Let me ease your distress." She tugged off his trousers and pants and cupped his erection.

He jumped. "What are you doing?"

She looked at him, confused. "Giving you pleasure, of course."

His eyes widened. "You're not going to . . ."

She licked her lips, her finger trailing the length of him. "Do you want me to?"

He flexed his fingers, fighting for control. Her hand on

him filled him with liquid fire. He wanted her to, but his mouth wouldn't form the words.

She shrugged when he didn't reply. "Maybe another time. Let me find another suitable way to relieve this condition." She lifted a suggestive brow. "I've very flexible." She winked. "You'll find out soon enough. Let me get my gloves." She grabbed a condom and rolled it on.

"Adriana—"

"Quiet. We want all our patients to be at ease. Now, Mr. Henson, are you ready for the remedy?"

He grabbed her arms and rolled on top of her.

She frowned up at him. "Eric, you're not playing by the rules. I'm the one in charge."

He kissed her neck. "Who cares about the rules?"

"I do." She tried to push him off her. "Do I have to tie your hands?"

They inched up her skirt. "No, they're busy at the moment. God, you smell good." He kissed her, then stopped when she didn't respond. "What's wrong?"

"Haven't you ever had a woman make love to you before?"

He sat up. "What are you talking about?"

She rolled away. "Question answered."

He watched her as she smoothed out her blouse. The V neck was so low her black bra peeked through. He wanted her. Naked. Now. He waved his hands, frustrated that talk was interrupting his goal. "What's wrong?"

"I want to please you."

He smiled. "You always please me."

"But you do all the work."

He hesitated. "If you don't like what I do—"

"That's the problem. You do everything." She sighed, exasperated. "Since you don't understand, I'll show you." She pushed him onto his back and saddled him. "Don't look nervous, this will be fun. I won't embarrass you."

"Adriana—"

She covered his mouth with hers for one wild moment and then stared at him. Her voice was low. "When a woman wants to please a man she finds his erogenous zones. Like his ears." She gently kissed each one. "Or his nipples." She fingered the hard bulbs, then followed with her tongue.

He jumped to his feet. "This isn't what I want."

She looked at him, startled. "Why not?"

He began to pace and shook his head. "I just don't want it."

"When have you had an aversion to sex?"

"This isn't sex and you know it."

She opened her mouth, then closed it. She finally said, "I don't understand."

He gestured to her costume. "You don't need to do this. All I want is sex."

She glanced down at her short skirt and tight blouse. "You're getting sex. Trust me."

He covered his eyes for a moment. "No, you're giving me something else."

His words finally became clear. "I get it," she said slowly. "I'm just supposed to lie there and offer you nothing, right? I'm not supposed to please you because that's a little too intimate." She slapped her forehead. "I'm sorry. I forgot that we're having an affair. I'm just supposed to show up."

He folded his arms and stared at her. "I thought you liked what I did."

She rested her chin in her hand. She loved what he did. Right now he looked incredibly sexy naked. He was intimidating like a menacing silhouette with the moonlight polishing his form. "I do, but a relationship is about give and take. Oops, there is that nasty word again, 'relationship.' We don't have that, do we? However, for your information, some people in affairs have fun like this. Perhaps we could consider this relationship unpaid prostitution."

"Adriana—" Her name was a low warning.

She ignored it. "I'm like one of those rides in front of department stores. Put your money in, ride for a short while, then get off. You're satisfied because you've had fun and the ride doesn't take you anywhere."

"You don't understand. I don't need anything from you."

"You need sex. That's why you're here."

"That's not why."

"Then why are you here? I must have misunderstood the basis of this affair."

"I want to be here with you. Isn't that enough?"

"No."

They stared at each other.

"What do you want?" he finally asked.

"More of you."

He turned away and said, "I don't want to be Nina's father."

Her temper ignited into rage. She grabbed her pillows and threw them at him one by one. "You bastard. How dare you! How dare you think I would try to sleep my way to getting my daughter a stepfather? What kind of woman do you think I am? Get out! Now!"

He dodged a pillow aimed at his head. "That came out wrong."

"Clever of you to notice. Get out."

He caught a pillow she threw at him and tossed it on the floor. He sat on the bed, his back toward her.

She pushed him, but he didn't budge. "You're a long way from the door."

He turned to her, his eyes full of regret. "I'm sorry. I didn't mean that."

His words weren't sufficient, but his expression was. "Jerk," she said.

"I know."

She looked away and tucked her feet underneath her. "I forgive you, you . . . slime chicken."

He frowned, confused. "What's a slime chicken?"

"I don't know. I couldn't think of anything else." She folded her arms. "You make me so mad sometimes."

He turned away, resting his hands on his knees. "Then why do you want to please me?"

"You know why."

He spun around. His eyes widened in shocked horror. "No."

"Yes."

"You're serious?"

"Yes."

He fell facedown on the bed and swore. "How did that happen?" His voice was muffled.

"I don't know."

He groaned. "Are you sure?"

"No, but I'm close."

"Then let's not go further."

"Is my love that repulsive?"

He rolled on his back and stared up at her. "No. It's not that." He threw an arm over his eyes. "I'm a simple man. I'm not hard to figure out. I like women and I like sex. I've never been in love my entire life."

"You asked three women to marry you."

He let his hand fall. "You know as well as I do that people don't always marry for love."

"But you could, eventually."

He studied her. "How would you know I wasn't marrying you for what you are, instead of who you are?"

"I wouldn't care."

"How would I know that deep down you don't want a stepfather for Nina? Or someone to finance your designs?"

"Why would you care?"

He reached to adjust his glasses, then realized he wasn't wearing them. "I don't know."

She searched his face, but his expression was unreadable. "Are we breaking up?"

He sat up and glanced out the window. He sighed wearily. "You'd be my first girlfriend."

"You've never had a girlfriend?"

"I usually called them lovers or—"

She poked him with her elbow. "I don't want to know."

A smile hovered over his lips. "I was always respectful."

"I still don't want to know."

He cupped her chin. "Do you want a boyfriend?"

She nodded.

"Okay, I'll help you find one."

She slapped his hand away. "Eric!"

He ran a tired hand down his face. "You're ruining my pattern."

"You're ruining mine."

He fell silent. So silent she began to worry he was withdrawing into himself.

"Eric?"

"I don't want you to pity me," he said in a brusque voice.

"I don't."

"You can't help it. You know that I have had two failed proposals, my last girlfriend cheated on me, my brother is considered the good-looking one, my immune system is so bad that I develop pneumonia from a seven-year-old with a cold, I'm afraid of heights, and my background is so low even dust mites snub their noses." His eyes swept her face. "You have a soft heart and that's what makes you wonderful, but I won't have a girlfriend that feels sorry for me."

"I don't feel sorry for you."

"Adriana—"

"I don't," she said firmly. She tugged on her blouse. "You don't make me feel useless."

"You aren't useless."

"I spend too much, have strange mothering habits, can't cook—"

"But you're clever, creative, and fun."

"And you're smart and solid and always there."

He pinched the bridge of his nose and began to mutter numbers.

"Are you adding something?" she asked.

"No, they're prime numbers. I mumble them when I'm going out of my mind."

"Thanks a lot."

He rubbed his forehead. "Adriana, we're crazy to think this can work as a real relationship."

She smiled sweetly. "It wouldn't be the first time you were illogical."

He sent her a hard glare.

She knelt behind him and wrapped her arms around his neck. "You're thinking too much." She let her hand slide down his chest, feeling his muscles constrict under her palm. "You want me and I want you."

He turned to her and hooked his finger in the V of her blouse, succumbing to his desire for her. He pulled her toward him. "Okay, then do your damage, Nurse Travers."

"I get to be in charge?"

He kissed her chin. "What do you mean by 'in charge'?"

"You'll have to trust me."

His lips brushed her forehead. "I don't trust anyone."

She paused. "That's a scary way to live."

He loosened her blouse. "You get used to it. I like to be in control."

"But—"

He suddenly grinned. "Nice bra. How do you undo it?"

She grabbed his hands. "You can't always be in control."

He frowned. "You weren't this talkative before."

She lifted a brow, tightening her hold on his hands.

"I don't mind risk, but only when the odds are in my favor. Think of life as everyone standing on the precipice of the unknown. I don't like falling."

"Even when there's someone to catch you?"

"There's never someone to catch you." He managed to get out of her grasp and undid her bra. "That's better."

"I would catch you."

His mouth covered her breast. "You don't know me."

For a moment she lost her train of thought. She arched into him. "I want to."

He fell back on the bed and looked up at her. "I can't afford to need you."

"You won't."

"I might." He cupped her breast and let his hand graze her side in a slow sensuous gesture. "You're very tempting."

"But, Eric—"

He swore fiercely. "I hate this. You don't understand. I can't have relationships."

"Why not?"

He sat up and tapped his chest. "Because I'm not normal. I don't feel things the way you're supposed to."

"What does that mean?"

It meant he felt too much. It meant that when he looked at her right now he felt a sense of possessiveness so strong it hurt. If he were to love her it would consume every part of him, body and soul, giving her the power to destroy him. He already stood on the danger precipice. Even when he was away from her, he longed to be near. The monster in him desperate for escape. Desperate to say, *Here I am. All of me. Would you accept me as this? This ravenous creature of darkness who could devour you with his need?*

She rested her chin on his shoulder. "Have you ever felt dead inside?" she asked softly.

He nodded. All his life.

"I have. When I was married to Laurence I felt as if I were in a play, given a role to act. And I acted well, feeling hollow inside, but not having the courage to break away. To stand up for myself and say: 'This isn't me. Sorry, but you have the wrong wife.' Instead I did as told. I had a baby though I didn't know what to do with one and went through the motions of domestic life, failing miserably.

"Then Laurence said he wanted a divorce." She rested her cheek against his back, his warmth giving her strength to share her painful past. "I was shattered because I didn't know what or who I was without being Mrs. Shelton. I know many women thought I was weak, I felt weak. But most people won't admit how it feels to have your identity taken from you, something you've struggled to build. I had nothing to hold me up after that.

"I managed, of course, by creating a new me. An Adriana Travers that I would have been if I hadn't met Laurence. I chose men that were his opposite—wild, rough, coarse. They filled me with emotions I had never felt before, did things to me I'd never imagined."

Eric cleared his throat. "I hope you're not planning to share them."

"No."

"Thank you."

"I soon realized I was acting again. Always on the go. Not staying still so I could think. Then I met you and for once I felt whole. Not because I'm with you but because I'm myself. You accept all of me. No one except Cassie has ever done that." She kissed his shoulder. "I'm not afraid of falling and I don't expect you to come with me."

"You shouldn't settle for less."

"Who says I'm settling?"

She touched his face with such tenderness he briefly considered the benefits of falling. Her soft hand grazed the stubble on his face. He felt as if he were a beast she was trying to tame, but he was a man who didn't need her affections. Didn't want them. He wasn't sure what he wanted. He couldn't understand how she could know nothing about him, yet would risk loving him.

Her hand fell to his chest. "I can feel your heart beating."

"Surprised I have one?"

She rested her head against him. "No."

He remained still, not daring to move. He was too close to the precipice; he could feel the earth trembling beneath him, but perhaps if he was careful he wouldn't fall. He had to stop talking, trying to put into words his apprehension. It made the danger of their relationship too real.

He said her name and she looked up at him. He kissed her, pulling her close. He held her as if she were a butterfly that had landed in his palm, careful to give her the choice to stay or fly away. Afraid that if he held too tightly he would crush her wings and hurt her.

He entered her with reverence as though he had been allowed through the doors of a sacred cathedral, its glorious, sanctified walls welcoming him. It washed away the filth of his past and the man he used to be, forgiving him his desire and making him worthy or this gift, this comfort.

His hands learned every part of her, her skin becoming a new and fascinating entity. Everything about her fascinated him. He kissed and held her as if he'd never been with a woman before.

Adriana closed her eyes, feeling the gathering of tears. Tears sweet with joy, ecstasy. She was floating on a cloud of pleasure, reveling in his masculine exploration of her, succumbing to the bliss of being one with him.

"You're crying." He brushed a tear away with his thumb.

"I know."

"Did I hurt you?"

"No." She held his face in her hands, determined to find a way to melt the ice in his eyes. "You healed me."

The sound of the doorbell crashed through Eric's peaceful slumber early the next morning. He grabbed his robe and answered the door.

"Do you know what time it is?" he demanded.

Keith took a step back. He glanced at the door number

to make sure he was at the right address. He seemed to have awakened a hibernating bear. "Sorry, I must have the wrong—"

"Hi, Keith," a sleepy, feminine voice interrupted. The sound of his name seemed to increase the man's scowl. He saw Adriana peeking behind the bear, who stood as a barrier. Either to block his entrance or her exit. "Come in," she said.

He stared at the man, unsure. "Uh."

She patted the man on the back. "Eric, go back to bed. I can handle this."

He folded his arms. "You haven't answered my question," he said in a low growl.

Keith cleared his throat. "Uh, yes. I know it's early, but Adriana is used to me."

Sharp brown eyes cut through him. "Uh-huh."

Adriana tugged on his arm. "Eric, go to bed. You're just tired."

"I'll make coffee."

"No. I'll not have you sending Keith into a diabetic coma. Go to bed."

He rested a hand on the door frame and sent him a cool, appraising look. "You do realize she has a little girl she has to get ready for school?"

Keith nodded. "Yes."

"Plus a full day of work?"

"Yes."

"So this won't happen again."

"Yes, I mean no. Uh . . ."

"Right."

Keith glanced down and saw Elissa. "Hey, kitty." He bent to pet her. She hissed at him.

"Take her with you," Adriana told Eric.

He scooped the cat up, mouthed, "Don't give him money," and turned.

Keith breathed with relief when Eric disappeared down the hall. "Who the hell was that?"

She ushered him inside and closed the door. "Don't worry about him, it is early. What do you want?"

"No need to be like that. I've come here early before."

"I know." But she had changed. She turned and headed for the kitchen, hiding a yawn.

He patted his portfolio. "I wanted to show you my new paintings."

She gestured to the table as she poured water into the coffeepot. Once finished she stood over his paintings. "Excellent."

"Thanks to your generous contribution, I've got an appointment with Lorna."

"What about Sartan?"

He hesitated, then shrugged. "Didn't work out. We didn't have the same vision. However, I think Lorna is my big chance. Unfortunately, the landlady is scratching up my back and I can't work with her screeching at me." He paused. "If I could just get a loan."

She sat, resting her chin in her hand. "I'm really tight this month. If you can't afford the rent, you may have to move."

"I can't move, it's the perfect location, the windows and the space allow my creativity to thrive."

She drummed her fingers. "I can't keep bailing you out."

"Just this last time."

"Is that a promise?"

"Yes."

"I believe in your work," she said, hedging. "But I'm not rich enough to be a patron."

"I know, you've been great. Last time. Promise."

"Okay, let me get my handbag." She suddenly groaned. "Which I left in the bedroom."

"Don't worry about it," he said, sensing her apprehension and having some of his own.

She stood. She would not be intimidated by Eric. He might be her boyfriend now, but her money was still her own. "Just stay here."

She peeked into the room and then quickly headed to her bag on the dresser.

A deep voice penetrated the darkness. "I told you not to give him money."

She turned on a lamp. "Yes, you've told me a lot of things I've chosen to ignore."

"Adriana—"

"This is none of your business."

"It is my business when I see you giving your income away to a lazy Samfi man."

"He is not a con."

"You should be spending it on yourself. What kind of friend is so selfish to have a hobby he expects others to pay for?"

"First of all, Keith has talent, and second, art is not his hobby, it's his career. Many artists struggle in the beginning."

Eric came over to her as she searched through her handbag. "How long has he been at this?"

"That doesn't matter."

"Does he know about your career, your sketches?"

"It's not the same."

"I guess you just enjoy throwing away your money on other people's dreams."

"You don't understand."

He turned her to face him. "I do understand. This gives you the perfect excuse not to reach your goal. Not to focus on yourself so you won't fail."

She yanked out of his grip and turned to her bag. "I'm not in the mood for a lecture."

"How about a lesson then? See what kind of friend he is. Tell him no."

She grabbed her checkbook. "Go back to sleep."

He seized her arm. "Adriana—"

She looked up at him, defiant. "Yes?"

He released her arm and watched her go.


"So you came back alive," Keith said, resting back in his chair with his coffee.

"Yes." She lifted her pen, then stopped. "I have one question."

"What?"

"Are these paintings yours?"

He looked unsure. "Yes, of course."

"Then who's KSY?"

"What?"

"One of your paintings had KSY as a signature."

"That's sort of a stage name."

"I didn't realize artists used them."

"I'm sort of in between a divorce. I don't want her to get any of the earnings."

"I see." She quickly wrote out the check and handed it to him. "This isn't just about talent. It's about friendship, trust."

He took the check and stood. "This is the last time, I promise. Thanks."

She chewed her lower lip. "You know, I'm having a fashion show in February the weekend of Valentine's Day."

"That sounds great." He opened the door. "I hope it goes well."

"You're welcome to come. I'll be—"

"February's going to be busy," he cut in. "You know Black History Month and all. Besides, I'm not really into fashion, but thanks for asking."

She managed an understanding smile. "Right," she said and gently closed the door.

"He's lying," Eric said behind her.

She spun around. "You weren't supposed to be listening in."

"He can't make your fashion show because he's a selfish donkey who doesn't want to appear anywhere where he won't be the focus."

"I think I can figure out my own friends."

"Every word that comes out of his mouth needs washing. It's covered in—"

"Eric!"

"I don't trust him."

Sya had said the same thing, but she'd had many friends others didn't understand. Besides, she liked being needed. She liked to know she was helping him. "That's your business. I know what I'm doing."

"We all make mistakes."

She walked past him.

"How much did you give him?"

"It was a loan."

"Has he ever paid you back?"

"He will—"

"Once he makes it," Eric finished in disgust. He swore.

"You have a filthy mouth."

"And a filthy mind. Do you want me to tell you what I really think of him?"

She dropped her robe and got in bed. "I don't care."

"Fine." He kissed her on the cheek.

"What was that for?"

"It was either that or slapping you on the rear for your stubbornness."

She kissed him on the mouth. "It was either that or strangling you." She switched off the lights.


Adriana woke with an odd sense of panic. It increased when she noticed Eric was gone. She found him in the living room tying his shoes.

"You're leaving?" It was a silly question. His bag sat next to him, his jacket hung over the couch.

He grabbed his bag and stood. "You didn't expect me to stay forever, did you?"

"No," she said quickly. "No, of course not. I'm glad you're better." She didn't know why the words sounded false.

He put his bag down and sighed. "You have that worried look on your face."

"Are you leaving because of this morning? Because of Keith?"

"No, I'm leaving because it's time."

She tightened the belt on her robe. "Right."

He watched her. "Moving in is a big step."

She jerked her head back. "I don't want you to move in."

He grabbed his bag. "Then that's that." He opened the door.

"Don't be angry."

"I'm not angry."

She leaned against the wall. "I enjoyed having you here. I'm just not ready—"

"I know. Don't worry." He turned.

She didn't want to see him go. She searched her mind for something to say. "Could you take Nina to work one day?"

"Why?"

"She's supposed to do a paper on a career."

He looked at her. "Why don't you take her to work?"

"I'd rather not."

He shook his head. "It's not like you run a bordello."

"Your job will be easier to explain."

"But—"

She held her hands together. "Please."

"Does she know what you do?"

"Yes."

He sighed. "Fine. I'll pick her up one day."

"Thanks."

They stared at each other, leaving certain thoughts and feelings unsaid so that they hung in the air between them, waiting to be revealed. He finally turned to go.


She missed him. She buried her face in his pillow and shook her head. It was ridiculous to miss someone like this. He had his place; she had hers. They were temporary lovers, nothing more. No, that was wrong. They were boyfriend, girlfriend now, but she still didn't know for how long.

She showered and changed and went into her office and switched on the stereo. Soothing jazz floated from the speakers. He had changed the station. Instead of being annoyed she laughed and switched it back to a rock station. She turned to her desk and stopped. "Oh no."

All her pencils had been sharpened, any eraser remnants swept away, scattered papers placed in the wastebasket. Her sketches were stacked. On top of them was a bad drawing of a bluebird. Underneath in Eric's barely legible handwriting he had written:

> Hope is the thing with feathers that perches on your soul and sings the tune without words and never stops at all
>
> —Emily Dickinson

"Damn you," she whispered without malice, brushing her tears away. She pushed the picture aside and began to draw.

She knew it wasn't in her budget, but she couldn't resist. It was a child's leather jacket that was the spitting image of hers. It had Nina's name on it. She could just imagine them walking down Sixteenth Street in their matching jackets, jeans, and black boots. It would be a wonderful gift for

Nina since she'd been such a good help with Eric. Plus their relationship had improved immensely.

Adriana examined the jacket, then looked at the price. She cringed, but her desire dampened any reservations. Nina deserved the best. She was used to it and Adriana wanted her to know her mother could get pretty things like her father could.

"It's really nice," Nina said, running her hand over the soft leather.

"I have a jacket just like it," Adriana said proudly. "We'll be matching, coordinated. Won't that be nice?"

"Yes." She hugged her. "Thanks, Mom."

"Try it on."

She did. She looked awkward, but Adriana was sure Nina would get used to it soon enough. She imagined getting her earrings and more fashionable jeans and tops. Nina needed something better than the old granny sweaters she wore when not in school. Perhaps she could even get her interested in fashion. She could buy her a teen magazine. Then they would have something more in common.

"You look wonderful," she said.

Nina smiled.

She'd meant to say "I love you," but Nina had already headed down the hall.

"Mom, the door," Nina called as Adriana cleared their dinner.

She opened the door and raised a brow. "Oh, it's you."

Laurence stepped in. "How are things going?"

"Fine."

Nina hugged her father. He patted her affectionately on the head. "Do you like it here?" he asked.

She nodded.

"How is school? Are you keeping up your grades?"

"Yes. I have a garden, do you want to see it?"

"Sure."

She took him to the kitchen and showed him her herbs. "Uncle Eric helped me set it up."

"Who's Uncle Eric?"

"A friend of mine," Adriana replied, answering both his verbal and his silent question.

He said in a low voice, "I hope you're being discreet."

She ignored the hint. "How are the wedding plans?"

"I think they're hectic, but Irene seems revived by them." He looked at Nina, who was whispering something to her garden. "What is she doing?"

"She talks to them. Eric says it helps them grow."

"She looks happy anyway. Perhaps you have a maternal instinct after all."

"Perhaps."

He strolled into the living room and stood in front of the balcony window. "Shame things couldn't have worked out between us."

"That's an odd thing for a new groom to mention."

"I'm just saying for Nina's sake."

"Yes. I know. We're too different."

"So who is this Eric guy?"

She rested her hands on her hips. "You're entering dangerous territory."

"I think I have the right to know the kind of men my daughter is being exposed to."

"Like I got to know Irene?"

"My women are harmless. What is he like?"

"She just showed you. He helped her plant a garden." She adjusted the cuffs on her shirt. "When he shows her how to load a .45, then worry."

"I can't help being curious. I know the kind of men you like." He leaned against the balcony door, shoving a hand in his pocket. "At least tell me how many earrings he has."

"None."

"Okay, then tattoos."

"None."

"Rings?"

"He doesn't wear jewelry."

"What does he do?"

"He's a financial adviser."

Laurence threw his head back and laughed. "That's a good one, Addie. You really had me for a second." He held up his hands. "Okay, you've made your point. It's none of my business."

She frowned. "But I'm telling you the truth."

He turned to his daughter, who had come to sit on the couch. "Nina, describe Uncle Eric for me."

She paused, thoughtful, then said slowly, "He looks a little scary at first, but he's really nice. He has glasses because his eyes are bad."

"Bad to the bone, huh?" Laurence laughed again. He walked to the door and then spun around and snapped his fingers. "I've got an idea."

Adriana clapped. "Congratulations."

He ignored her. "Why don't we all have lunch? Irene wants to meet you anyway."

She narrowed her eyes. "Why?"

"Curiosity, I suppose."

"And you're curious to meet Eric, right?"

"This weekend okay for you? Saturday?"

"I'll—"

"Good. See you then." He opened the door. "I'll call and give you directions to her place. Unless you want to be picked up."

"I said—"

"We'll figure it out later." He waved at Nina, then left.

"That man," Adriana muttered, staring at the door.

"Aren't you going to call Uncle Eric?" Nina asked when she continued to stand there.

"I'm sure he's busy." Why would he want to suffer through an experience with her ex and his fiancée? She certainly didn't want to.

Nina tugged on her sleeve. "You have to ask him."

"I have things to do."

"Then can I call him?"

Adriana sighed. There was no use avoiding it. "Fine. Go and call him."

He shouldn't have mentioned living together. Eric watched his dinner heating in the microwave and fumed. The relationship had already gone into a direction he hadn't planned. Why would he say that? He'd never lived with a woman. He liked his freedom. Why would he want to change that?

The phone rang. "Henson."

There was a brief pause. "Uncle Eric?"

His voice softened. "Hello, Nina."

"Can you come to lunch with us on Saturday?"

He pulled his dinner out of the microwave. "Sure."

She said something to Adriana, then spoke to him. "Mom wants to speak with you."

Adriana picked up the phone. "Eric, the lunch is with my ex-husband and his fiancée."

He stuck a fork into his spaghetti. The entire meal came out of the carton. "Trying to warn me off?"

"I don't even want to go, there's no reason why you should."

He pulled the frozen meal off the fork and shoved it back in the microwave. "Moral support?"

"That's not enough."

"Fine, then curiosity. I want to meet the man capable of persuading you into marriage."

"I was naive. Partially brain-dead."

He laughed. "I'll see you Saturday."

\* \* \*

Lunch was on the covered lanai. November sunshine crept along the surrounding greenery in a dim haze. Bowls of fruit, santorini salad with grilled shrimp, chick-pea salad, sliced fresh guava with coconut, and ginger punch decorated the table dressed in a lace tablecloth and hand-painted dinnerware.

"I can't believe I'm doing this," Adriana mumbled, staring out into the rock garden, listening to the bubbling of a small waterfall. She glanced over her shoulder at Eric, who was trapped in the corner with Irene. She was pleasant enough as Laurence's women went. She had an animated face, not too animated naturally. Subtlety was paramount in his crowd. She was dressed in classic wool trousers and a peach sweater set. Her movements were young and energetic, but would eventually be tempered by maturity and marriage. It was clear that Irene did not take to Nina, whom she avoided like an unwanted crease.

Laurence had yet to make his appearance. If he didn't come soon Adriana would start lunch without him. She shifted to her other leg, her suede red skirt brushing against the iron rail. Nina entertained herself by walking through the garden. Adriana glanced at Irene again. She was the very reason Nina's life had changed.

Adriana suddenly set her glass down and went up to Eric. She looped her arm through his. "Excuse me, I need to borrow him for a moment." She drew him away.

"You didn't have to save me," he said.

"I'm saving myself. Her voice is getting on my nerves." She glanced at her watch. "I should have known."

"Known what?"

"That Laurence would be late. He always is. It makes him feel important to make an entrance."

Irene approached them. "I don't know where Laurence could be."

"I'm sure he'll be here soon," Adriana said. "He's always late. It's a chronic disease with him."

Her voice turned cool. "You don't need to tell me about him."

"Retract the claws, I am not interested in him."

"Then why did you want to have this lunch?"

She let Eric's arm go. "Me? He was the one who invited us. I don't know what's running in your mind, but Laurence and I have been over for a long time. There's no need to be jealous."

"I'm not." She sipped her drink and looked Adriana up and down. "I graduated from Brown. Where did you go? "

"Screw U. Heard of it?"

Her mouth fell open but no words emerged. She spun on her heel and went into the house.

"Insecure little—"

Eric rested a hand on her shoulder. "Don't say anything you'll regret."

"I won't regret it."

"You were a little harsh."

"Tacky and vulgar. I know. My parents would have killed me." She grinned. "It would have been worth it."

"Don't let her get to you."

Laurence made his entrance then. He stood in the doorway and glanced around as if he expected applause. "So where's this Eric I've heard so much about?"

Eric set his drink down and held out his hand. "That would be me."

Laurence's eyes swept him in one incredulous stare. He looked at Eric and then looked down at himself. He had expected leather or denim, not the dress shirt and trousers before him.

"It's nice to meet you," he said, recovering.

"Likewise. I'll tell Nina you're here." Eric disappeared into the garden.

Laurence nudged Adriana. "Returning to your old staples, huh?"

Adriana poured herself another drink. She couldn't drink enough to make this day end. "Let's eat. I'm starving."

Surprisingly, the lunch went well. Eric had a skillful ability to direct the conversation, so it went smoothly. All potentially dangerous topics were either avoided or redirected. One tense moment threatened to destroy the calm atmosphere. Irene didn't like a prepared dish and threw the food away. For a moment Eric looked physically ill at the sight of such waste. Adriana touched his sleeve and he averted his gaze. She requested that they take home any unwanted leftovers.

As the staff cleared the table, Irene came up to her. "I am sorry about earlier."

"Don't worry about it," Adriana replied, flippant. "I believe I played my role well."

"Your role?"

"Yes, the first wife is suppose to be a bitch."

"No, I didn't mean—"

"Relax. Laurence tricked us both. But it was time we met each other."

Irene's eyes fell. "He talks about you and Nina a lot."

"That's because he's grateful he doesn't have to live with us anymore."

Irene raised her eyes. "It doesn't seem that way."

"He may talk about us, but he loves you. There are plenty of women dying to marry him and he chose you. That makes you important to him. Nina and I are part of his past. Soon you'll be the only one he talks about."

Irene glanced at Eric, who was talking to Laurence near the garden. "Your boyfriend seems like a decent guy. From what I've heard, you like bad boys."

"Eric is really a bounty hunter, but I just dressed him up for the occasion to impress you."

Her eyes widened.

"That was a joke."

"Oh, right," she said, but she looked unsure. "Excuse me." She went to instruct the staff to wrap up the dishes.

Laurence came up to her. "Your Eric is quite a guy."

She sipped her punch and imitated his tone. "And your Irene is quite a girl."

His voice lowered. "There's no reason to be jealous of her."

"Why would I be jealous?"

"Because you're still in love with me."

She choked on her punch. It took a lot of effort not to be ill. "What?"

"Admit it, Addie. It's obvious. You've chosen a guy who's just like me."

Her voice was tight. "He is not just like you."

"Look at him."

Her eyes remained on his face. "He is not like you."

"You can deny it all you want, but the evidence is right there for everyone to see. Of course it goes deeper than that. You constantly try to rebel, but keep choosing men like your father."

"Will you be charging a fee after this consultation?"

He shrugged. "I'm just trying to help you break a bad pattern. You won't last long with him. He's a smart man and he's going to get bored eventually."

"Like you did?"

"Why don't you stop trying to prove yourself and get someone on your level?"

Her lips thinned. "Because I have to wait for him to graduate from nursery school."

"You're taking this the wrong way. You don't understand."

"Unfortunately, I do." She pushed past him and stumbled to the bathroom, afraid she would really be ill and embarrass herself. Thankfully, she managed to keep her lunch down. She sat on the toilet and held her head.

She let the tears fall then. She tried to combat Laurence's words, but feared there was a hint of truth. What if he was right? Could she fall for another man like her father? Was that why she had married Laurence in the first place? Would Eric be the same? Someone she would care for, try to please, and ultimately fail?

Her uncertainty made her feel stupid. She wished she could argue with Laurence instead of feeling like a confused child. She wished she could engage in witty banter with the Irenes of the world, that Laurence would consider his first wife to be someone to brag about like, "Yes, the marriage didn't work out, but she's a researcher at NIH or a professor at Hopkins." She doubted he even mentioned her name.

She clenched her fist. He was wrong. She wasn't trying to marry her father. Their relationship was complicated, but she accepted it for what it was. She loved him, accepted him, despite the shadow of pain that came with thoughts of him.

Christopher Travers was a dynamic man who was the ultimate master of his fate and others'. A calculating, domineering force who loved with discipline. He used to make her tremble with just a breath. He was a brilliant cardiologist who expected nothing less from his offspring.

She had failed him. He made allowances because she was only a girl after all, but he would have liked her to be clever so he could brag to others of her achievements. Her fashion scholarship didn't count, or the design club she developed, and her Master Pattern award was of no consequence. She only offered lousy SAT scores and an ordinary college degree. Nothing to recommend her.

She was ordinary, but not inoffensively so. She didn't blend into the background. She liked loud music, loud clothing, and people who made her family cringe. Would

Eric ultimately look down on her also? He already didn't like Keith and her ideas about money. What other parts of her life would he disapprove of? What would he want her to change?

A soft knock on the door interrupted her thoughts.

"Are you okay?" Eric asked.

She stood and wiped her face. "Yes. Yes, I'm fine." She stared at her reflection in the mirror, then fixed her makeup. She took a deep breath and stepped out. Eric stood against the wall.

"I'm ready to go," she said.

A muscle in his jaw twitched. "Who made you cry?"

She blinked. "What?"

"I heard you."

Heat touched her cheeks. "I made myself cry."

"I don't believe you."

She didn't care. She glanced around the hallway and stared at the curving staircase. "Laurence and I lived in a house similar to this. He had many dinner parties. I smiled a lot because he didn't want me to say anything that would embarrass me." She laughed without humor. "Of course he meant him. I spent most of the evenings trying to disappear. At times I wonder if that was why he grew bored with me. Originally he liked my vitality, and then he asked me to tone it down. Now he's found a young woman as I used to be."

"He grew bored with himself. He thought that by divorcing you he was changing his life. But he's boring and will continue to be so. It has nothing to do with you."

"I want to believe that, but a marriage takes two people and I contributed to its failure."

"Maybe because it wasn't meant to succeed." He took her hand. "Let's go."

* * *

"Are you free tomorrow?" Eric asked on the drive home. "I'm teaching a class for young entrepreneurs."

She wanted to decline, but he had come to the disaster they had escaped. "Yes, I'm free." She glanced at his profile, wondering how their relationship would end. Would it be bitter? Amicable? Eventual? She pushed the thought aside. Right now she didn't want to think of a future without him.

Damn, she was running late for Eric's class. She had dropped Nina at Cassie's and gotten stuck in traffic and then missed her way. She glanced down at the room number he had given her and raced up the stairs. Her high heels echoed on the tile floor as she hurried down the empty hallway. She finally reached the room and peeked inside. She saw Eric in front of the blackboard. She inwardly groaned. They had already started. Sneaking in would be impossible. She took a deep breath and carefully opened the door. Thankfully, the hinge didn't squeak but the ungauging of locks caught everyone's attention. Twenty heads turned to her. She smiled, apologetic, and glanced up at Eric, expecting a frown. He was grinning so broadly her knees trembled.

He said, "At last our special guest speaker has arrived."

# Eleven

She didn't get a chance to ask him what he was talking about. He was too busy describing what she did. When he mentioned she owned lingerie stores, a few snickers followed, but she was welcomed with applause.

She went up to him and spoke under her breath. "Is this some sort of cruel joke?"

He handed her the chalk. "No."

She seized his arm before he walked away. "What am I supposed to do?"

"Tell them about business."

"I don't know much."

He pushed up his glasses. "You successfully run three stores. I'm sure you know more about business than they do. You're a success, share the wealth."

She had never thought of herself as a success. The chalk began to crumble as she twirled it between her fingers. "I can't do this."

"What was the idea behind Divine Notions?"

"I—"

He sat in the front row. "Don't tell me, tell them."

She couldn't believe she was in a classroom. In the *front* of the classroom. Images of standing at the blackboard flashed through her mind. She remembered staring at a math problem she couldn't solve or a sentence diagram she couldn't understand as sweat trickled down her back. She didn't belong here. She looked at Eric. She didn't want to let him down either. She'd make him pay later.

In a halting voice she described how she got started. She related special considerations such as location, need for advertising, merchandising, customer service, loss prevention, and visual display. When she was through, eager hands shot up and waved for attention. The class went a half hour over its designated time. Eric finally had to dismiss the class, promising that Adriana would come again.

"You set me up," she accused once the classroom was empty.

"I knew you wouldn't come otherwise."

"That was still underhanded."

He shrugged. "You got your revenge. I was afraid you wouldn't come."

"Would have served you right."

"You were excellent up there."

She grinned, pleased with herself. "Yeah, I wasn't so bad."

He placed his chin in his hand. "I have a few questions about loss prevention."

"I'm sure you know something about that."

"Not much. I'm not in retail. I don't know everything."

"How shocking."

They discussed shoplifting issues, then hiring and firing staff. Later, Eric said he needed to pick up groceries so they walked to a store nearby.

"I look like I'm fasting so I thought I'd better pick up a few things," he explained, taking out his list. It was organized by sections, of course.

She frowned as he tossed two cereals in his cart. "Corn Pops and Fruit Loops?"

"Breakfast is the most important meal of the day."

"Yes, and should be healthy. Try Special K or Shredded Wheat." She handed him the box.

He looked at it and frowned. "Twigs."

"You can put honey on it or in your case pounds of sugar."

He took the box and tossed it in the cart. Adriana smiled, pleased. "You can stop grinning," he said. "These are for you in the morning."

"Don't forget pineapple soda."

"Cassie gets them for me at the Caribbean Market along with grata cake."

"I'm surprised you still have your own teeth."

He flashed a wicked grin. "Who says they're mine?"

She tried to pull her eyes away from the tabloids (WOMAN EATS HUSBAND FOR INSURANCE) as they stood ready to check out. "I really enjoyed this afternoon," she said. "I was actually in a classroom and didn't feel stupid."

"Why would you feel stupid?"

She shrugged. He wouldn't understand.

He winked at her. "You can't fool me. I know it's all an act. You don't want anyone to feel insecure around you, so you play down your intelligence so they can feel adequate. I saw you do it with Laurence."

"That's not—"

"It's all right. I understand that women do that a lot. The man's an idiot, so you have to make him feel better. I'm glad you don't do that with me."

"Laurence went to MIT."

He pulled out his wallet. "Yes, he told me—twice."

The clerk spoke up. "That will be fifty-four dollars and twenty cents."

"No, it's not."

"Sir, the monitor says—"

"The monitor is wrong. The chicken, oranges, and cans of soup were on sale, the total should be about forty-seven eighty-two."

The clerk looked down at the receipt and noticed the sale items had not been reduced. She made the appropriate changes.

Adriana watched amazed as he handed the clerk the right amount. This man who could calculate in his head thought she was smart?

She pulled out a small calculator from her handbag. "What's six hundred forty-seven times seventy-four?" she asked as they stepped out of the store.

He thought a moment. "Forty-seven thousand, eight hundred seventy-eight. Why?"

"Divided by two?"

"Twenty-three thousand nine hundred thirty-nine." He suddenly grinned. "What's this about? Are you working on a new budget or something? Doing comparative shopping?"

"No, I'm trying to figure out how brilliant you are." She'd expected him to look arrogant or at least proud. Instead he looked annoyed. "Did I say something wrong?"

"No. I just . . . they're simple parlor tricks, Adriana. I'm far from the brilliant mathematician you think. If I were, I'd probably have a few more degrees behind my name and would be molding in some ivory academic tower."

So he had been haunted by the towers of academia too. She couldn't understand his insecurity. At least he was smart. "But I could never do what you just did."

"You could with practice."

She looped her arm through his. "I doubt I'd live that long."

He laughed. "It's possible."

"I don't have the interest. I'd rather believe you're brilliant."

They stopped in the parking lot ready to part ways. It was cold, but she didn't want to leave. "Thanksgiving is coming up. I'm not the best cook, but I'm sure I could put something together."

He reached out and curled a strand of hair around his finger. "I'm volunteering at Memorial Church."

"How about Friday?"

"I'm going to Drake's."

She knew her cooking couldn't compare. She smiled, masking her disappointment. "Oh well, I'll see you after the holidays then."

"You're invited to come. You've never come before."

Yes. Cassie had asked her, but *he* had been there so she'd declined. Amazing how feelings could change.

He touched her face. "I'd like you and Nina to be there. We have fun and there's no reason to eat your cooking on a holiday." He kissed her frozen nose and got into his car. "I'll pick you up."

Nina looked like an administrative assistant behind the table in his office, Eric thought, watching her. All she needed was a pair of glasses hanging around her neck and an in-box. He had worried that he wouldn't be able to keep her busy at work, but he had no reason to. With her trusty coloring book and *Charlie and the Chocolate Factory* she managed to keep herself occupied. After his last client, he would treat her to a snack.

"Come in," he said when someone knocked.

Carter entered. "Hello, Henson." He glanced at Nina as he took a seat. "Your help is getting younger. Are you trying to cut costs?"

"This is Nina Shelton."

"Hello," she said.

"Shelton?" Carter asked. "Your father wouldn't happen to be Laurence Shelton, would he?" He meant it as a joke. He nearly swallowed his tongue when she said yes. He looked at Eric, impressed. "You know Shelton's kid?"

"Yes," Eric said.

He gave a low whistle and crossed his ankles. "Remember what we used to call guys like him?"

Eric's eyes met him with eloquent warning. "No."

They used to call them marks or targets. But Eric's look

convinced him to skip memory lane. "Right. So what school do you go to, Nina?"

"Brenton Girls' Academy," she said.

He nodded. It was expected. "Play any sports?"

"No."

"Do you plan to be like your dad?"

She shrugged. "I'm not like him really. Do you think I'm like him, Uncle Eric?"

"No."

"You met him?" Carter asked.

His voice was short. "Yes."

"What's he like?"

Eric twirled a pen in his fingers; his eyes darkened dangerously. "Why?"

Carter let the subject drop.

Eric placed his pen down and sat back. "Do you have my money?"

Carter uncrossed his ankles and sat forward. "That's why I'm here."

"There's a problem?"

"I wouldn't call it a problem."

Eric's voice was soft. "If you don't have my money, I would."

"You will get your money. There's just been a delay. I need more time. That's all."

"Time?"

He nodded. "Yes. Nothing more than a couple more weeks."

Eric picked up his pen and studied it. Carter knew it was a ploy to get him to relax. "Am I the only person you owe?"

"You'll get the money."

"That wasn't my question."

He smoothed out an eyebrow. "You're the only one."

Eric looked at him, his eyes sharp. "You're losing your touch. I usually can't tell when you're lying."

"There's only one more guy. He's not a problem."

He looked pensive, then nodded. "I'll give you time. Three months. After that, no excuses."

"Thank you."

Eric didn't acknowledge his gratitude. Instead he stood. "Nina, I'm going to walk Mr. Carter to the front door. I'll be right back."

"Okay," she said.

He opened the door and gestured Carter ahead of him. They walked to the building's front glass doors in silence. When they reached the street Eric asked, "Are you in trouble?"

"Why would you ask that?"

"Your questions about Shelton."

Carter couldn't help a grin. "You've gotta admit it's tempting."

Eric's voice hardened. "Not to me."

He shrugged. "I was just curious."

"You're only curious when there's a payoff. What's going on?"

"Nothing."

"We both promised to stop."

"I'm not scamming anyone."

"True. You're in a new game."

"Why would you say that?"

Eric adjusted his glasses. "You never used to sweat then."

"I'm not sweating."

"Your upper lip is glistening."

Damn his eyes. Carter thought fast. "It's Serena."

Eric folded his arms. "What's the problem?"

"She's spending me into the ground. I'm thinking of divorce, but I have to get everything in order first. You know how vindictive women are. I want my deal to go through before she gets wind of it."

"I see."

Carter hoped he didn't.

Eric turned. "I'll call you in a few months." He patted him on the back. "I hope you're not lying to me."

"Would I lie?"

Eric just looked at him.

"Bad choice of words."

He held up three fingers. "We're clear?"

"Yes."

"I don't like losing money."

"You won't."

They both nodded, then parted ways.

Eric returned to the office and saw Nina coloring. He sat behind his desk and tapped a pen, thoughtful. The gleam in Carter's eyes had worried him. He knew what he was like, knew the temptation to get in the game again. But if Carter did anything that involved Nina he would kill him.

Carter hoped his investment would pay off soon. He didn't like that Henson didn't believe him, though he was lying. He wasn't a bad guy and when he made his money he would prove it. Fortunately, he had more time now so he could relax.

At home he hung up his jacket and grinned. So Eric knew money. He remembered the days when they had dreamed of days like that. Serena would definitely be impressed, she liked dropping names. He headed to the kitchen where he knew she would be.

"Hey, babe. Henson knows Laurence Shelton's kid. Can you believe it? I just met her. She's—" He came around the corner and stopped. Serena was eating lunch with three other women. "Sorry, I didn't realize you had company."

She waved her hand. "Don't worry about it."

He flashed a sheepish grin and took a step back. One cute, petite woman caught his eye. He wasn't sure why she did, there was just something about her. He pushed the thought aside and went to the basement.

\* \* \*

Drake stared at his brother across the desk as they sat in his main office. He couldn't put his finger on it, but Eric had changed. He seemed more real, as if his existence was more than that of a moving shadow, drifting in and out of life and relationships.

"Adriana and Nina are coming for Thanksgiving," Eric said suddenly.

Drake scribbled something down to look busy. "Okay."

"Schedule to make something where you can use basil or chives."

Drake glanced up. "Why?"

"Because Nina has been growing them."

He nodded. "Okay."

After a few moments Eric said, "And make sure there's nothing too hot. Adriana doesn't handle spices very well."

Drake hesitated. "Okay."

Eric tapped his pen on the desk and then pointed at him. "And make sure to use candles. She likes candles."

"Fine." Drake sat back in his chair ready for more instructions. He was not disappointed.

"And could you use your china dishes, the ones with the geometric patterns?"

"I think you should talk to Cassie about that."

"Right." He turned away, missing Drake's smile.


"Did Eric call you?" Drake asked his wife that evening as she washed dishes. He liked simple times like this when the children were asleep in the nursery and they had time alone.

Cassie nodded. "I don't know what has gotten into him. He had so many requests I felt like saying, 'Very good, sir.'"

He took a towel and dried a plate. "He likes her. It's going to be awkward when things don't work out."

"Stop saying that. They might."

"Those two are about as good together as Cheez-its and caviar. They have nothing in common."

She took the towel from him and dried her hands. "People could say the same about us."

"We have plenty in common. We both love food. We both think I'm incredibly attractive."

She rolled her eyes. "Oh yes, and humble."

"And we both love . . ." He wiggled his eyebrows suggestively.

She hit him with the towel. "I'm sure they have that in common."

"Doubt it's as good."

"Your humility is faltering." She opened a cupboard, then quickly shut it, guilty. She turned to him and smiled, hoping he hadn't seen what she had been hiding.

He had. He narrowed his eyes. "Did I just see what I thought I saw?"

"No."

He opened the cupboard and picked up a can. "What is Slim-Fast doing in my kitchen?"

She reached for the can. "Drake, don't be silly."

He moved the can out of reach and frowned. "I can't seem to make clear how much I hate these things."

"I just bought it today. I've been exercising, but the fat from Ericka is still clinging on."

He shoved a hand in his pocket, unconvinced.

"It's been six months."

He rubbed his nose and sniffed.

"I just want to lose—"

He lifted a brow and measured her body. "When you want a workout, you can just come to me."

She frowned. "I don't like your workouts. Torturous machines, running until my lungs threaten to burst."

"This involves lying down. I—"

She snatched the can and tossed it in the bin. "I'm in."

He smiled and grabbed her.

Adriana dumped the *Washington Post* advertising inserts in the trash bin, but their glossy covers and bright colors remained in her memory. The Thanksgiving sales were calling her like the Sirens. She had to resist them. Most of the stores were closed today, but tomorrow would be sale heaven. She had to try and think of something else.

She missed shopping. Missed the feel of shopping bags, their logos stamped on the bags signs of a successful hunt. She missed clothes wrapped in tissue paper, the rush of crowds, spotting a bargain, seeing the red dash slashing through the price tag. Her palms began to sweat. She had to think of something else. It was Thanksgiving Day. There had to be something she could think of.

"Nina, we're going to volunteer."

She arrived at the Memorial Church just as the meal ended. She glanced at the black and orange streamers on the walls, the remnants of food on paper plates, and trash bins overflowing with rubbish.

"It smells funny," Nina said, wrinkling her nose.

"Remember what I told you," Adriana whispered as they walked past the row of tables. "Many of these people don't have homes so they don't get the chance to shower."

"Isn't this a surprise!" Cassie said. She approached them wearing a plastic cap and an apron.

"I'm surprised myself."

"Eric's over there." She pointed to him in the kids' corner, helping a little girl with a puzzle. Nina ran to him.

"He volunteers with the kids every year," Cassie said. "I don't know why. He doesn't seem the type."

"But he is," Adriana said. "He understands them."

"Are you going to say hello?"

She hesitated. "He looks busy."

"He's never too busy to say hello."

She shrugged and watched him. He didn't seem as distant with kids. Probably because he remembered what it was like to be a child, the uncertainty and private insecurities that most adults chose to forget.

Cassie took off her cap and sat at an empty table.

Adriana sat in front of her. "Where are the kids?"

"At home with a baby-sitter. I love them, but sometimes I have to get away before they drive me crazy."

"How do you do it?"

"Do what?"

"Be a mother, wife, and Cassie."

"It's a struggle. Drake helps a lot. It's really about planning and getting help when you need it. There are those women who are meant to be stay-at-home moms and that's great, but I'm not one of them. If I stayed home I would only end up resenting the very thing I love most—my family."

"Do you feel guilty?"

She looked sheepish. "I'm supposed to say yes, but I don't. I'm so happy with everything about my life—my husband, my kids, my career. It's all about priority. I love them more by loving me first. I'll always be Cassie in every role I have."

"You're brave to admit that."

"Sure, and if you repeat it I will deny every word." She drummed her fingers. "You're doing the same thing. You're a mom in a relationship also running a business."

"I keep waiting to mess up."

"We all mess up, but we try our best. Should I ask how things are going with you and Eric?"

Adriana glanced at a streamer that was slowly falling from the wall. "I'm scared to think about the future."

"Why?"

"Because I know it will be without him."

"It doesn't have to be."

She wished she had Cassie's optimism. "I'm not marrying Laurence again, you know that."

"Eric is not like Laurence and it's unfair to compare them. It's downright cruel, really. I know he's a nerd, but—"

"He's not a nerd," Adriana cut in. "He's a little brainy but not that."

"Those were your words, not mine," Cassie reminded her.

Her voice dropped, ashamed. "I know. I've changed."

"I've noticed." She switched topics. "I'm glad you'll be joining us for dinner tomorrow. Eric has made sure it's to be a fantastic affair."

Adriana stared, amazed. "He has?"

"Yes." Cassie smiled, pleased. "He's fussed over every detail—the table setting, the food. Don't tell him I told you." She stretched the elastic rim of her cap and chose her words carefully. "He really cares about you and Nina. I think if you want him, you can have him. He's officially on the marriage market."

Adriana shook her head. "You know marriage changes things."

"Yes, sometimes for the worse, sometimes for the better. I didn't let a first bad marriage stop me from enjoying a second one."

She lowered her eyes. "Truth is. I don't think I'm the wife he's looking for."

"How do you know?"

"Past experience. You've met the women he's gone out with."

"He wouldn't have married the ones I met."

"He asked Lynda."

"He did?" She made a face. "Then you'd be a nice change."

"You didn't like her either?"

"No."

"He doesn't want to be Nina's father," Adriana said.

Cassie blinked. "He said that?"

"Yes."

She was quiet a moment. "Perhaps he meant he doesn't want you to be with him for that reason."

Adriana shrugged.

"Sometimes we don't know what we want until we find it. And who says he wouldn't want you?"

"I don't know why we're having this conversation. I don't want to get married."

"Aren't you going to say anything to him at least?"

"No, not yet."

Cassie stood. "Then you can help me clean up."

Adriana glanced at a young man gloomily sweeping the floor. "What's wrong with him?"

Cassie turned. "Cedric?" She sighed. "Pamela won't be coming home for the winter holiday. He's very disappointed."

Drake passed them humming the death march.

Cassie hit him. "Be quiet."

He stopped in front of them. "The end is near," he said in ominous tones.

"She had an opportunity to travel to France and took it."

"I'm not faulting her choices. Unfortunately, she's leaving Cedric behind. Even if she does come back—"

"She will."

"I bet we won't recognize her." Drake watched him, pensive. "I'm surprised he hasn't started to cheat."

Adriana and Cassie sent him a venomous glare.

He held up his hands in surrender. "It happens. I'm not condoning it but—"

Cassie pushed him away. "Go before you shame me further. I'll give you a lesson on appropriate conversations in mixed company later."

Adriana watched Cedric put the broom aside, wondering if his relationship would last. Educational differences was a big hurdle to climb, especially when you're young. Perhaps it would be better for them to break up as friends.

To date people who had similar experiences so that there would be no awkward moments, no instances when one would be regarded as better than the other.

Cassie nudged her. "Let's work. I see a table with your name on it."

The trash bag was an anchor, but she wasn't emptying out its contents. She took a deep breath and swung it over her shoulder, teetering backward. She was saved from falling over when the load was suddenly lifted. She turned and saw Eric.

He didn't smile, but looked pleased to see her. "Cassie is working you so hard you didn't have a moment to say hello," he said with mock annoyance.

"It's not completely her fault. I wanted to help."

"Thanks for coming."

She felt shamed into honesty. "A Hecht's Thanksgiving's sale was calling me." She shoved her hands in her pockets. "I felt safe to come here."

He nodded with sympathy. "I'm sure that must hurt. All those designer blouses fifty percent off, Tayrn Rose shoes buy one, get one free."

She frowned. "You're not helping."

He tossed the bag in the bin. "That's because I know the secret."

"What?"

"Sales always come back."

"But it's not the same," she said, gloomy.

"True, but considering how quickly trends change, that's a good thing, right?"

She sighed. "I miss shopping."

"Don't worry. Christmas is coming up. I'll be sure to give you my list."

"Come on, Nina, time to go," Adriana said once the clearing had been completed.

Nina came up to her smiling. "This was fun."

"I'm glad you enjoyed yourself. Where's your jacket?"

Her smile faltered. "Tamara needed it."

"Tamara?"

She nodded.

"You gave your leather jacket away?"

She wrung her hands, sensing she was in trouble. "She needed it. She doesn't have anything, not anything, and it's so cold. I can't take it back."

"But I gave you . . ." She stopped. It was gone and it was no big deal. She shouldn't feel betrayed. "Forget it." She took her hand to go.

Eric approached them, zipping up his coat. "Hey, Nina, where's your jacket?"

She lowered her eyes, but her words were defiant. "I gave it away."

"That was nice of you." He glanced at Adriana and could see she didn't agree. "Why don't you let Aunt Cassie give you something for your special deed?"

She turned to her mother for permission. Adriana nodded and she left.

Eric said, "I can see that Mom doesn't approve."

"Do you know how much that jacket cost? I bought it especially for her and she just gives it away like it's nothing."

"Adriana, she has plenty of coats. She did a good thing."

"Yes, now some homeless kid is going to look good in—"

"Adriana," he warned.

She moved her hand in a quick dismissive gesture. "Callous of me, I know. She did a good thing. Very much in the holiday spirit. I shouldn't care she gave away the very coat I bought especially so that we'd look like mother and daughter. My gifts never mean anything. They're just shallow, materialistic baubles. Your gifts, of course, are gold. Heaven forbid she should give one of your beloved books away."

He shoved his hands in his pockets.

"No, don't explain the reason," she said, sarcastic. "I forgot that I'm not as deep as the rest of you. My cares and concerns are frivolous, or had you forgotten? I wouldn't even be here if there hadn't been a sale. The only time I volunteer involves clothes and makeup to help women look beautiful for an interview. Not deep stuff like feeding them." She turned.

He grabbed her arm. "Stop it."

"I probably shouldn't even give her a Christmas gift. Just offer a donation."

"Are you finished?"

"What? You're not enjoying my little tantrum?"

"It was just a jacket."

She yanked her arm away. "No, it wasn't. It was a symbol of how much I loved her and she didn't care."


"I didn't mean to make you mad," Nina said in the car.

Adriana stared at the traffic lights. "It doesn't matter. You did the right thing."

"But you're still mad."

"Only at myself."

"Are we still going to Aunt Cassie's for Thanksgiving?"

"Sure." But Nina would be the only one staying.

Eric picked them up around seven. He looked handsome in a black jacket, gray trousers, and navy dress shirt. His eyes were remote. She smiled and he relaxed.

"Everything sorted out?" he asked, studying her face.

She kept her smile. "Yes."

"Good."

He complimented Nina on her rose dress and they headed out. Adriana was quiet on the drive. Nina and Eric were so busy guessing all the food they were going to eat that they didn't notice.

Drake met them at the door. Marcus followed, shouting,

"Awety Anna, Uncow Ewic!" He abruptly stopped when he saw Nina. His stocking feet didn't. They slid on the slick wood floor and he fell backward, hitting his head. Everyone rushed to him, ready to offer comfort. Nina reached him first.

She saw ready tears swimming in his big amber eyes. He was trying to be brave. She quickly rubbed the back of his head. "Ow, that must hurt." She gave him a quick hug. "But you're all right, aren't you?"

His chin trembled but he said, "I'm aw-wight."

She took his hand. "My name is Nina. Do you want to show me your toys?"

He smiled, the tears forgotten. "Come on, Nina."

They went down the hall, leaving the surprised adults.

Drake spoke first. "That was an artfully diverted disaster. Nina should go into damage control."

Adriana nodded. Yes, Nina, her little diplomat.

Jackie walked past, holding Ericka. "Hi, guys."

"Hi," they greeted.

Clay, Cassie's half brother, followed her. "May I please have a go now?"

"No, I'm holding her." She disappeared into the living room.

Clay looked at Eric and Drake in disgust. Since he was six five with the body of a bouncer he managed the expression well. "You can't go round raising women like that. It's just not on. She's spoiled rotten," he said, his annoyance giving a hint of his Manchester accent. "You know you two have done the men of this world a great disservice."

Drake patted him on the back. "You'll get to hold Ericka after dinner."

"I doubt it," he mumbled and followed Jackie into the living room.

"Hmm, the house smells good," Adriana said. "Is Cassie in the kitchen?"

"Since morning," Drake replied, taking their coats.

She went into the kitchen where Cassie was chopping zucchini.

"Everything smells delicious," she said, taking a seat. "Good job."

"What lies has Drake been telling you? Most of the credit goes to him. I was with the kids."

"No matter who cooks it, I'm sure it will be good."

"You'll see. Just stay away from the chicken, it's hot."

She hesitated. "Actually, I'm not staying."

Cassie turned. "What do you mean you're not staying?"

"Shh! You don't have to shout."

"Answer my question or I'm going to scream instead."

"Cassie, don't make this a big deal."

She put the knife down and leaned on the table. "It is a big deal. Do you know how many people you'll be hurting by leaving? Not to mention offending your best friend."

Adriana shrugged, helpless. "I don't even know why I said yes. You know I haven't done traditional dinners since I left my parents' house. Last Thanksgiving I spent at the movies. The year before at a club in Atlantic City."

"Point?"

She gestured to the kitchen and the dining room. "This isn't me. Drake will carve the turkey."

"We don't have a turkey. You're not leaving and that's final. I'll have Clay guard the door if necessary. It's just one night. You can break up with him tomorrow."

Adriana furrowed her brows. "I never said anything about breaking up."

"I thought since you'd like to hurt him by leaving, your relationship mustn't mean much."

She rested her forehead against her fist. "I don't mean to hurt anyone. It just happens."

"Then leave."

Eric entered the kitchen. "Who's leaving?"

"Adriana," Cassie said, returning to her chopped vegetables.

"Why?"

Cassie continued chopping, leaving the explanation to Adriana.

"Because I forgot to bring a gift," she said.

Drake walked in and grabbed some napkins. "Don't worry, you can bring a gift tomorrow wrapped in a five-page apology."

"Don't tease her," Eric said. "Can't you see she's upset?"

Drake shrugged. "It's not important."

"It's important to her."

Adriana stood. "Perhaps I should just—"

"You don't have to stand up for her," Drake said. "She knows us."

Eric frowned. "Don't start giving me orders."

"Hell, I knew you two dating would make things awkward."

"What do you mean by awkward?"

"It means—"

"All right, enough!" Cassie said. "Adriana, you want to give us a gift? Fold the napkins into pretty shapes. Eric, put the glasses on the table. And, Drake, check on Nina and Marcus. They are too quiet and it's making me nervous."


"Drake didn't mean anything," Eric said as they set the table. "If you really feel bad we can swing by—"

"I'm okay," she said. "It's just . . . I'm uncomfortable."

"Why?"

"I'm not sure how to behave. At my house everything had a rule: how to hold utensils, how to sit, how to eat, how to approach a guest. I could never get it right."

"You know everyone eats differently. We're very casual."

"I've only had a sit-down dinner at Cassie's house twice, but her mother criticized her so much I stopped going."

"You're among friends now. We pretend to be civilized."

He lowered his voice. "Remember I've seen you spear a shrimp and send broccoli flying."

She smiled.

"We don't always used the right utensils and sometimes even eat with our fingers, so don't be too judgmental."

His light tone made her feel more at ease. She remembered when she had hated his tone, feeling that he was looking down at her. She finished folding the napkins, then stared at him. "Eric, how did we end up here?"

He thought a moment. "First I picked you up in my Volvo, and then I took the—"

"You know what I mean. A year ago we hated each other."

He caught her eyes. "I never hated you. I thought you were flighty, a little vain—"

"I am vain," she said, ashamed. "I was going to leave."

"Why?"

"Because I wanted to be missed. I wanted to punish you for yesterday. I thought my absence would hurt you and Nina."

He nodded. "It would." He was silent. "Why did you stay?"

"I'm trying to be a grown-up." She pulled out a chair and sat. "I can't make Nina into me any more than my mother could make me into her."

"Why would you want Nina to change?"

"So we would have more in common."

"Sometimes our differences make us more common."

"Is that supposed to make sense?"

He sat next to her. "When you told me about how you felt about the salon, saying that it was something you loved, something you couldn't imagine not doing, I understood the passion and thought about my plants. I understood you because we had the feelings in common."

"So I'll understand her more by letting her be herself?"

"Yes." He held her hand. "Have you ever noticed how

often she wears the shirt you made for her Halloween costume?"

"No."

"You should take note. You've given her things of importance that you've never noticed because they hold a different meaning to you."

She swallowed building tears. "So I'm a good mother? She knows I love her?"

"Yes."

She hugged him and went into the kitchen.


Eric approached Clay, who sat and watched TV. "I need to find out something about an artist named Keith Trenton."

Clay didn't look at him. "Description?"

"Looks like a bottom feeder, but then again I'm biased."

"One of Adriana's?" Clay asked, familiar with her choice of men.

Eric nodded.

"I'll see what I can find."

"What's the fee?"

"We're family." He turned to him and grinned. "I'll think of something."

When dinner was announced they all headed for the table, which was dressed for the festivities. There was an elaborate array of votive candles set on a mirrored tray, red goblets, silver-plated cutlery, and red-beaded silk place mats. The food was just as decorative: the vivid green of sautéed zucchini, the fluffy whiteness of mashed potatoes, the deep brown of jerk chicken.

Marcus raced in front of Adriana and climbed onto a chair next to Nina. It was clear it was not his placement. Aside from the table setting, his eyes could barely be seen above the table.

"Honey, you know that's not your seat," Cassie said.

He settled in his seat. "I wanna sit with Nina."

"That's nice, but perhaps she wants to sit next to her mom. You didn't ask if she'd mind."

"No. She likes me."

Cassie sent Drake an eloquent "he's your son" look. He shrugged, then winked.

"It's all right, I'll move next to him," Nina said. She sat next to his booster seat and all was well.

"So how's business?" Clay asked Adriana as everyone began to eat.

"It's fine," she said vaguely, not wishing to elaborate.

"Must be an interesting field."

"It has its moments."

"Did you read about the lingerie designer who created matching bra and knickers out of human hair?"

Cassie laughed. "You're joking."

"What are knickers?" Nina asked.

"Panties."

"Eww!"

"I agree," Jackie said, scrunching her face. "Eww."

"They're being sold at two thousand pounds a set," Clay continued.

Eric pushed up his glasses. "The scary thing is that someone will buy them."

"No, what's scarier is that someone would wear them," Drake said.

Clay laughed. "I hear you, mate. Imagine chatting up a woman and finding that."

The men shivered. Cassie tapped her glass.

"Excuse me, gentlemen, and I use the term loosely, please remember that there are children present."

"So I guess I won't mention about the—"

"Clay," she warned. "If you don't behave, I'll tell Mom you want to visit her for Christmas."

He returned to his meal properly scolded. "The chicken is great."

"You can thank Nina," Drake said.

She looked up, surprised. "Me?"

"Yes, I used your chives for the jerk marinade. It gave it that extra-special flavor."

"Let's give her a round of applause," Clay said.

Everyone clapped, Marcus the loudest. He wasn't sure what was going on, but he liked to clap. Nina smiled, both embarrassed and pleased.

After the main course, Adriana excused herself. As she returned to the table, she walked past the kitchen and saw Cassie stacking the dishwasher. She ducked behind the corner when Drake entered. He said something in a low voice and Cassie flicked him with water. He wrapped his arms around her waist and kissed her neck. Adriana sighed at the tender moment.

Drake was a very affectionate husband without being distasteful. He would tuck a strand of hair behind Cassie's ear, touch her cheek, or whisper words meant only for her, demonstrating small gestures of devotion. They looked at each other with such love it made everyone around them feel good.

She and Eric probably made everyone feel nervous. He would glance at her, but there was nothing in his look, no hidden desire, no secret message in his gaze. He barely touched her when others were around. If her leg brushed his, it might as well be a piece of board. He was a kind and thoughtful lover when they were alone, but that didn't stop her from wishing he were a little more like Drake when it came to affection.

"Is the coast clear?" a male voice whispered behind her.

She spun around and slapped Eric in the chest. "You shouldn't sneak up on people."

"Why not? It's fun." He peered around the corner. "What are you looking at?" He saw Cassie and Drake preparing the dessert: mixed fruit with ice cream. Drake fed Cassie a melon ball. "He loves her very much."

"I know. It's nice."

He adjusted his glasses. "Making some comparisons?"
She nodded.

His eyes grew wary. "I see."

She thought about how he had planned the food and table settings. How Nina's herbs were used. And he did it to please her. He might not be physically affectionate, but his tenderness was clear. She kissed him on the cheek. "I like you better." She grabbed his hand. "Come on. Dessert looks good."

After dessert they all sat in the living room. Nina and Marcus played with blocks, Jackie coddled Ericka. Clay scowled at her.

"So, Adriana, do you think we can convince you to come next year?" Drake asked, sitting next to Cassie on the couch.

She sat on the floor next to Eric's legs. "Certainly. I'll probably become a nuisance."

"Or we could go to your place," Jackie said.

"I'm not the greatest cook."

"Don't worry, Eric can help you."

Silence fell, dropping so suddenly even the children sensed something was wrong.

Would they be together next year? "Yes," Adriana said finally, to fill the air.

Cassie spoke up. "More dessert, anyone, or something to drink?"

Eric stood. "No, I think we'd better leave."

"Bigmouth," Drake scolded Jackie as Eric, Nina, and Adriana went to the closet. He took Ericka and handed her to Clay. "Go find a foot to chew."

She blinked, innocent. "What did I do?"

"You just couldn't leave it alone."

She kissed her teeth, annoyed. "It's obvious they are in love."

"No, it's not obvious. Leave it alone."

She rolled her eyes, but said nothing.

* * *

Nina put on her jacket. Marcus watched with building tears. She buttoned up her jacket and stared at him. "Don't cry." Eric hid a grin, recognizing the tone. "I'll come back and visit, okay? So don't cry."

He nodded. However, when they opened the door he grabbed his father's trouser leg and burst into tears as if his little heart would break.

Nina looked at him, sad. "I said I'd be back."

Drake saw her distress and smiled. He touched her cheek. "Don't worry, he'll cry for a while, then go to bed and wait for your return."

Nina was only partially comforted. Nobody had ever cried when she had left before and he looked so unhappy. Eric took her hand. "He's young. He still has to learn that people will come back."

"Marcus is so silly," Nina shared on the drive home. "He says his father makes clouds."

"Clouds?" Adriana asked.

"Yes, he takes a white stick and makes clouds with it when he's on the balcony."

Eric frowned. "He means his smoking."

Nina's eyes widened. "Uncle Drake smokes?"

"Sometimes."

Her voice grew anxious. "But smoking kills people. Uncle Drake's to nice too die. I don't want him to die."

"He's not going to die."

"Yes, he is, I've seen it," she said, adamant. "He's going to get black lungs and die." Her voice wavered.

"He's not going to die."

Adriana saw Eric's tense profile and said, "He's trying to quit. Eventually, he won't smoke anymore."

Nina nodded, satisfied. "Good."

\* \* \*

Eric walked them to the apartment, then stood in the doorway, wondering the best way to end the evening. Elissa came up to greet him.

"Don't you want to come in?" Adriana asked.

He patted the cat, then straightened. "No, I think I'd better leave." He hesitated. "About what Jackie said—"

She waved his explanation away. "Jackie is Jackie."

"Yes." He shoved his hands in his pockets. "I want you and Nina to spend Christmas with us. We—"

"Yes."

He frowned. "I haven't explained it to you yet."

She shrugged. "Call me impulsive."

"We spend the night Christmas Eve and stand on our head till morning."

"Fine. I'll see you then."

He smiled. "Thanks for deciding to stay."

She brushed her lips with his. "Thanks for giving me a reason to."


She would not overspend, Adriana coached herself as she stepped into the mall. Everything was dressed in the holiday tradition, urging you to spend more than necessary only to suffer a mild stroke at the sight of your credit card bill in January. She had a budget and she had a list. She stared down at the items. She would only give one gift to each person, not three like last year.

On Christmas Eve, they scattered birdseed around a tree and everyone named a blessing for the coming year. Inside they shut off the electricity and sang songs by the fire.

Adriana stayed up after everyone had gone to bed. She sat in the living room and stared at the Christmas tree. Handcrafted glass ornaments hung on the branches, red and gold satin ribbons, white lights, and silver candy canes

decorated it. Wreaths hung in the windows. She sat in front
of the dying light of the fireplace.

In the distance Eric watched her, the glow of the fire
touching her dark skin, illuminating her face. She looked
serene like a queen draped in her blue silk robe, a gift Laurence had given her on a trip to Milan. The emeralds in her
ears were twinkling like green flames.

She was like a doll in a toy store he could not afford. No
matter how he pressed his face against the glass and
dreamed . . . she was meant for someone else. Someone
who could take care of her, provide for her. But he'd let the
dream last a little longer. He stared at her, wanting this moment to burn into his memory. Right now he could pretend
that what he gazed upon was his.

She suddenly turned. He took a step back, ashamed of
staring. She held out her hand and smiled. "You couldn't
sleep either?"

He sat next to her. "I wanted to make sure you were
okay. You've been quiet."

"I was just thinking about family." She took his arm and
draped it over her shoulders, cuddling next to him.

He turned to her, the firelight catching the dark purple
highlights of her hair, the silk of her robe whispered
against his skin, her scent as alluring as a falling star. Her
warmth and vibrancy called him home. He felt the earth
shift beneath him and he fell.


There was no snow on Christmas morning, but cold had
gripped the city, creating frost on the windows and trees.
The adults watched the kids dive into their gifts. To Adriana the feeling of home and family was as euphoric as any
shopping high. She bought Nina a picture book on the rain
forest and saw her face light with joy. As Nina hugged her
she saw Eric wink and knew she had gotten it right. Nina

had painted a mug for her and Eric bought her an orga-
nizer. She gave him a purple sweater.

"I have to get you out of gray and black," she said when
he frowned at it.

"Good luck," Cassie said in a stage whisper, glancing
at Drake. "I've only recently gotten him to wear white."

"You're island men," Adriana said. "You've been in the
U.S. too long."

Drake looked at Eric. "Should I bring out mi shirt wid
de palm leaves?"

"Don't forget the Panama hat."

After breakfast they told stories, and played games.
When evening came, they ate Christmas dinner, filling the
house with sounds of love and laughter.


"What are you working on?" Drake asked when he
found Eric at his dining table working. Eric had been acting strange since New Year's Day.

"It's a business plan for Adriana."

"Why are you doing that here?"

"I had to ask Cassie a few questions. I've done some
research on the fashion industry and think I could give her
some direction. She needs to approach this goal with organized steps."

Drake sat down in front of him, amazed. "You're in love
with her."

He scratched out a few numbers.

"Are you going to tell her?"

Eric crumbled up a sheet of paper and tossed it away.
"You're as nosy as an old woman."

Drake ignored him. "Try to make it romantic when you
do."

"Have you forgotten who I am?"

"Try."

"How?"

"Good question." Drake rubbed the back of his neck. "Food?"

"Not everyone sees food as an instant aphrodisiac."

"Poetry?"

"I already gave her a poem." He reached for his checkbook, then stopped. He looked at Drake.

Drake grinned, reading his mind for the first time. "Perfect."

Adriana paced in Rita's studio as the woman looked at her designs. They were surrounded by stacks of fashion magazines, sketches by various young artists taped to the wall, flyers for different shows scattered about, and ashtrays positioned on every flat surface, flooding with ashes and cigarette butts.

"They're awful," Rita said at last.

Adriana halted as if she'd been slapped. "What?"

Rita tapped her cigarette in a nearby ashtray. "I said they're awful." She took a brief drag and set it down. "There's no originality." She gestured to a mannequin. "This male robe is much too effeminate for any man to wear. And the color." She just waved her hand, the gesture eloquent enough. "You have no vision, no voice." She shrugged. "But it isn't like this is New York so you can show your designs at our little fashion show without any fanfare."

Instead of disappointment, Adriana felt a rage that was blinding. Rage at having her work verbally slaughtered without cause. She might not be smart on many things, but one thing she did know was what would sell. Her vision might not be unique, but she knew her consumer and she knew her talent. She took her clothes and gathered up her designs.

"I worked for months on these patterns," she said quietly. "Getting every detail right. Every seam is perfect. These are quality items and I'm going to show my designs at the fashion show if I have to call them out myself. And I will succeed because they will sell." She marched to the door.

Rita laughed. "Good girl," she said, picking up her cigarette. "You'll make it after all."

Adriana frowned, recognizing the test. It did not improve her mood. "I'll get you for this."

Rita laughed harder. "Like to see you try."

"I'll see you at the show." She slammed the door.


He was lost. He knew he should have waited until after the fashion show to see Adriana, but he wanted to wish her luck. Eric searched through the crowd of half-dressed women, but couldn't see Adriana anywhere. He should have brought her flowers, he thought, frowning at the envelope in his hand. It would have been more romantic and perhaps he wouldn't look so out of place. He shoved it inside his jacket. He looked as if he were delivering a summons.

He sighed and took off his glasses, wiping them with a cloth. Someone bumped into him and he lost his grip, sending his glasses crashing to the floor. He bent to pick them up, but someone kicked them away. He swore and dropped to the floor, searching for them. He crawled on the tile floor, unnoticed through the chaos of legs. He swept his hands across the floor, finally finding his glasses near a clothes rack. He grabbed them, relieved, and shoved them on. A pair of hot-pink high heels came into focus. They were attached to long legs. He glanced up.

"Thank God!" the woman said in a deep, smoky voice. "You just saved me from having a coronary. I thought you hadn't made it." She seized his arm and helped him up.

He began to protest. "But I'm not—"

"Honey, right now I don't care who you are. I was so scared we'd be a man short. You'll be wearing these." She held up red silk boxers and a robe. "You'll escort Laviana out on your second changing." She pointed to a woman getting her makeup done.

Eric stared at the items she'd given him, his heart accelerating. She couldn't possibly want him to go out in these. "But—"

"Hurry, we're about to start. Don't worry, you'll look fabulous. They're from Divine Notions." She looked him up and down. "You'd have thought they were made just for you."

"But—"

"See you out there." She spun away and began barking orders at a hairdresser.

He swore. He couldn't do this. He was a financial adviser for God's sake. He glanced at a man in boxers getting the shine taken off his nose. He caught his eye. The man winked. No, he definitely couldn't do this. He put the items down and walked to the door, then stopped. Adriana would be disappointed if her new design wasn't shown. He swore fiercely, snatching the items.

# Twelve

"Will you relax?" Cassie said as they sat facing the runway. "I'm sure he'll be here."

Adriana tried to keep calm. The seats around them were quickly filling up while the seat next to her remained empty. She looked toward the stage at the cream curtains, red carpet, and technicians working on the lighting. There were reporters setting up in the back of the room. It wasn't a large event, but some minor celebrities always showed up, giving the event some exposure.

"It's strange, he's usually on time," Jackie said.

Adriana toyed with one of her gold hoop earrings. "Perhaps he changed his mind."

"He didn't change his mind," Cassie said.

"He wouldn't dare," Sya added with emphasis. "He gets to see women in their underwear. What man would miss that?"

Adriana frowned. "That's not all this fashion show is about."

"That's all he'll care about."

"Eric isn't like that."

"No," Jackie agreed. She glanced at her watch. "But it is strange."

Adriana felt tears of disappointment building, but set her jaw firm. She wouldn't cry. It didn't matter. It just showed how different they were. How could she have expected him to come? She didn't need him to be there anyway. She didn't care. Hell, her family had yet to attend one of these events and only her mother had ever visited her shop.

"He will be here," Cassie repeated, trying to assure her.

She shrugged as the lights dimmed. She glanced around the room and sighed. Damn it, it did matter and she did care. He knew how important this was to her. He should have been there with her, his dark eyes surveying the crowd, his jaw like steel as he watched the women parade in front of him.

She couldn't focus when the show started. The models were a blur, the announcer's voice a buzz in her ear. Suddenly, she heard Cassie gasp. She turned and saw Sya and Jackie with their mouths open.

"What's wrong with you?" she asked. "Did someone's brassier slip?"

"No," Cassie said, breathless. "Look on the stage."

Adriana glanced at the stage at the line of male models strutting their wares. All delicious. "Yes, the men do look yummy." Perhaps she could meet one.

Cassie shook her. "Adriana, you're not looking."

She measured one of the men—a blond with a prominent bulge. "Yes, I am. Trust me."

Cassie grabbed her chin and directed her face. "The one in the red boxers and robe. Your design."

He was breathtaking. Withdrawn but sexy. "I'm sure I've seen him at other fashion shows. God, what a presence he's like—oh my God!" She leapt to her feet. "What is he doing up there?"

Cassie pulled her back down. "At least he came."

"Why isn't he wearing his glasses?" She stood again.

This time Jackie pulled her down. "I'm sure he won't fall off the stage."

"He's recovering from pneumonia."

"That was months ago," Cassie said.

She wasn't sure she breathed through the entire event. Every time he came out she saw no one else. As if everything fell away and became out of focus. At last it was over. The four women sat in stunned silence.

"Well," Jackie said.

"Well," Cassie replied.

"I'm sorry, Adriana," Sya said. "But I think your boyfriend is going to end up in my dreams tonight."

Adriana couldn't reply, still too shocked. Her pounding heart seemed to block out all sound.

"I had no idea he looked like that," Cassie said. She began to grin. "But it explains a lot."

"I love him," Adriana said, her voice barely a whisper.

"I'm glad you figured that out."

Sya said, "I'd love him too. Imagine a man walking half naked onstage for you. How romantic."

It wasn't what he had done. It was the fact that he had come. He had been there for her.

"At least we know what he'll be wearing on the honeymoon," Jackie teased.

"Quiet," Cassie ordered. "Here he comes."

The women watched him make his way to them with a placid, commanding presence, ignoring the eyes that followed him.

Sya frowned. "It's like he's a different man."

"I know he's the same one," Adriana said.

"Try to act normal," Cassie instructed.

Eric stopped in front of them. "Hello, ladies."

They all stood. "Hello." They glanced at each other. Sya said, "I've got to speak to Rita" and left. Cassie and Jackie also thought up excuses and soon did the same.

"Looks like tonight was a success," he said.

Adriana nodded. "Yes." She didn't know what to say to him, or how to look at him. Her feelings were so new and powerful, she was afraid he would see them in her eyes and run from them.

"I hope you raised enough money."

She swallowed, trying to dislodge the lump in her throat. "I'm sure we did."

Jackie walked past, whistling at him. "Hey, baby. Do you—"

Cassie grabbed her arm and dragged her away. "We'll see you later."

They left the ballroom and walked down the hall in silence. Adriana kept her eyes on the ornate pattern of the carpet.

He sighed. "You have every right to be angry with me."

She looked up at him, shocked. "But I'm—"

He held up his hand. "Just hear me out. I was the only guy around when she picked me to fill in. I know I looked ridiculous up there. I never felt like such an idiot, but I wanted to make sure all your clothes were shown. I knew it was important to you. So I—"

She held his head and kissed him. "Now shut up before I start to cry."

He raised a brow. "I looked that bad?"

She wrapped her arm around his. "You looked irresistible. I'm going to ask the photographers for copies."

He colored a bit. "It was the clothes."

"It was you." She stopped walking, the need to tell him how she felt rising in her throat. "Eric, I—"

"Here." He handed her an envelope.

"But, Eric—"

"Open it first."

She did. Inside was a business plan and a check for twenty thousand dollars. She looked up at him, stunned.

"It's just a start," he said. "A few ideas to help your business venture. I don't know much about the field, but I think you're a great investment."

She loved him and he thought of her as an investment? She smiled at him as her heart gently cracked.

* * *

"He gave you twenty thousand dollars?" Cassie asked as they sat in the Golden Diner.

Adriana stared at a woman, sitting at another table. She was young, but her breasts threatened to touch her knees. "I wonder if she would be offended if I told her where to get a good bra," Adriana muttered.

"Pay attention."

"I am. I have this terrible urge to go up to her and say, 'Sit up, sweetie, it helps the girls defy gravity.'" Cassie kicked her; Adriana turned. "What?"

"We're not talking about breasts right now. We're talking about Eric and his twenty-thousand-dollar check."

"Do you know most women don't wear the right bra?"

Cassie glared at her.

"I don't want to talk about Eric."

"Why not?"

"Because it hurts. He thinks of me as an investment. Doesn't that have a cold ring to it?"

"It's his way of showing that he cares."

Adriana stared at the envelope. "But what does it mean?"

"I just told you."

"I know, but this is serious. Does this mean we've reached another level? I'm not sure I can accept this. What if things don't work out? Will I have to pay him back?"

"No, this is business. He really believes in you."

"Or perhaps his libido is talking."

"We're talking about Eric and money."

"True." She put the envelope in her bag.

"Why don't you tell him how you feel?"

"Because it won't change anything. I knew I was falling in love with him and he knew it too."

"So what? Now it's for real."

"Doesn't matter. There's no reason to tell him, because a part of me will want to hear him say the words too and that's not fair."

"Give yourself time to think and if you feel uneasy about the check, wait awhile before you deposit it."


"Has she deposited the check yet?" Drake asked as they walked to Drake's second restaurant, the Red Hut. The February wind was fierce and they both held their collars up against the cold.

"No," Eric said, his words coming out as a puff of air.

"Perhaps she's a procrastinator."

"Or maybe she just doesn't want to." The prospect made his insides feel as cold as the weather. He knew her. She was impulsive. She would have deposited the check by now.

"It's only been a week. She could be nervous. Women act in strange ways. Take her to dinner and drop some hints. From there you'll find out how she feels."

Eric shrugged.

Drake pushed open the doors to the restaurant, then stopped. "Bring her here with Nina. I'll reserve one of the special tables and have a dinner set up for you. With the mood set you could talk things through."

Eric shrugged again.

Drake patted him on the back. "It will work."


It didn't work. Eric stared at Adriana across the flicker of candlelight, her orange cashmere sweater a bright contrast to the subdued maroon walls of the restaurant. She was quiet. That wasn't like her. Already his grasp on her had robbed her of her vibrancy, her passion—the very thing he loved about her.

It was time to set her free. He wasn't the one to care for her. He could never please her the way she deserved to be. He glanced around the restaurant imagining it through her eyes. The serene atmosphere, a well-dressed couple displaying the pretense of elegance and refinement in the corner, waiters full of deference with ready smiles. She was a high-energy woman.

Adriana stared at her glass. She wished she knew what to say. Eric looked expectant. As though he wanted her to say something. No doubt he wanted to discuss his business plan, but she couldn't. She hadn't been able to look at it, because it turned her heart cold. She didn't know where the relationship could go from here. She didn't want to do or say anything that would betray her feelings and send him running.

Yet he must know. He had been able to read her before and stayed. She took a deep breath. After tonight she wouldn't be so awkward. Her feelings for him would melt into something natural, becoming a part of her and not feeling like a foreign entity invading her heart. She stole a glance at him. He looked so handsome—his features strong, distinguished. But his eyes still bothered her. Would the ice never melt?

"Are you okay?" he asked her.

"I'm fine."

"It's a lovely place," Nina said.

He smiled at her. Even she could feel the tense energy hovering above the table like a rain cloud.

"You don't like it here," he said bluntly.

"No," Adriana quickly denied. "It's not that. It's just when you said you had a surprise—"

"You expected something more than the Red Hut?" he guessed.

"It's a wonderful restaurant," she said, trying to soften her criticism.

After a few moments he asked, "What did you think of the business plan?"

"You worked hard. Thank you. It will give me plenty to consider."

"I don't know much about fashion, but—"

"I appreciate the effort."

The conversation fell flat from there, becoming strained and painful. Soon the meal was over.

At her apartment, Eric accepted her offer of a drink. He sat on the couch, wondering the best way to phrase things. The best way to let her go.

She handed him a glass. "It's pineapple soda."

"Thank you." He took a sip, then tapped the side of the glass. "I think we should start seeing other people."

His words fell on her like an anvil. She took a step back. "What are you talking about?"

"Us."

She gripped the couch. "I know you're talking about us. What do you mean?"

"We should see other people."

She stared at him, but his face was unreadable. "Do I get an explanation for this revelation or are you just going to leave?"

His intense eyes swept her face. "You knew as well as I did that we wouldn't last."

She turned away. "That's not an explanation. What have I done?"

His voice was gentle. "You didn't do anything but be yourself."

She spun around, her eyes burning. "You're speaking in code. Have you forgotten I'm not as smart as you?"

His voice became as hard as his eyes. "Don't pull that crap with me. You know damn well that I'd never be able to make you happy."

"What are you talking about?"

He opened his mouth, then shook his head.

She pounded the couch with her fist. "Tell me!"

"At the restaurant I finally realized that I would never be able to afford you."

"I don't need you to afford me. I'm not some high-ticket item at an auction."

"I'm not saying you are."

"I admit to being a little disappointed at the restaurant. I expected a big surprise. Did you get a family discount?"

His jaw tensed. "Yes."

"What do you have against splurging every once in a while? About being impulsive and free?"

He pushed up his glasses in a quick angry gesture. "Impulsive behavior can lead to ruin."

"No, it leads to unexpected joys."

"And tragedies. If my parents had just planned their journey to America they might still be alive and we wouldn't have had to suffer their folly."

"Yes, but you survived it and look at you now. Where is your passion? Where is your romance? You have money, but guard it like a miser. Afraid it will disappear. You do everything with a goal in mind. You've never given me anything of sentimental value—a locket or a rose. It would have been a nice change if you had given me chocolates or champagne at the fashion show, but no, my solemn suitor writes up a business plan and becomes my investor."

His eyes pierced the distance between them. "Did you deposit the check?"

"No."

"Too much of a commitment?"

"Yes." Since money was all he cared about, he could have it back. She grabbed the check, crumpled it up, and stuffed it in his shirt pocket. "There, now you're free to leave."

Raw hurt flashed in his eyes; a layer of ice quickly covered it. He took the check out of his pocket and smoothed it out. "The money—"

"I know what the money represents and I don't want it. I don't need a lecture to explain it. Go and find someone you can afford. Someone who won't mind feeling that you can conveniently squeeze her into your budget. Someone—"

"You've made your point," he said quietly. "Good-bye." The door closed with a soft click.


She didn't sleep that night. Not that she expected to. It was over, finished. Just when she'd discovered she loved him, he wanted to see other people. Fine. Let him. It was good that he was gone. She could meet someone else too. She would miss him, but habits were usually missed until they were replaced by something else. Now she was free to find someone like her. Someone who didn't look for the best bargains, someone who could be impulsive and frivolous. Someone unpredictable.

After work, she sat at her drafting table and glanced up at the drawing and poem Eric had given her, posted on the wall. Suddenly the gravity of what she had done hit her. She had accused him of giving her nothing of value when he'd given her the priceless things, the intangibles: Hope, strength, courage, friendship.

He had come to her fashion show, cared about her daughter, supported her dreams, and she had been blinded by convention. Their argument hadn't been about money. She hadn't made him feel worthy. She had ignored his business ideals to tout the advantages of a romantic ideal. Of course he would want to find someone else. She would have to convince him not to.


Eric stared at the doodles of numbers in front of him and scowled. This definitely was not like him. He knew better than to get too close. He tore up the paper and stared down at the fresh sheet below. He would start again. Learn from his mistake. He had let a woman shatter his life once, he wouldn't do it again. He glanced up when someone knocked on his door.

"Come in," he said.

Adriana entered. "Eric—"

He leapt to his feet and grabbed his coat. "What's wrong? Is Nina hurt? Is your store in trouble?"

"No," she said quickly. "Everything is fine. I just wanted to talk to you."

He fell into his seat. "I wish you wouldn't look at me like that."

"Like what?"

"Never mind," he said, irritated with himself. "Sit down." He folded his arms, and his voice was neutral. "So how can I help you?"

"I owe you an apology. I—"

He shook his head. "No, you don't." He looked down at the sheet of paper in front of him; he had started doodling again. He scrunched up the paper. "Things were said in anger, but most of it was true."

"You've given me things of immense value. Things that are priceless." She leaned forward, desperate to convince him. "I was wrong and I want you to forgive me. I want us to work."

He glanced away, unable to look at her. His desire threatened to overcome sense. He couldn't go back. "I left you out of hurt pride. I had everything planned, the table, the food, the setting." He turned to her and managed a smile. "I forgot that my hummingbird deserves to fly."

"But, Eric, I want you."

He pounded the table with his fist in sudden impatience, surprising them both. "I can't be what you want." He took a deep breath and sat back. He lowered his voice, fighting the need to say what was in his heart. That he loved her, that she would haunt him for the rest of his life. "I would give my right eye to be the man you deserve. A man who thinks of roses instead of rosemary, who will take you out for no reason, who will shower you with jewelry and presents." His eyes fell. "Unfortunately, I know myself too well to pretend to be one of those. I will lecture, I will worry, I will plan, and I can't be any other way."

"But I don't want you to. I like you just the way you are. I want to keep seeing you."

He barely heard her. Catherine's rejection of his proposal rang in his ears. If only he'd been Drake. If only he had more passion, more heart, more romance. "I'm not going anywhere."

"I want to be with you. I love you."

He took off his glasses and rubbed his eyes. "What does that mean?"

"What else could it mean?"

*Does it mean that you pity me? That you see my heart bleeding and want to fix it?* He opened his top drawer just to give himself something else to do. "Do you want to marry me?"

She hesitated.

That was answer enough. He slammed the drawer shut. "Let's just try seeing other people to find out if we would really work. You just may discover that I'm not the one."

She stared at him.

He stared back. Her eyes were his weakness, cutting his heart open every time he thought it had closed. "Don't look at me like that."

Her voice was soft. "Like what?"

"Like I'm abandoning you."

"You are."

"No." His voice was firm. "I'll always be there for you."

Adriana gripped her bag. He would always be there for her. It sounded like the mission statement of a bank. She didn't want him to be *there*. She wanted him to be with her. "I won't let anyone take my place."

"Nobody will." He held out the check. "I want you to have it."

She pushed his hand away. "I don't want it! I want you.

Don't you understand?" She tapped her chest. "It's not about the money, it's about us."

His tone was level. "Just take the check."

She stood, feeling the ice in his eyes as he created a distance between them. "No. You're not listening. I want—"

He rose to his feet, propelled by anger. "I know what you want, but this is all I can give you! I know it's not enough, but it's all that I have. Why can't you—" He rested his hands on the desk, gathering his temper. His voice became quiet. "Accept what I can give you. I want you to succeed."

"I will succeed, but—"

"Take the check. Don't worry about what's on . . ." He adjusted his glasses. "Just take it, no strings. No commitment. As friends."

She reluctantly took the check and put it in her bag. "Are you free Saturday?"

He shook his head, his throat preventing any words.

She stared at him; he stared at her. Her gaze fell first and she went to the door.

"Adriana—"

She gripped the handle. "Don't say good-bye," she said and walked out the door.


Adriana sat in the car and watched snowflakes land on her windshield. They were small and melted quickly, touching the window and then streaming down like tears. She didn't want to go home or to work or talk to Cassie. She didn't want to cry or think. She just wanted to disappear.

She drove out of the city and ended up in Virginia. She stopped at a mall. In a haze she walked past the stores where there were blouses that promised a fresh new life, dresses that avowed to catch a man's eye, and shoes that swore they would add a spring to your step. She felt beaten, but knew she was going to be fine.

They just needed time apart and then they'd be together again. She wanted to believe that, but in her head a vicious little imp whispered that it was over. That he'd grown tired of her. Tired of her need for him. Tears threatened, but she fought against them. That's when she saw it. Her tantalizing demon. Neiman Marcus was having a sale.

# Thirteen

Drake, Clay, and Eric sat in Eugene's Bar with beers and a bowl of chips on the table in front of them. They watched a basketball game on the TV as a few regulars shouted out the plays.

Drake stared into his mug. "So it's over?"

"Yep," Eric said.

"Why?"

"Why are you surprised? You knew it wouldn't last."

Drake shrugged. "I wasn't sure. I hoped it would."

"Well, it's over now." Eric lifted his glass. "We're friends."

Drake winced. "Friends? Why don't you just break up?"

Eric swallowed his beer.

Clay said, "You're in luck because I met this woman—"

Drake scowled at him. "He doesn't need a woman right now."

"Why not?"

"Have you lost track of this conversation? He's just broken up with his girlfriend."

Clay nodded. "Right, so it's time for some medicinal bonking."

"What?"

"Therapy sex."

"What the hell is that?"

"It's like pity sex except more intense," Eric explained.

Clay leaned forward. "Right, and only some women can do it well. Fortunately, I met this woman—"

"No," Drake said. "He needs time."

"Time's relative, mate."

"He loves her."

"You're thinking like a married man. You're thinking of loyalty. But we reside in the single guy's realm. The rules are different. Once you've broken up, it's over. You and your willie are free."

"So it's okay if Adriana suddenly finds another man?"

The sound of crushing metal interrupted Clay's reply. They both turned to Eric's demolished beer can.

"I'm sure that won't happen," Drake said quickly, moving the can out of view.

"I said single *guys*," Clay clarified. "Single women operate by different rules." He scratched his chin. "Unfortunately, I haven't quite worked them out yet."

Drake turned to Eric. He was too quiet, becoming a shadow again. He sighed. "You make me worry sometimes."

Eric glared at him. "I'm not a damn drug addict. You've a wife and two kids to worry about. When am I going to get off your radar?"

"Never. I've known you all your life."

Eric shook his head, solemn. "No, you haven't."

"You're right," Drake agreed. He ordered another beer. "I could never figure you out."

"Don't try."

"Why not?"

"You don't need to pretend anymore."

Drake thanked the waitress for his beer, then turned to him. "Pretend what?"

Eric glanced up, his eyes like stones. "I know you've despised me since Dad died."

"That's not—"

"You can deny it, but I know how my illness affected

you. I know how much you had to sacrifice. I know how you had to keep me out of trouble all the time. When you thought I wasn't looking, I'd see you staring at me as if you wanted to put a pillow over my head while I slept. Do you deny it?"

"Yes. I never despised you. What put that in your mind?"

Eric set his glass down with a thud. "Because I despise myself. I was pathetic and weak with bad eyes and bad lungs and could do nothing to help you."

Drake pulled out a pack of cigarettes from his jacket. Eric snatched the pack. Drake flashed a slow, dangerous smile. "You're in a fighting mood today."

He didn't deny it. He held up the cigarettes. "I want you to stop this. Not just for me and Jackie, but for your family. Do you think it will be fair to put Marcus through what we did? You sick in bed with emphysema or lung cancer and he having to watch you die and not be there for him and his sister."

"I'm not going to get sick."

"You don't know. You've always been healthy. If you knew about illness you wouldn't risk it." He tossed the cigarettes down in disgust. "I made you become this."

"No, you didn't."

"I remember the way you used to look at us. It was—"

"Guilt. I felt guilty. Every time you got sick or said you were hungry, I felt guilty because I wanted to keep you instead of giving you over to the system. You were my family. The only thing of value that I had and I made you suffer for my own selfish need." He raised his drink, then set it down. "It preys on a man's conscience." He frowned at his drink. "Who knows? You might be healthier now if you'd been brought up in a good home and a clean environment instead of what I could get for you."

"But my scams . . ."

"Your scams kept me going. They gave me the motivation to work harder and provide a better life so you would stop."

Eric grabbed a handful of chips. "I didn't stop."

"Did I ever turn your money away?"

Eric turned toward the exit, his voice a raw whisper. "I nearly got you killed."

Drake sat back and shook his head in regret. "How could you still blame yourself for that?"

Eric couldn't stop. It was a virus eating away at his mind, every year the memory becoming more clear, more gruesome. He had scammed the wrong guy. The man had seemed a good mark: weak, unassuming, naive. He didn't look like a guy with connections to an underground gang that had slipped under the radar of police for fifteen years.

Eric had discovered his mistake quickly. The man hadn't been pleased to lose five hundred dollars in Eric's counterfeit money scheme. He had gotten reckless and Drake had paid for it. The gang grabbed Drake as he left for work, beat him until his face was barely recognizable, and hung him upside down over the side of a building.

They made Eric watch. They held him and forced his eyes open. Time stood still.

It was spring. He wore a T-shirt with the arms cut away and jeans. The spring air was warm and brought a gentle breeze, but his insides were frozen. His heart was crystal, his lungs icicles. He could hardly breathe. They held him a few feet away from Drake so he could see the bottom of his brother's sneakers—so worn the grooves were smooth. He was sixteen but nearly wept like a baby, talking fast, trying to come up with a bargain.

They finally dropped Drake on the concrete roof and offered a warning. Eric didn't hear it, he didn't need to. His eyes remained fixed on Drake, who lay motionless only a few feet away. He'd seen death before and felt its presence. He wondered if it would sweep down and take his brother away. Soon the gang was gone. The sound of traffic was heard below, voices carried up from the streets. But he stood paralyzed, trapped by invisible restraints.

Something in him had died that day. He was never the same again.

"It was better me than you," Drake said, cutting through his thoughts.

"Why?"

Drake looked at him. Eric knew the answer then. He would have killed them and probably gotten killed in the process. That was Drake—passionate and ready to defend and protect those he cared for. Either way he would have been involved—either as sacrifice or defender. Eric swore, the fierce love for his brother annoying him.

"It's over," Drake said. "It's the past. It taught us both a lesson. That you were playing a dangerous game and that I had to keep a closer eye on you."

Drake tried to make light of it, but Eric couldn't. His real fear shadowed him every day. "I'm like Dad," he admitted, ashamed. "I have his rashness, his optimism, his willingness to risk it all. And I fight that part of me every second."

"Why fight it?" Clay asked.

The two men looked at him, surprised. They had forgotten he was there.

"What?" Eric asked.

"Why fight it? Isn't life a gamble?"

"I've taken risks. I've asked three women to marry me."

Clay gave a low whistle. "That is a risk. One of them might have said yes."

"How come you never did marry?" Eric asked him.

"What are the acceptable excuses? Never found the right woman, didn't want to, I'm gay, fear of commitment. Personally, I think I'm too old now. I'm too set in my ways."

"Should guys like us get married?"

"Don't see why not. If you can convince a woman to marry you, what's the harm in that?"

"Your past. Who you used to be."

"I used to drink. Was completely legless for years. I hardly remember my twenties. I can assure you I'm not that man anymore. Whoever meets me is meeting Clay now, not then."

"You told me once not to be ashamed of my past," Drake added.

"Your past is different than mine."

"Is the man who accepts dirty money cleaner than the one who makes it?"

"He has a point," Clay said. "You—" He stopped when Eric looked past him and swore.

Bruce approached the table. A large and predatory menace. "I've been looking for you."

Drake leaned back. "What is the problem?"

Clay flashed a cold smile. "We might be of service."

Bruce pointed at Eric. "I owe Four Eyes a broken nose."

"Really?" he said slowly.

Drake stood. "Why don't you practice on me first?"

Bruce kept his eyes on Eric. "This isn't about you."

"Yes, but I can make it about me."

Eric spoke up in a lazy voice. "I can handle it." He rose to his feet and threw some money on the table. "I've been waiting for this moment."


March pushed into February with ice, snow, and wind. When Adriana stepped into Divine Notions she was too busy trying to get warm to notice Sya's excitement.

"You won't believe this," she said as Adriana hung up her coat.

"What?"

"A woman came in and ordered three of your boxer and robe sets."

Adriana looked at her, confused. "That's nice. Did you give them to her?"

Sya shook her. "She wasn't talking about the store, she

was talking about your design. She saw it at the fashion show and—"

Adriana didn't hear the rest. She fell into a chair. "She liked them?"

"Yes. Adriana Travers, you're in business."

Adriana looked at her; Sya looked back. They took a deep breath and screamed.

She had to tell someone. Adriana was so full of energy she thought she could float. First she had survived a Neiman Marcus sale, actually walking away with nothing, and now a woman wanted to buy her clothes. She went to Cassie's house and saw a man stumble down the steps. She raced up to him.

"Eric! What happened?"

"Bruce found me." He pulled out something from his shirt pocket. "This time he did break my glasses."

"That's awful." She reached for him but stopped herself.

He shrugged. "I have another pair at home."

"Will you be able to find your way?"

He squinted at the ground. "I know I scattered crumbs somewhere."

She wrinkled her nose. "Are you drunk?"

He shook his head, mournful. "Tried but it didn't work."

"I think it did."

He looked at her. His eyes were clear. "I'm fine. I don't get drunk. I told you I like being in control."

"I'm so sorry about Bruce."

He tenderly touched the bruise on his cheek. "Don't be. He only hit me twice."

"You counted?"

He nodded.

"What do you mean? How can he only hit you twice?"

"Are you sure you want to hear this?"

She made a face. "Is it bloody?"

He nodded.

"Very violent?"

He nodded again.

She bit her lip. "Is Bruce conscious?"

He paused.

She held up her hand. "No, I don't want to hear it."

"Okay." He walked past her.

"I have news."

He turned. "You found someone?"

Her voice fell. "No."

"I was trying to be funny."

"Don't."

He rested against the railing. "What's your news?"

"I did it!"

He blinked. "Did what?"

"I sold a design! A woman wants three boxer and robe sets. Can you believe it?"

He held out his arm. "Congratulations."

She hugged him. "I hardly feel like myself."

He stifled a groan. "Careful. Not too tight."

She looked up at him. "I thought you said he only hit you twice."

"That's right, but he threw me a couple of times. Concrete is not good for the back."

"Are you sure you're okay? Will he be looking for you again?"

"Doubt it."

She frowned. "I don't like this. How could he be angry with you after all these months?"

"He knows how to hold a grudge."

"Did he mention Lynda?"

"We really didn't get a moment to chat," he said dryly.

"I wonder if they're still together."

"I really don't care." He pulled away, realizing he was still holding her. It felt too natural.

She studied him. He looked tired. "Are you coming down with something?"

"No, I've just had a lot to do." He turned and slipped on some ice. Adriana grabbed his arm. They both fell.

"Are you all right?" she asked, hovering over him. His eyes were closed.

He smiled. "You smell good."

"Are you sure you're not drunk?"

"I'm sure."

"How hard did you hit your head?"

"I didn't." He sat up and opened his eyes. "I'm fine." He winced. "Stop worrying."

"You could have twisted an ankle, broken a leg."

"Busted a skull."

"That's not funny."

He shrugged. "No, but this is." He pulled the back of her shirt and dropped in snow.

She squealed and shook it out. "Why, you—" She tried to catch him, but he ran. She made a snowball and threw it at him. It hit him in the back of the head. He spun around and grabbed some snow.

"I love you," she said.

The snow fell through his fingers. "I wish you would stop saying that."

"I'll say it until you believe me."

His shoulders fell. "It's not enough."

She walked up to him. "What else do you want? Proof?"

He wiped the snow off his gloves.

"Nina wants to know when you'll stop by."

"Some day."

She searched his face. His nose was red from the cold, the bruise on his jaw turning purple. She thought he looked beautiful. "Are you seeing anyone?" she asked softly.

He sighed. "No."

"Then you might as well see me."

"Adriana—"

"I've proven that I don't need to spend impulsively, I will

be grateful for anything you have planned, I've accomplished a goal—"

"I don't want you to change because of me."

She bit her lip. "And I don't want to lose you because of me."

He groaned and turned. "I'll think about it," he called over his shoulder.

"Don't think too long," she said. "I'm not as patient as you think."

Carter gripped the phone, fighting the wave of panic that threatened to drown him. He'd lost the money. His investment was gone. In three weeks the family would discover three thousand missing from the fund and Henson would demand his money. The receiver slipped from his hand, clattering into its cradle. He needed money now. Fast. Serena would never forgive him for this. Her family would never trust him.

They wouldn't understand. They'd never had money troubles. It was always there. For him money troubles had haunted him all his life. Even in elementary school he was aware of the differences between the haves and the have nots. He grew up with kids like Nina Shelton who never had to worry about money, or even about getting a job after graduation. Their lives were planned out and if they made a mistake, they had a big cushy trust fund to land on. Their parents invested in them like property. Something valuable.

Something valuable. He repeated the words, as their meaning became clear. He began to smile and jumped to his feet.

"Where are you going?" Serena asked as he packed his bags.

"Not far. I'm just going to put something on the market."

\* \* \*

Eric sat in the back office of the Blue Mango, randomly adding numbers in his calculator, when someone knocked on the door. Outside, the wind howled. It was the last week of March and there was no sign of the coming spring.

"Come in."

A tall dark-skinned young woman with smiling brown eyes entered. "Hi, Mr. Henson."

Eric leapt to his feet. "Pamela! What are you doing here?"

"I'm on spring break."

He glanced out the window at the melting snow. "You should have gone somewhere warm."

She smiled shyly. "I like it here."

Drake came into the room. He looked at Pamela, spun on his heel, and left.

She frowned. "What was that about?"

Eric sat on the edge of the desk with a secret grin. "Just wait."

A few moments later they heard hurried footsteps. Cedric burst into the room. "You're here," he said.

"Yes."

"You didn't tell me you were coming."

"I know. Surprise."

He pulled her into his arms and spun her around. They both laughed.

Cedric turned to Drake. "Mr. Henson, do you think—?"

"Finish your tables and enjoy yourself."

They left the room surrounded by the glow of young love.

"I can't believe it," Eric said. "You let him off early?"

"It's a slow day," Drake grumbled.

"You're getting soft."

"Shut up."

Eric left the office and spotted the young couple in the corner. Pamela rested against the wall; Cedric leaned toward her. Their different backgrounds were evident by their shoes. Pamela's stylish leather flats made Cedric's dress shoes look like rubber. But somehow to them it didn't matter.

With all the college guys she had met, Pamela had come home to him, and of all the available girls for Cedric to choose from he had waited for her. Eric heard the whispered words of love and wondered if it was easier for the young. Easier because they had no notice of the eventual heartache that would follow. Yet they might be lucky to have found each other, their path already destined to be together.

Pamela and Cedric had taken the risk of falling completely, holding on to each other on the way down. Adriana loved him and he loved her. It might not seem like enough, but it would do for now.

Adriana adjusted her scarf as she stood at the bus stop. It was not like Nina to sit at the back of the bus. But that must have been the case since a number of children had disembarked before her. Then the doors closed. Adriana felt the rise of mounting horror as the bus pulled from the curve. Nina was gone.

Adriana called the school. Everyone said they saw Nina get off the bus in the morning or rather that she had attended her classes. However, no one could definitely say they saw her get on the bus in the afternoon. Adriana hung up the phone, then dialed Eric.

"Henson speaking."

"Is Nina with you?"

There was a pause, then, "How long has she been missing?"

She gripped the phone, her sweaty palms making it slippery. His words made the situation too real. Nina was missing. "I'm not sure. The school officials say she attended school but . . ." Her words died away, a sob replacing them.

She heard the phone disconnect and knew he'd be there.

She paced the living room, trying to think of various harmless scenarios. Perhaps Nina had made a new friend and once she reached the friend's house she would call. Or perhaps she had stayed after school and the teacher would soon call.

The doorbell rang. Adriana opened the door and Laurence stormed into the apartment. "Tell me Nina is here. I received this ridiculous ransom note and I want to know what's going on."

She fell into the couch, all hope gone. Someone had taken her. "Nina's not here."

"I can't believe you let this happen."

Her mouth fell open. "You can't blame me."

"If she hadn't been taking the bus we would know where she is."

She stood up and faced him. "I work, Laurence. I can't afford a driver or to chauffeur her back and forth to school."

"If you took my money you could."

She turned away from him and threw up her hands, exasperated. The argument was illogical. He just needed someone to rage at.

"The school will hear from me. How could a child disappear under their watch?"

"Let me see the note."

He handed it to her. The letters were made from magazine cutouts. It said: *Ten thousand for your daughter. Deliver at Rock Creek Park at 1:30 A.M.*

She frowned. "Ten thousand? That's not much."

"It's a damn insult."

The doorbell rang.

"Who the hell is that?" Laurence opened the door and scowled at the visitor. "What do you want?"

Eric ignored him and went to Adriana. His stoicism, though in stark contrast with Laurence's vehemence, came with more menace. "Are you okay?"

"I'm about to go into hysterics. Look." She gave him the note.

Eric scanned the note. Ten thousand? That was how much Carter owed him. He swore.

"What?" she asked.

He tucked the note in his coat. "I think I know who has her."

Adriana and Laurence stared at him, hopeful. "Who?" Laurence demanded.

"I'm not sure, but I'll check it out." He opened the door.

"I'll call the police," Laurence said.

"No."

"Why?"

"I can deal with him."

Laurence's voice deepened. "How do you know that?"

"Because he's my friend."

Laurence's voice was cold. "Don't think I'll ever let you forget that." He slammed the door shut before Eric could leave. "Why should we trust you?"

"Laurence!" Adriana said, embarrassed by his suspicion.

His gaze remained on Eric. "An acquaintance of mine encouraged me to check up on you. So I did. You're not as clean as you would like people to believe. Now you and your dirty past have put my daughter's life in danger."

Adriana touched his arm. "We don't know that."

He turned to her. "Why is he here?"

"Because I called him."

"How do we know he's not in on it? I know him better than you do."

Eric's voice, though soft, pierced the air like a missile. "I would never do anything to hurt Nina. I love her like a —"

"Like a daughter?" Laurence sneered. "But you're not her father, I am. And do you know *who* I am? I am Laurence Adom Shelton. Son of Reginald, grandson of Stephen. Our roots traced to Ghana where my line can be linked back to the times of Shakespeare. I have a major in physics and a Ph.D. I am Adriana's first husband and Nina's father. No matter how much time you spend with Nina, she will always belong to me. I will be the one watching her graduate from high school and college. I'll be the one walking her down the aisle. I'll be the grandfather of her children. Not you."

Eric opened the door, his voice laden with steel. "Until we find her, you won't be anything."


He wouldn't touch him, Eric promised himself as he drove up to Carter's Georgian-style home. He'd just take Nina and leave. If he touched him . . . He clenched his fist and parked his car. He counted to ten before ringing the doorbell.

Serena answered. "Hi, Eric. Haven't seen you in a while."

"Where's Carter?"

"In the basement. He—"

"Thank you." He walked past her. He found Carter at his desk. "Where is she?"

Carter spun around, his smile of welcome fading. "Who?"

"Don't play games. I saw your ransom note. I knew you were asking too much about Shelton."

"Ransom? What are you talking about?"

"You sent a ransom note to Shelton."

Carter shook his head. "Kidnapping is dirty business. You know I'm too clean for that."

Eric folded his arms.

"You're tense."

"I'm trying not to hurt you."

Carter held his arms open, a gesture of innocence.

"Come on, when have I ever had to use a child to get money? It's not my style."

Eric swore and let his arms fall. Carter was right. Using kids was not like him. But at that moment he wished it were. He didn't want to face Adriana without Nina. Face that he had failed her.

"It was a ransom note, not a phone call?"

"It's a note."

Carter held out his hand. "You have it with you?"

Eric gave it to him.

He studied the note and frowned. "Ten thousand? That's it?"

"Yes."

He held the note up to the light. "Are you sure this is real?"

"Nina is missing. It can't be a prank."

He spread the note on his table and sniffed it. "Who did the note go to?"

"Her father. He showed it to Adriana."

Carter looked at him, confused. "Why not the police?"

"I don't know." He shoved his hands in his pockets, resisting the urge to break something. "Perhaps he thought it was a joke like you did."

"Unless he's pulling the joke."

Eric glared at him in disgust.

"Human nature never surprises me. Was the divorce amiable?"

"It's not him. He wouldn't hurt Adriana this way."

Carter tapped the note, considering that. Eric usually read people well. "Something's strange about all this. Are the police involved now?"

"Not yet."

"Because you thought it was me, right?"

Eric didn't reply.

"Loyal till the end."

Eric pushed up his glasses. "No. I wanted to get to you first."

Carter folded the note and headed for the stairs. "Hmm. We're back in business."

"Why?"

"I think someone's trying to pull a scam. Fortunately, I got the string to hang them."

When Eric and Carter returned to Adriana's place, Laurence grabbed Carter by the lapels of his jacket. "Where's Nina?"

Carter held up his hands. "I don't have her, but I think it's someone you know."

"Why?"

"Usually is. Nina isn't the type to go with a stranger. I met her. She's smart."

"She's just a kid," Adriana said. "Kids make mistakes."

"It's the amount that bothers me."

"Perhaps it's a druggy who needs fast cash," Laurence said.

"They usually don't steal children."

"She could have been snatched randomly."

"But they knew she was worth money," Carter said.

Eric rubbed his chin. "Most girls at Brenton are worth money."

"They knew where to send the note."

Laurence picked up the phone. "I'm calling the police."

"You think the exposure won't get her killed?" Carter asked. "You're a big name. The media will be all over this."

Laurence dropped the phone.

"When kidnappers get nervous they get sloppy," Eric said.

Carter nodded grimly. "Yes, and they'll start to clean things up."

Adriana covered her ears. "Stop it!" She glared at them.

"You're acting as if this were a game. There is nothing to be 'cleaned up.' We're talking about a child, my daughter. Her name is Nina. Understand? You don't need to be so cold and calculating about it."

Laurence drew her close. "It's all right, Adriana."

"No, it's not all right," Eric said coldly. "We can't have you falling apart on us. We can't afford to get emotional. We need to think and plan and organize. That's what's going to get her back. Not falling into tears."

Laurence cut in. "Wait a—"

Eric glared at him. "Shut up until I'm finished." He looked at Adriana. "You think we're not worried? Do you think our insides aren't turned into knots wondering where she is, wondering if she's safe? We feel too, but that isn't going to help her. You're a woman. You could put a different angle on things. We need you to think."

She stared at him, wanting to hate him for being so callous, but knowing he was right. "Fine."

Carter folded his arms. "She's insurance. They'll hold her until they get the money."

"Let me just pay it," Laurence said.

Eric shook his head. "And let him win? No, Nina would never be safe after that. He needs to be caught."

"How do you know it's a he?" Adriana asked.

The men looked at her, then each other.

Carter clapped his hands and swore, pleased. "That explains it. Nina might be more likely to go with a woman."

"Then I'm calling the police," Laurence said.

Carter looked at him, curious. "Why didn't you do that when you got the ransom note?"

Laurence ignored him and began to dial. Carter stopped him. "Forget it. I already called."

Chaos soon followed. Everyone was interrogated. Police officers riddled them with questions exposing Adriana's marriage, divorce, and current arrangement. The police delved into Eric's and Carter's backgrounds.

As night turned into morning, tensions mounted. Eric returned home with Carter since Laurence made sure their presence was unwanted. Eric searched his mind for answers, hating the helpless feeling of being out of control. A half hour later Clay and Drake arrived at his house.

"What are you doing here?" Eric asked as they stepped into the room.

"Carter called us," Clay said.

Eric turned to him. "What are you up to?"

Carter grinned. "I'm pulling a scam of my own."

"What the hell are you talking about? This is a kidnapping, not a con."

"Let's look at the facts first."

The four men sat at the kitchen table.

Carter spoke. "Nina is missing. Her parents appear not to know where she is."

"Why do you say appear?" Clay asked.

"Can anyone say Susan Smith?" A mother who drowned her children and reported them missing.

Nobody argued.

"Okay, so we've established Nina is missing either knowingly or unknowingly," Drake said.

"Right," Carter said. "And Eric is the prime suspect."

Eric shook his head, amazed. "How could I be the prime suspect?"

"If the police built up a case you could be arrested."

"Why?"

"Because the clues point to you."

# Fourteen

Eric leaped to his feet, outraged. "But I don't have Nina."

"We know, mate," Clay said. "That's not the point. You're being set up."

"But the police—"

"The police aren't involved yet," Carter said.

Eric stilled. "But we just spoke to them."

"No, we didn't."

He swore. "You got fake cops? You mean no one is out there looking for her?"

"I have a reason for this. Nina is safe."

"How do you know?"

"First the note. You use very distinct paper at your office. It's the same as the note, same thread, same watermark. Second, it will be easy for any witness to use the 'I saw a black man walking a little girl fitting Nina's description' statement. Third, you're on the list of authorized adults to pick up Nina from school, right?"

Eric nodded. "That's right. Adriana made sure just in case I needed to get her."

"So you could slip under the school's radar. Fourth, you didn't go to work today."

"It's the end of March. I always go to . . ." His words died away. He always went to the building where his life had changed.

"Did anyone see you?" Clay asked.

"No."

Drake sighed. "So no one can vouch for you."

"No."

"Someone knows your pattern," Carter said. "Someone knew you'd be there. Who else knew you would be away from your office?"

Eric shook his head, too angry for words.

"This isn't about money or Nina. It's about you."

"Do you have any old enemies?" Clay asked.

Eric glanced at Drake and Carter and suddenly felt ill. Drake took out his cigarettes. Eric glared at him. "I'll quit when this is over," he said, igniting his lighter.

Eric didn't blink. Drake swore and gave him the cigarettes.

"So what do we do now?" Clay asked, ready for some action.

"We wait. Since Eric is the villain of this little game, someone's going to play the hero."

They fell into silence. Nearly a half hour later Eric's phone rang. "Yeah?" He listened for a moment, then hung up. "That was Adriana. They have Nina."


Only Carter and Eric went to Adriana's. Eric's joy and relief plummeted when he saw Lynda standing with Laurence. Two officers approached him at the door. Carter touched his ear, signalling that they were his.

"We'd like to ask you a few questions," one asked.

His jaw twitched. "I answered your questions."

"And we thank you for your cooperation, but we have a few more."

He paused. "Am I under arrest?"

"We just have a few questions."

"Am I under arrest?"

"We could—"

His eyes darkened. "Does that mean no?"

"Yes."

Eric opened the door. "Then I suggest you leave."

The cop pushed his face so close their noses touched. "If you have something to hide, we'll figure it out."

Eric stared back, unmoved. He closed the door behind them.

Nina ran to him. "Uncle Eric."

Laurence grabbed her before she reached him. "Go to your room."

She looked up at him, shocked. "But—"

"I said go."

Her eyes filled with tears. She nodded and left.

Eric said, "Don't make her feel like this was her fault."

"Why? Because it's yours?"

"I haven't done anything." He looked at Lynda. "What is she doing here?"

"She has my eternal gratitude. She found Nina."

Eric pushed up his glasses. "What a coincidence. You know she used to be my girlfriend."

"Yes, she told me all about you. While you were not directly responsible for Nina's kidnapping, you couldn't help bragging about your advantageous connections. You told Carter about her."

"She met him in my office."

"How convenient. Lynda overheard him talking about his supposed introduction with his wife. He has always had money trouble. He owed some guy money and convinced him of a bigger payoff if he used Nina as bait."

Eric looked bored. "Only ten thousand?"

"Ten thousand is a lot when you're desperate. He already knew where Nina went to school, thanks to Carter, and set his plan in motion."

Eric narrowed his eyes. "And Lynda just happened to know all this?"

He shrugged as a way of excuse. "She admits to liking bad boys. Her current boyfriend, Bruce, heard of the plan and agreed to be part of it. He took Nina and brought her to Lynda."

**Carter spoke up.** "Why didn't he just call the police to prevent the kidnapping in the first place?"

"Who cares why they did what they did?" Laurence asked, agitated. "Because of them Nina is safe."

"Ah, yes, the heroes," Carter muttered.

"She's lying," Eric said.

Laurence's voice was ice. "And you used to make a career out of it. I know her family. She has a sterling reputation. You have nothing but your name. Who do you think I'll believe?"

"Don't be a snob," Adriana said. "We know even blue bloods can lie."

He turned to her, angered that she would question his logic. "Why would she make this up?"

"Because she's a vindictive bitch."

"Who knows how to twist information," Carter said. "It will hang you one day. I'll provide the string." He opened the door, touched his sleeve with two fingers as a sign of revenge, then left.

Lynda burst into tears. "I knew you wouldn't believe me. I just wanted to help. I know it's far-fetched but it's true. When Bruce brought Nina to me she was so scared. I did everything to make her feel safe. I held her and took care of her and brought her here to you and this is the thanks I get."

"No, we're very grateful," Laurence said gently.

Adriana's voice was cold. "I'm not."

"Adriana!"

"She set this entire thing up. You're being blinded by your prejudice."

"Facts are facts."

"All I see is smoke. The only thing we have to grasp is her word."

Lynda straightened, wiping her tears. "I know when I'm not welcome." She raced out of the room.

Eric followed her to the elevators. "Lynda."

She stopped and slowly turned, all signs of tears gone. A cruel smile marred her pretty face. "I guess you deserve an explanation since you just lost your ticket up." She touched her hair, making sure it was in place. "You insulted and dumped me, Eric. I told you, you would regret it." She stepped into the elevator and held his gaze until the doors closed.


Adriana rested her hands on her hips, tapped her foot, and glared at her ex-husband. "You're wrong."

"She told me all about him," Laurence said.

"She doesn't know him."

"She dated him. He asked her to marry him. She refused because of what he is."

"She's lying. I was—"

"She has pictures of them dating. He has asked wealthy women to marry him before. Don't you understand? He's trying to marry up."

"I'm hardly wealthy."

"But you have a name and Nina, which connects you to me."

"Laurence—"

"This isn't a discussion. He's a con artist. You have to make a choice. You can do whatever you want with your life, but not my daughter's."

"So now she's an interest to you? The love of your life doesn't matter?"

"Go ahead and be childish. I can fight you on this. In the courts you know who will win. However, you do like to be impulsive. Perhaps you would like to try," he said in a mocking voice.

"You're so damn arrogant and selfish. You only care about yourself."

"Selfish?" His voice cracked. "I'm trying to keep you safe. You're a train heading for disaster. You argue with me out of habit, not sense."

"That's not true."

"Why won't you accept alimony?"

"Because I want to be independent of you and your money."

"Money is money, it holds no chains."

"Of course it does. It comes with a price." She waved her hands. "Look at us! I'm not even taking money from you and you're still trying to control my life."

"I'm not trying to control your life. I've never said anything about your men before. But this time I must. Eric is dangerous, he's clever."

"Too clever for me?"

He softened his voice and held her arms. "I've known you since you were nineteen. You were my wife, you're the mother of my child. I'll always care for you, about you. It's my job. You deserve better than some guy trying to marry your name or what you can give him." His voice grew hard. "You're not used to men like him, but I am."

"Just because your sister married a gold digger doesn't mean I will."

"You don't know that. No matter how exciting he seems to be, he is no good. Look at the danger he put Nina in. Who knows what other unsavory 'friends' he has? Maybe you could be next. You could disappear and he would come to me to get the money to rescue you. I won't sit by and watch you make a mistake like this again. It's either him or Nina."

"No." She yanked away from him and went to her room, slamming her door.

Eric came into the room then. He could feel Laurence's eyes on him, but chose to ignore them. His concern was with Adriana and Nina.

"I came to say good-bye," he said in a casual tone, taking off his coat.

"Permanently, I believe."

He swung his coat over his shoulder. "How much are you going to offer?"

Laurence looked smug. "I knew this was about money."

"No. I just wanted to see how far you would go to insult me."

"I want you out of their lives."

"I'm not going anywhere." He headed to Adriana's room.

"You have a brother that owns a few restaurants, don't you?"

Eric halted and turned.

Laurence smiled. "Good, you're beginning to understand me."

Eric adjusted his glasses, saying nothing.

"They're very popular restaurants, the Blue Mango and the Red Hut," Laurence said in a conversational tone. "Don't restaurants live on their reputations? It would be unfortunate to give them a bad one. Think how quickly business will falter. I would hate to have to say something awful about the service or the food. However, a man in my position has to do his duty."

Eric glared at him. "You can't win."

"I think I have." Laurence went to the door. "And if my little scenario didn't make up your mind, think about this. If Adriana continues to see you, I'm taking Nina." He opened the door. "I'll give you a chance to say good-bye. But I'm returning later to make sure you're gone for good."

Eric stood paralyzed, gripped in rage. Laurence had beat him. He was going to take Nina and ruin Drake's business. But Laurence wouldn't do anything if he left. Yes, he would leave. He could start fresh away from his brother, away from Adriana and Nina. Go somewhere where his past wouldn't hurt those he loved.

"He can't threaten you," Adriana said behind him.

Eric didn't turn. "He did pretty well."

"He can't do this. He can't control our lives."

"He can. Damn ginnygog. He's a powerful man. Drake and I may have money, but not the prestige. He has influential friends. He could crush us like beetles." He sat on the edge of the couch. "How's Nina?"

"Why don't you see her?"

He shook his head.

"She thinks this is her fault."

"It's Lynda's fault." He laughed bitterly. "No, it's my fault. Mine alone."

"I'll handle Lynda and—"

"Doesn't matter."

"It does. People like Lynda and Laurence think they can do whatever they want."

"Probably because they can. We're the little people. The few ways I could get back at him would be illegal. Satisfying but illegal."

"In this game it's who you know." She toyed with her earring. "Who do we know that is as rich as Laurence with the same background?"

He shrugged.

"This isn't hopeless. I just have to think." She grabbed his hands, pulling him to his feet. "Please say something to Nina. She wants to see you."

He walked into Nina's room and found her on the bed with her knees drawn to her chest, her head held down.

"Hello, Nina."

"It's all my fault," she said in a tear-soaked voice.

"No, none of this is your fault."

"Dad says that a small pebble can create a big wave."

*Yes, and your father's a baboon.* "You're not a pebble. You're a little girl who had a very horrible thing happen to her. It shouldn't have."

She peeked up at him. "I didn't cry when it happened."

He sat on the bed and touched her hand. "Do you want to cry now?"

"No." She hesitated and straightened. "Aren't you happy I'm back?"

"Of course I am."

"You don't seem it. You seem sad and Dad was angry with you. Why?"

He stood, needing to create a distance from her. "I can't see you anymore."

Tears threatened. "Why not?"

He went over to the window and pulled the curtains aside to stare out. *Because your father doesn't think I deserve you.* "Your father loves you very much and—"

She sat up, her feet falling to the floor. "But don't you love me too? Just a little?"

He felt his throat close. He nodded.

"Then why do you have to go away?"

He swallowed and turned to her. "Your father wants to keep you safe."

She frowned. "But you'd never hurt me."

"No, but . . ." Why couldn't she just understand so he could leave? He removed his glasses and pinched the bridge of his nose. "You know how in stories there are good guys and bad guys?"

"Yes."

"Your father is a good guy and—"

"So are you."

"No." He leaned against the wall and shook his head, shoving his glasses back on. "I wasn't always. I used to play tricks on people."

She tilted her head to the side. "Like Anansi?"

"Exactly."

Understanding dawned. "Oh, that's bad."

"I know."

She paused. "But that doesn't mean *you're* bad." She

stood, staring up at him. "You don't play tricks anymore. Right?"

"Right."

"I used to play tricks but you said I was good."

"It's different. I'm—"

"It's not different. People change."

He rested on one knee so they were at eye level. "People don't always think like that."

She stomped her foot, angry. "But they should. It's not fair that you have to go away. It's not fair at all. And it's all my fault."

"It's not your fault."

She turned from him and fell on the bed pounding her fists. "It is! It is! I shouldn't have gone with him. But he told me you were hurt and I went with him when I shouldn't have. They tell you not to go with strangers and I did. I'm stupid and dumb and I ruined everything." She began to pound the bed harder. "Everything's my fault. Everything!"

"Nina." He said her name gently, cutting through her tantrum. She stopped pounding but didn't look at him.

He grasped her shoulders. "You aren't stupid. He was a trickster. You can't blame yourself." He lifted her up to face him. "You're home safe now and you'll never go with a trickster again."

Her eyes swam with tears. "I don't want you to go away." She wrapped her arms around him. "Please don't go away. Please."

For the first time in years moisture built in his eyes. "Nina, you already have a dad, you don't need me."

"You're my friend. Please. I'll tell Dad you're not like Anansi. I'll tell him you're good. Please don't go away. *Please*."

He held her close, unable to say yes.

# Fifteen

He left her room and leaned his head back against the wall. He tried to gather the pieces of the foundation to re-build the brick wall, but they continued to crumble. He took off his glasses and covered his eyes, fighting against tears. He didn't belong here. He had nothing here he could claim as his own.

"Eric," Adriana said softly.

He couldn't look at her. He turned away. "Don't say anything."

"Eric," she said again in the same soft voice, drawing him to her as if she were an oasis to a man lost in the desert.

He resisted the need to be close to her. She romanticized him, felt sorry for him.

"Laurence thinks of people as part of his inventory, but we're individuals. Nina loves you and so do I. We want you to be a part of our lives." She cupped the side of his face. "Look at me please."

He shut his eyes. "I can't."

"Why not?"

"Because if I look at you I won't be able to leave."

She slapped him across the face. He sent her a venomous glare.

"Go ahead and be angry at me," she said. "But don't re-build that damn wall. You shut people out, afraid of being hurt. Well, you're hurting now, right? The pain is real, burning. No layer of ice will heal it. But we can together."

He turned away.

"We're already falling, Eric. There's no turning back, but there's nothing to fear at the bottom."

"There's separation, loss—"

"Or renewal. Look at me."

He did. The ice had melted into a river of such anguish, tears stung her own eyes. She held him. "Stop punishing yourself."

"It's what I know. Because of me Drake's business is at risk and you could lose your daughter. I've hurt Nina. And for what? Because I—" His voice faltered. "I was reckless once and will never be again."

"We both know survival creates different rules, different codes of conduct."

"That doesn't matter. The results are the same. Someone gets hurt."

She bit her lip. "I have an idea."

His voice hardened. "You're not listening to me."

"No, you're not listening to yourself. You're as bad as Nina. People mistreat you and you blame yourself. Laurence is wrong. He doesn't trust you partly because of what Lynda told him and partly from his own prejudice. I won't stand for that and neither should you. He's no better than you are, though in the hierarchy of things it appears that way. If they want to use their background as a weapon, I know someone who can handle them."

"Who?" he asked, curious in spite of himself. The tempting allure of risk was calling to him again.

"Kevin Jackson."

Eric lifted a brow wary. "The rich playboy? The one who had nearly every woman at Drake and Cassie's wedding drooling?"

"Yes."

He shook his head. "No."

She ignored him. "I'll get Cassie to talk to him. He would do anything for her."

"And the fact that Drake hates him doesn't bother you?"

"He doesn't have to find out." She smiled. "No worries. Do you trust me?"

He glanced up at the ceiling. "I don't trust myself."

She grasped his shirt and forced him to look at her. "That wasn't the question. Do you trust *me?*"

He gazed down at her. Her caramel eyes were full of mischief. A ghost of a smile touched his mouth. "Yes."


Kevin Jackson owned three homes, but he loved his Maryland estate the best. Especially in the spring. He sat on the patio watching the cardinals darting through the trees, as the blue sky melted into the lush green lawn.

"Mrs. Henson is here," his assistant said.

His heart accelerated. Cassie had arrived. He knew a part of him would always love her. "Great, I'll meet her in the living room."

Cassie came onto the patio and said, "Too late, I'm already here."

He was a handsome man who used his good looks to his best advantage. He used them now to flash a heartrending smile. She looked lovely in a pink floral slip dress that hugged her luscious figure, which could fill a man with sinful thoughts. He didn't discourage them. No one would mistaken him for a saint.

He stood and kissed her on the cheek. "Hello."

"Thanks for seeing me."

He gestured to a chair and sat. "Always a pleasure."

"I need your help."

He grinned. "You want to leave that bully of a husband and run off with me."

"No."

He sighed. "A man can dream." He snapped his fingers and pointed to their glasses. They were instantly filled.

"You should treat people with more regard," she said, glancing at his assistant.

"He's being paid. What's the problem?"

She sipped her drink. "Adriana's ex-husband has threatened to ruin Drake's business if his brother Eric continues to date her."

He frowned. "I thought you didn't watch soap operas."

"Kevin, this is serious. His name is Laurence Shelton."

"And you want me to do what?"

"Stop him."

A slow smile spread on his face. "With a little gentle persuasion?"

"I don't care how you do it, but Adriana's happiness depends on you."

He raised a brow. "As well as your husband's business?"

"Not really. I know Eric will not do anything to risk the business."

He looked disappointed. "Damn. It would have been nice to have Drake in my debt again."

"Again?"

"I let him have you, didn't I?"

"Behave yourself."

"I stopped that years ago." He tapped his knee, thoughtful. "I suppose his brother's gratitude will be good enough." He suddenly paused. "You're telling me Adriana is involved with Drake's brother? The android with glasses?"

Cassie scowled. "He is not an android."

"It's the best description I could come up with." He shook his head, amazed. "A man leaves for the winter and all hell breaks loose. Adriana and *Eric*," he murmured. "I can't believe that little elf is related to them."

"Elf?"

"You know . . ." He snapped his fingers, trying to recall

her name. "Jasmine, Jennifer . . . Your brother Clay kept frowning at her during the baptism."

"Jackie."

"Yes, that's right. Jackie. Cute little thing."

Cassie pointed a finger at him. "You stay away from her."

He began to grin. "It would probably upset Drake if I—"

"I'm warning you."

"I like warnings."

She rolled her eyes. "Kevin, will you help?"

"Of course. I have to see this new couple for myself."

"Do you know Laurence Shelton?"

"Probably," he said casually. "I know a lot of people."

"Mostly women."

He winked. "The best kind of people."

"Not always."

"Tell me what you know and I'll see what I can do. Does he have a sister?"

"Yes, an older one. She's divorced."

"Perfect."

Cassie looked at him, concerned. "You won't seduce her, will you?"

"Only if she's attractive."

"Kevin!"

"Don't worry about my agenda, tell me more about Larry."

"Laurence," she corrected. "Don't under any circumstances call him Larry."

"Fine."

After she gave him some more information about Laurence, he picked up the phone. "Let me call my gardener."

"What? Now?" she asked, appalled.

He raised his hand and she quieted. "Hello? Yes, I'm fine. Get your shovel. I need some dirt." He glanced at her; she smiled.

* * *

Kevin tugged on his tie, annoyed. He felt as if he were in a business meeting. He hadn't attended one of those mind-numbing sessions in years. He lifted his glass and thought of Cassie. She was the reason he was here. It had only taken him four days to get all the information he needed. Wooing Laurence's sister was pathetically too easy. She was a shy, desperate thing, eager for attention and swallowing up his like a thirsty giraffe. It was evident how she had become a pawn in the Shelton game.

"You wanted to see me," Laurence said, slipping into the booth.

"Drinks first," Kevin said.

They chatted until there was a semblance of camaraderie.

"I had dinner with your sister last night," Kevin said.

"I see."

"Sweet girl."

"If you're interested in her, I have no objections."

"If you knew me better, you would."

"Why?"

Kevin looked at him, amazed. "You mean my reputation hasn't preceded me? That's disappointing. I've worked hard at it."

"I know you like women. As long as you treat my sister well . . ." He shrugged, leaving the rest of the statement understood.

"Yes. I believe your sister has been treated badly by men. She told me about her ex-husband. However, I found it unfortunate that she didn't know why he had divorced her. She said it was so sudden."

Laurence's eyes became hard, his bitterness toward his ex-brother-in-law clear. "He was a conniving gold digger and she was better off without him. I told her that. She chooses to remain naive and not believe me."

"Perhaps she would believe you more if you told her that your father paid him three hundred thousand to get out of her life. Don't look surprised. I had a little chat with him before I came here."

Laurence slowly stiffened. "Why did you really ask me here? What's this about?"

"This is about using influence to run other people's lives. Warren's great-grandfather used to work for your family, right? Oddly he disappeared just when the family business made a profit."

"There's no proof."

"Of course not. But there's always time to find some."

Laurence finished his drink.

Kevin leaned back in his chair. "It seems to me that Sheltons have a hard time letting go of what they believe belongs to them. Adriana isn't yours anymore and the thought of her being another man's wife bothers you."

"No. If he was worthy—"

"Adriana loves Eric."

"He put my daughter's life in danger."

"And you watched your father set your sister up as a sacrifice. Who are you to judge?"

Laurence stood.

"Don't go yet. I want you to learn a little lesson about threats."

# Sixteen

Adriana sat on the couch as Cassie talked on the phone. She could hear the kids giggling in the nursery and smiled to herself. Cassie finally hung up the phone and turned to her. "That was Kevin. You don't have to worry about Laurence anymore."

"Good. I suppose shallow, superficial womanizers have their use in this world. I'll have to thank him."

"Now you can tell Eric."

Her joy faltered. She hadn't seen him since he left her place that day. He didn't want to do anything to jeopardize the plan. When Laurence had visited to make sure Eric was gone, she had to do everything not to bare her teeth. Now they could be together, but she wasn't sure what that meant. Would he feel obligated because she had fought for him? "Let's go shopping," she said. "You buy and I'll pay you back."

Cassie shook her head. "No."

"Okay, then you shop and I'll watch you."

"No."

She rested her head back. "I need a distraction."

"Have you cashed Eric's check yet?"

"No." She took the business plan and check out of her bag. "I've been carrying it around with me. A reminder of what I'm worth to him. I might as well sign it." She flipped the check over and screamed.

Cassie rushed over to her. "What!"

Her hand trembled as she held the check. "Oh no!"

Cassie shook her. "Adriana, what is it?"

"He loves me! He wrote it on the back of this check." The sight of his face when she'd crumbled it up and stuffed it in his shirt flashed through her mind. He had thought she was rejecting his love. Her gut clenched. "I'm a jerk."

Cassie looked at the check, shaking her head. "You wouldn't have known."

"I should have looked at it."

Drake came home. "Hello, ladies," he greeted.

Cassie pointed a finger at him. "Your brother is an idiot."

"Is that a news flash?"

"He wrote 'I love you' on the back of a check."

"We thought it'd be romantic."

"We?" She covered her eyes and groaned. "I should have known you would have been part of this. What do you know about romance?"

He wrapped an arm around her waist and kissed her cheek. "I got you, didn't I? I wrote you poetry."

"That you had read while I was on a date with another man."

"All that matters are the results. Eric found out that Adriana doesn't love him."

Adriana held the check to her chest. "But I do."

"Then why did you crumble up the check?"

"Because I hadn't looked at the back."

"Hmm." He rubbed his chin, recognizing their error. "We hadn't accounted for that."

Eric counted the money, then glanced at Carter across his desk. "This is twice what you owe me."

"Just call me Rumpelstiltskin. I turn straw into gold."

He narrowed his eyes, suspicious. "How?"

"Nina gave me an idea. I thought of something people would buy. Then the product came to me. Used cars. I bought several at an auction and sold them—"

"Double the price bought." He handed him the extra money. "I'd rather pull my teeth than take money from a used car salesman."

Carter winced. "At least they move."

"For how long? A day?"

He shrugged.

Eric shook his head. "How does your crooked little heart beat?"

"One sucker at a time."

"Thanks for what you did."

"Glad to help."

They both nodded, the gesture saying more than words. The phone rang. "Henson."

"You wanted some information on Keith Trenton?" Clay asked.

"Yes. You have something for me?"

"He's definitely an artist."

He glanced at Carter. "A con artist?"

"Correct. Five names, three Social Security numbers. Known for choosing women to finance different projects. He's too clever to be caught on fraud."

"What's his address?" He scribbled the number down, mumbled, "Thanks," and hung up. He looked at Carter and stood. "I have to go. I'm thinking of buying some art." He opened the door and stopped. "How are you and Serena?"

"I think I'll keep her awhile longer. With women like Lynda out there I'll stick with what I have. Speaking of Lynda—"

"Forget about her."

Carter looked confused. "Why?"

"She's a witch, but she did me a favor. She forced me to face some of my demons."

Carter shivered with the memory of her. "Yes, she was one ugly demon." He sighed. "Revenge would have been sweet, but if you want to let this go, fine."

"I do." He hesitated. "Uh, say hi to Serena for me and if you ever want to . . ." He left the statement unfinished.

"I'm not really a talker."

Eric adjusted his glasses. "I know a good bar. If you get drunk enough, you can talk about anything."

"You never get drunk."

"I wasn't talking about me."

Carter laughed and stood, following him out the door.


At home, Carter cleaned up the living room, gathering all of Serena's magazines. A bunch of papers fell out of *Home and Garden*. He picked them up and stared at them stunned. They were advertisements for baby items.

"What are you doing?" Serena asked, coming into the room.

He held up an advertisement, his heart pounding. "What's this?"

"What does it look like?"

"You're not—" He couldn't finish, thoughts of money going to diapers and hospital costs filling his mind. He quickly calculated when they'd last had sex.

"No, I'm not," she said. "But hopefully one day."

His heart returned to its normal rhythm. "Why didn't you tell me?"

"You said you didn't want kids until we had enough money. I wasn't sure the day would ever come. So I dreamed about it."

"You never gave me the chance to make any money. You spent what we have and ignored anything I said."

She shrugged. "I'm just used to getting my way, I guess."

It was a lame excuse, but at least it was honest. He put

the papers on the table. "Money's important to me. I never had any and you knew that when you met me. If you want a rich man who will give you lots of babies and provide for you, you have the wrong husband."

She lowered her eyes. "I know."

A heaviness settled in his chest. "Do you want a divorce?"

"No." She looked at him and for the first time in a long while he didn't feel invisible.

"I haven't been fair to you. I wanted to compete and impress my friends so much that I lost sight of our marriage, but I'd rather change my friends than my husband."

The heaviness began to ease. "What made up your mind?"

"I saw you had circled an ad for a divorce lawyer."

"I guess I was dreaming too. Dreaming of a wife who loved me, admired me."

She wrapped her arms around his neck. "I do love you."

He drew her close. "I love you too." He kissed her, his mouth giving credence to his words. "I'd love you more if you'd stay away from on-line shopping."

"I will." She rested her cheek against him. "I would like a family some day."

He gently stroked her hair, wondering how they had become strangers. "Okay, some day. Right now let's get to know each other again."

"How?"

"I know one way." He took her hand and pulled her toward the bedroom.

Keith swore when he opened the door and saw Eric. "Hell, I was scared you'd come here one day," he said, kicking the door wider.

Eric walked into the studio. "If you were truly scared, you would have disappeared by now."

Keith grinned. "And miss you at work?"

"I'm not working."

He smoothed his goatee. "True. From what I've learned, Lonely Hearts aren't your thing. More like the Jamaican Hustle."

Eric glanced at him, but said nothing.

Keith continued. "But don't knock what I do. It's really easy and you don't get caught. Women like Adriana . . ." He shrugged. "You know. They're an easy mark. I saw her at a gallery and just *knew*. Took me less than a month for the first check."

Eric looked around the room.

"Junk, isn't it?" Keith asked, trying to read his thoughts. Eric's silence was beginning to make him nervous.

Eric's voice was soft. "I have another word for it." He looked at one picture where Keith was painting over the signature. "KSY?" Eric turned to him. "Another name?"

"Yes. Adriana nearly caught me. Never had to think so fast." He shrugged. "It was an old painting I hadn't adjusted." He cleared off a stool and sat. "I'm just a businessman. I'm not hurting anyone. Actually, I make them feel good. Adriana needed someone to help and I volunteered."

"Hmm."

"So I play the role of protégé. And it's easy money." He looked around his well-furnished studio. "You won't believe how easy this is."

"Unfortunately, I can. You could vomit on something and fetch a good price." He frowned at a picture. "I see you've already done that."

"Careful with your criticism. I recently sold a painting for six thousand dollars. A widow with a nice inheritance."

A slow, wicked grin spread on Eric's face.

Keith read the expression and swallowed, then swore. "No, you can't . . . But—"

"Don't worry, I'll cover for you and explain why you suddenly had to leave."

Keith narrowed his eyes. "How do I know you won't take the money?"

"You don't, but that's not your problem."


Eric sat in his kitchen, trying to create the best story to give Adriana about Keith, when his doorbell rang. He answered it.

Adriana stood there, tapping her foot. "I don't know whether to kick you or kiss you."

"Do you take requests?"

"No." She opened her coat, revealing a blue blouse, plaid skirt, and thick-heeled black shoes. Glasses hung around her neck. She pulled a ruler from her jacket.

Eric's eyes widened with pleasure. "You're a teacher."

"Yes, and you're about to learn a lesson."

"Great." He pulled her inside and closed the door. He grabbed a chair from the kitchen and set it in the living room. He sat and looked up at her. "Now you pretend I'm your favorite pupil that you had to keep after class." He pointed to the TV. "That's the blackboard, right? And I'm sitting in the front seat and you—"

"Eric—"

He shook his head. "No, not Eric. Try something different like—"

"Eric!"

He looked up at her and frowned. "What?"

"I'm in charge." She rested a foot on his lap. The stance inched up her skirt.

He peeked at her panties and grinned. "No Fruit of the Looms."

"No."

His hand inched up her thigh, stopping between her legs. His voice deepened. "Crotchless, even better."

She saddled him, undid his buttons, and took off his shirt. She reached for his trousers. "You've been a bad boy and—"

He held up his hand. "Wait, before I forget."

"But—"

"Just wait." He lifted her off his lap and disappeared into the kitchen.

Adriana fell facedown on the couch and moaned. "I don't believe this."

"Adriana?"

She rolled onto her back and glared at the envelope in his hand. "That had better not be another business plan."

He held it out to her. "No, it's from Keith."

She opened the envelope and pulled out a check. "This is from your account."

"I deposited the money just to be safe." He unzipped his trousers.

"Why?"

Her pulled them off and tossed them on the floor. "I spoke with Keith. He told me he had sold a painting and wanted to reimburse you for your help."

"Keith sold a painting? Isn't that great!" She smiled, smug. "I told you he had talent."

"Hmm." He scratched his chin. "He's moving to New York."

"That's to be expected." She tucked the envelope in her bag. "Now will you trust me to choose my friends?"

No. But he wasn't in the mood to argue. He pulled her onto his lap instead. "Let's finish what we started."

"Oh yes. Your first lesson . . ." She took a piece of paper out of her bra and unfolded it. "Is this."

"You haven't cashed it yet?"

"No."

"Why not?"

She flipped it over. "Because of this."

He stared at her, blank.

She shook the check. "Eric, this says 'I love you.'"

He nodded slowly. Then shook his head. "What's your point?"

"The day I crumpled up the check I hadn't looked on the back. Don't you see? I didn't know you loved me."

"Okay, but do you realize how much this is?"

"I don't care. The words mean more than the amount. Why didn't you just tell me?"

Because saying the words made them too powerful. "I wanted to show you."

She took off his glasses and stood. "I am very disappointed with you, Eric." She set his glasses on the TV and grabbed her ruler. "I had such hope for you, you demonstrated such promise." She slapped the ruler against her palm. "I usually can spot the students with the most potential."

"But I—"

She directed the ruler at him. "You will not speak unless I give you permission. Is that understood?"

He nodded.

She slapped the ruler again. "Good." She circled around him, continuing to slap her palm. "So why did you behave so bad? Why did you push me away when you knew that you loved me? I suggest you close your mouth, Eric, unless you want it rinsed out with soap."

He sent her a glance but said nothing.

She stood behind him and used the ruler to trail a sensuous path down his arms and chest. "I believe I know the answer. You were afraid of what you felt." She whispered the words, her lips brushing against his ear. "It was something you couldn't control and you like being in control." She gently nipped his lobe. "But this time you weren't and that upset you. So at first you didn't say anything about your feelings because you thought I didn't love you. Then when you discovered I did . . ."

She stood in front of him and cupped the back of his

head. "You still punished us." She undid her blouse. "Yes, and I do mean *us*." She brought his head to her chest. "You hurt me by denying what you felt."

His tongue darted between her breasts. "Feel that?"

"You're talking, Eric."

He wrapped his arms around her, bringing her closer. "Sorry."

"As I was saying, your denial—"

He shook his head.

"You weren't in denial? Fine, let's call it lack of communication."

He shrugged and kissed a path up her chest.

"You didn't think our feelings were enough. To you feelings are annoying, uncontrollable things and not a strong enough foundation to stand on. You've wondered about them for years. Is love strong enough?" She tugged off his boxers. "Fortunately, I have a theory. Love is as strong as the people who claim it. Some people's love, while genuine, is as durable as flint. But that's not us." She eased onto him. He looked anxious. "Relax, love, I'm wearing one." She moved against him, tightening around him as he filled her.

"When we love, it consumes us, seeps into our smallest vein. But there's no reason to be ashamed, because we're both strong enough to accept and cherish the gift from each other. We will never use it to hurt." She kissed his forehead. "Therefore you have nothing to fear. Because any time you fall it will always be into my arms." Her mouth swooped down to capture his. He surrendered willingly, his body eager and open to her, her body ready to honor him, adore him, please him. As their moment together slipped into the night he learned that love was not a weakness and that it took the greatest courage to trust.

\* \* \*

Later, they lay together on the couch wrapped in a blanket, their bodies languid with pleasure. Adriana rested her chin on his chest and looked at Eric. His eyes were closed, but she knew he was awake. "What does KSY stand for?"

"Keith Simon Yothers." He opened his eyes. "Why?"

"Your story was clever except when you said, 'I spoke with Keith.' My brother's spoken to a lot of people and always ended up bloody afterward."

"I didn't touch him."

"I'm glad. I liked his face."

They fell silent. A bus rumbled past, pigeons cooed outside the window, and something scurried through the grass. Adriana looked around at all of Eric's plants and felt as though she had found her own private Eden.

"I think it would be beneficial to get married," he said.

Adriana shut her eyes and fell face foward on his chest. "Oh, Eric," she said, disappointed.

"What?"

She turned on her cheek. "I imagined the ways you would propose to me, even the boring ones, but that was the worst. It's so horrible I can't repeat it."

"I want you to marry me."

"That's a bit better. However, that's not how we agreed a proposal should go."

He sat up and lifted her in his arms. His eyes captured hers. "I love you."

Joy fluttered through her, tears glistened in her eyes. He was completely hers, the ice was gone.

"You're going to cry?"

"No." She cupped his chin. "That wasn't a proposal."

"I just wanted you to know."

"Thank you." She waited.

He looked at her.

"Eric," she warned.

He smiled. "I wanted to see how long you would wait."

She jumped to her feet and began to dress.

"Will you marry me?"

She sent him a glance and slipped into her shoes.

His smile fell. "I was only teasing, don't be angry."

She pulled on her coat and opened the door.

He grabbed her wrist. "Adriana, wait. It wasn't a spur-of-the-moment thing. I've been waiting to ask you." He pulled a small box from a flowerpot and opened it. Inside was a band with an emerald, a ruby, and a diamond. "I chose the emerald and ruby because I fell in love with you Christmas Eve. I know we'll have our differences but I'd like you to be my wife."

She closed the door and slipped the ring on her finger. She looked at him and winked. "The answer is yes."

He snapped the box closed, recognizing her ploy. "You're a wicked woman."

"Just what a bad boy deserves." She wrapped her arms around his neck and kissed him.

The spring morning crept into her room with the promise of a fresh new day. Adriana stretched her arms and turned to the empty space beside her. She could still smell Eric's scent on the sheets. She looked at the ring on her finger in wonder. It had been three weeks and the sight still made her feel giddy. No weight or burden came with the symbol of devotion, just love and commitment.

She looked at Elissa, who sat on the ottoman looking smug.

Adriana made a face. "I know you're a cat, but you don't need to look so pleased with yourself."

Elissa blinked.

She put on a robe and slippers, then checked on Nina, who was still asleep, clutching the pendant Eric had given her—two spiders on a rose. Adriana thought it was a rather creepy gift, but wisely said nothing when Eric had wrapped it around Nina's neck. She watched them share a mischievous look, but instead of feeling excluded she felt proud of their special bond. Already they were planning what their new place would be like. Adriana wasn't picky as long as there was plenty of closet space.

She headed for the kitchen and opened a cupboard. She stopped when she heard city sounds, seeping through an open window. She went to the living room and saw Eric fully dressed, standing on the balcony. His hands rested on the railing.

She went up behind him and wrapped her arms around his waist. "Congratulations."

"You're right. The view is nice."

She stood beside him and looked down. "Yes."

He paused. "So you won't mind living out here?"

She turned to him, alarmed. "Why?"

"Because I can't move."

She glanced down at his hands. His knuckles were pale. She bit her lip to keep from grinning.

His jaw twitched. "Go ahead and laugh."

"I love you too much to laugh at you." She sat on the rail. "I could do my little trick again."

"Don't you dare."

She swung one leg over.

He narrowed his eyes. "You promised."

She sighed and stood. "You're right." She ducked into the circle of his arms and looked up at him. He didn't meet her gaze. She could feel his shame. "It's going to be okay." She hugged him, her head resting against his chest. She abruptly let go, stunned. "I didn't realize you were terrified. Your heart is racing."

His mouth twitched. "No, that's your fault."

She giggled, pleased. "Oh." She tilted her head. "Then that's strange."

"What?"

"Why would you hold on to the railing, when you can hold on to me?"

His gaze went to her face, his eyes melted into hers. "You're right." He kissed her with his eyes and then his lips, all fears of falling dissipating into a feeling so strong he felt he could fly. He let go and gathered her in his arms.

## ABOUT THE AUTHOR

Dara Girard's love for the written word began with the many picture books her mother read to her. At an early age, Dara was a vocracious reader, and was delighted with the seventy-five-book limit at the local library. *Table for Two* was her first book for BET/Arabesque. Born to a British West Indian mother and Nigerian father, Dara loves to travel and hear from her readers. You can reach her at:

dara@daragirard.com or

PO Box 10345
Silver Spring, MD 20914

If you would like a reply, please send a self-addressed, stamped envelope.